Imperfect

Circle

Robert L Mason

**The third book of the
FORBES TRILOGY**

The other books are
Black Diamond and
Isosceles Triangle

authorHOUSE®

AuthorHouse™
1663 Liberty Drive
Bloomington, IN 47403
www.authorhouse.com
Phone: 1-800-839-8640

In this work of fiction, the characters, places and events are either the product of the author's imagination or are used entirely fictitiously.

First published by AuthorHouse   10/24/2011

ISBN: 978-1-4670-0191-5 (sc)
ISBN: 978-1-4670-0193-9 (ebk)

Printed in the United States of America

This book is printed on acid-free paper.

I dedicate this book to
my Great Grandson

Charlie Mason White

Contents

Glossary

Althing	The Icelandic Parliament
Astrakhan	A fur coat made from wool
BTF	British Trawlers Federation
CIA	The Secret Service of the United Sates
CG	The Icelandic Coast Guard
DFA	Designated Fishing Areas
FO	The British Foreign Office
GDP	Gross Domestic Product, a measure of national prosperity
GI	Government Issue (Term used for the ordinary US Soldier)
HMG	Her Majesty's Government
KGB	The Russian secret service
The Mission	The Royal National Mission to Deep Sea Fishermen
MAFF	Ministry of Agriculture, Food and Fishing
MHQ	Maritime Head Quarters at Pitreavie, Fife
MI5 and MI6	The twin arms of the British secret service, home and abroad.
NATO	North Atlantic Treaty Organisation
NHS	The British National Health Service
OTC	Officer in tactical command
PM	Prime Minister
RoE	Rules of Engagement
Side Winder	A trawler having the trawl net streamed over the side
VHF	Very High Frequency radio, i.e: Line of sight.
Wavy Navy	The Royal Naval Volunteer Reserve
Wavy-stripe	An officer in the Wavy Navy— The naval reserve
Wilco	By radio meaning 'I will co-operate'
Sitrep	Situation Report

Dramatis Personae

CREW of the ACE

		After Sean and Saxon resign
Saxon Mac Donald	Skipper	Chas Forbes
Sean Bowyer	Mate	John Fowler
Chas Forbes	Bosun	Mike Campbell
Doug Mills	Cook	Doug Mills
Taffy Picton	Engineer (ex Mirlees)	Taffy Picton
Tim	2nd Engineer	Tim
Sparks	Radio Officer	Sparks
John Fowler (ex RN Lt)	1st Hand	Scot
Mike Campbell	2nd Hand	
Scot	3rd Hand	
Robbie	4th Hand/ Cook's assist	Robbie
Plus eight more deck hands		plus six more deck hands

FAMILY

Charlie Forbes
Susan, his wife
Chas, his son
Charlene, his daughter
Sir David Brown, Charlie's brother in law
Lady Brown, David's wife, identical twin with Susan
Hugo and Violet Robinson (both deceased), parents of the twins
Jack Forbes, father of Charlie
Eliza Forbes, mother of Charlie
Peggy Petrie (Eliza's sister, deceased)

ICELAND

Reynir Josefsson	Minister of Fishing
Haraldur Gunnarsson	Best Friend of David
Captain Georg Baldursson	Harbour Master and Deputy Prime Minister
Captain Bjann Liefsson	In charge of the Ace while under arrest
Captain Gudmundur Kjaernested	Head of the Coastguard and Skipper of Aegir
Captain Throstur Sigtryggsson	Skipper of Thor
Vilbert Agnarsson	Chief of Police
Jon Petursson	Chairman of the Trawler Company

OTHER CHARACTERS

Marjory	Saxon's wife
Oskar Krause	A Russian Secret Agent (see Isosceles Triangle)
Zap Winterton	The Calligraphist
Col. Rostovski	Head of Security at Harz (see Isosceles Triangle)
Vladimer Maikovitch	Captain of the Lenin (see Isosceles Triangle)
Max	Oskar's Assistant
Celia	Max's Mistress
Jonny	Chief of Kingston upon Hull's Police, Retired
Claus	Pilot of the Helicopter
General Hank Thorne	Commander in Chief of the NATO Base

Felix   The CIA agent working for
                               Hank Thorne
Kay   Charlie's receptionist and
                               nurse

ILLUSTRATIONS

Prologue

My name is Abraham Goldstein, Abe for short. Some of you will have heard of me already but in case you haven't let me give you a brief run down. I was born in 1870 into a large family. Although I have only one brother, our cousins are, or rather were before the second World War, scattered all over Europe. Based in Bern we had offices in most major cities supplying finance for business, underwriting insurance and many other services. Since 1945 and the demise of Adolf Hitler and his evil gang of criminals, I have been engaged in tracing and offering help to the remains of my family.

Nothing will ever remove the memory of my escape from Antwerpen in 1940, right under the noses of Nazi officers. After hearing that our good friends, the Smidts, had been arrested I realised that my wife, Gerda, and our granddaughter were in imminent danger. Help came from another close friend who arranged a passage to Switzerland on a Rhine barge for us and the Smidt's two daughters, Gretchen and Rita. Much later, when we were nearly at our destination, poor Gretchen was shot by a German soldier.

Our plan would have been discovered but for the action of a courageous young man called Charlie Forbes. His quick thinking in diverting the attention of the sentries enabled the crate, inside which I was crouching, to be hoisted onto the barge. Having lost my own son in the early days of the war I took Charlie into my paternal care right up to the moment when he graduated in medicine in 1951 at Manchester University. Charlie proved himself to be honest and brave beyond the call of duty. He well deserved the George Cross for helping British and US airmen escape through the minefields on the Swiss/Franco frontier. I adopted him as if he was my own son.

He was charmed by the identical twins, Lucy and Susan Robinson, whom he met in Switzerland and who helped the escaping airmen also. He admired their beauty and vivacity; so did I, even though their three sided relationship was somewhat unconventional. In times of war, when so much fear and hatred abound, love remains the solid rock beneath our civilization. Charlie married Susan, not so much because he loved her more than Lucy, but because she was having his baby.

My dear Gerda died last year and was laid to rest in the family's mausoleum where I shall soon join her. Now, lying here, tears well up within me as I realise that I shall never see her or my Charlie again. His recent visit came as a complete and wonderful surprise. For a week he brought the twins and their two children, Chas and Charlene to my home in Bern. I hardly recognised him after a gap of nearly twenty years since the end of the war. The slim youth I remembered had grown to be tall and strong but gentle when we shook hands. His striking blue eyes shone out from a face tanned by the action of salt and sea. His smile, as ever, was warm and infectious and despite my misery drew one from me.

According to the doctors, I have only a few more weeks to live. I am not able to stand any more and I wear suitable plumbing and feeding attachments to prolong my stay on earth, though for what purpose it is hard to say. Nathan, my brother, says all my affairs are in order. My will leaves the bulk of my considerable fortune to Charlie. I am confident that he will invest it well for the benefit of his family. I entrust this deposition to the care of Charlie's biographer, Bob Mason, so that the story will be faithfully recorded for future generations.

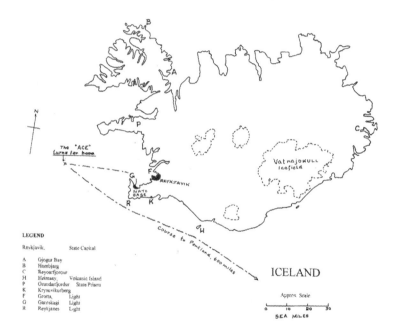

N

The "ACE"
turns for home

G
REYKJAVIK

NATO
BASE

R   K

P

B

A

C

Vatnajokull
Icefield

Course to Pentland, 600 miles

ICELAND

Approx Scale

0   10   20   30

SEA MILES

LEGEND

Reykjavik,   State Capital

A   Gjogur Bay
B   Hornbjarg
C   Reyoarfjorour
H   Heimaey,   Volcanic Island
P   Grundarfjordur   State Prison
K   Krysuvikurberg
F   Grotta,   Light
G   Garoskagi   Light
R   Reykjanes   Light

xviii

1   The Ace Of Spades

Once again angry words spilled out from the house on the Chorley road. In spite of the large garden surrounding their home, Belvedere, their shouts could be heard by the neighbours.

"Well, I don't agree with a word of it. The boy's crazy," Susan shrieked.

"Stop there." Charlie Forbes held up his hand as if to stop the traffic.

"I will not stop," she went on at maximum pitch, "and for you to go along with it. Words fail me. You spoil that son of yours."

"Better not let Chas hear you say that. He thinks Charlene is the one we spoil."

"You're making me angry again. Every time I try to discuss this we end up shouting."

"I'm making you angry? What about him then? It's for Chas that I'm doing this."

"I thought that when we agreed to be married and . . ." She slumped into the kitchen chair and buried her face in her hands hoping that things would soon calm down. They usually did.

"We are married Susan," Charlie said slowly. "Don't ever say we're not. We are. That was the vow you and Lucy made to each other when you swapped identities." Charlie felt his gut wrenching guilt rising once more. It hardly seemed possible that after all the years of love and hatred, he longed to take her in his arms and smooth away her tears. Even now he remembered the slim beauty of his wife as she was, over twenty years ago. Where had the years gone since that crucial night when the Robinson twins swapped their identities in the course of true love? His former wife had gone to live with his friend, David and called herself Lucy and David's wife of a few hours had become his wife, Susan. 'What is happening to my life?' he wondered and not for the first time. Susan was only too happy with their lifestyle but the dull routine of general medical practice over the last twenty years had gradually worn away his enthusiasm and devotion. He needed something new, something dramatic to wake him from his present torpor. Sometimes he wished he was back in the Medical Corps.

"Listen." She broke his brief reverie. "Well then, if we are as you say, I've got an equal stake in all this. Chas will be mad to buy a trawler in these times, and you know it. Just because Abe's money is sitting there, in the bank, he thinks he can go out and spend nearly half a million pounds on a lost cause."

"He's not spending; he's investing. The Ace of Spades will be built to the latest specifications and for her size will be equal to any trawler afloat. Have faith and trust. He will have a vessel capable of handling any weather and with all the latest equipment."

Calm now, Charlie drew up a chair and put his arm round her slender shoulders. She turned her face towards him. He smiled. She wiped her eyes and at last they were reconciled once more.

"Equipment. What do you mean? What equipment?" she said.

"We'll go into all that this evening when Chas is back from the Beverley Yard."

"Why did we go to the Beverley Yard in the first place? Every vessel they ever built there has to be floated down the river Hull for fitting out."

"Well, for one thing they quoted a very keen price, much less than the other yards. That's why, plus the fact that they have a very long tradition."

"What's that got to do with it?" Her throat tightened with the effort of keeping calm. She knew a wrong word or even a raised voice might spark another row.

"Oh. No need to pick me up on every word. Experience then," he said somewhat testily. "With tradition comes experience. I've heard good reports of CD Holmes and Company. When Chas gets back he should have a copy of the latest spec. with drawings, the lot. It's a long time since Holmes had an order like this and he's revelling in it."

"Of course he's revelling in it. All the yards are having a tough time. Don't you think you're leaving too much to Chas. He's barely twenty two and looks younger."

"He's a strong intelligent man. He may look young to you but at six feet three he out-reaches his contemporaries. He's had plenty of experience, ever since he was eighteen, and now he is negotiating the best possible agreement for the realisation of his dream, a modern trawler incorporating all his wish list."

"That's all very well but the Icelanders are not just going to stop at the 1961 settlement. The grapevine has it that their next dictat will be for 50 miles."

"I know that. The yards are buzzing with it but I take it with a big pinch of salt. The present deal doesn't run out until 1971. We'll worry about it when the time comes. At the very worst, there's still at least five more years of uninterrupted fishing on the Iceland shelf to go for. In any case there's no reason why Britain shouldn't get better treatment than the rest of Europe."

"That seems unlikely. You're a dreamer Charlie, always were and always will be. You're just like your father."

"The world needs dreamers. Chas is a dreamer too. How do we get ideas, make progress?"

"I wouldn't have thought fishing was an occupation for dreamers"

"Well that's where I think you may be wrong. Chas has more to offer than just dreaming. He's a practical man, blessed with a tough attitude. He'll make good in the industry and what's more he's inherited Dad's outlook on life. They didn't give Jack Forbes the nickname 'Fearless' on the Grimsby dock without knowing the man. He gets his ideas from the Forbes and his strength from your side. In my opinion he's the ideal man to join the industry in crisis. Innovation and imagination will see it through."

"You're all talk."

"Have more faith Sue. Don't forget our export trade. It's not just fishing. Britain sells a mountain of stuff to Iceland."

"Ha, you've got to be joking. The war's over now. Europe's back on its feet."

"We're best placed to do deals."

"Maybe but I still think, from all I've read, that fishing is a dying industry. The future is in fish farms, surely." She rose and went to the sideboard. "I'll make us some coffee."

Charlie, conscious of having won the argument at least for the moment, went on.

"It will be another century before farms can fully replace traditional methods, if then. Besides, fishermen are not so stupid as to hunt fish to final extinction. It's going to be the job of the navy to catch pirates but for licensed boats, with the latest developments in nets etcetera and proper control, the future will be assured. Let's see what proposals Brian comes up with next week and then we'll go to Beverley."

"Who's Brian?"

"You've met him. Mr Haslam, our naval architect."

"What makes you think Chas can handle this?"

"We've talked about this already. He's physically strong and with a personality to match it. He may not be a genius but he's well qualified both technically and practically. Those weeks he spent with the trawlers have given him experience some men never pick up. I have every confidence in his enterprise and judgement."

"I'm coming to Beverley too. I don't mind sitting in the back so that you and he can talk boats."

"Of course you are. I hoped you would come. Chas has got a day off work."

With that Charlie reached for his coat. "I'm late again. My patients will be queuing in the street if I don't get going." He gave her a quick kiss. "I'll get Kay to phone if I'm going to be late. Back to the grind. Bye."

"Bye." She said turning away. "Charlene should be home soon."

"Please don't involve her in any of this. Our daughter's got enough on her plate with her entrance exam."

"I won't. Of course not. Bye."

****

The Forbes' journey to Beverley and Hull was conducted mainly in sulky silence. They left Bolton before dawn hoping to reach Beverley in time for a light lunch before meeting with Holmes. Susan, well wrapped in her astrakhan, rested her head on the rear cushion and closed her eyes, wishing the tedious journey was at an end. Expressions of disapproval and anxiety passed across her face in equal measure though she kept her thoughts to herself. After Rochdale the road climbed steadily to cross the Pennine Hills putting the Lagonda through her paces.

"Some fine views up here on a clear day. You should find time to take Mum for a drive, Dad, one day when you haven't much on."

"I can't imagine when that will be Chas. I haven't had a day off in eighteen months. This outing is a real treat for both of us. Eh dear?"

There was no reply from the rear seat.

"I'll drive after breakfast if you like Dad."

"Good idea son. You could do with a bit more practice, especially if you'll be coming this way a lot from now on. Have you thought about buying a car of your own? Its not going to be possible for me you lend you this one. I need it."

"Yes I have, unless Mum lends me hers. I fancy an MG."

"Second hand maybe. You can charge it to the firm. Get a copy of Autocar."

"OK Dad, I will, as from next week. Thanks."

"What's that about?" Came from the back seat.

"Chas needs a car, dear."

"So we're going to be a three car family, are we? Next we'll have to get one for Charlene."

"Be reasonable. He's going to be making frequent trips to Hull from now on. As for Charlene, there's no question of that. When the time comes, maybe, if she has a job which demands it."

"So that's settled then." Susan closed her eyes as a signal that the conversation was at an end."

Descending into Yorkshire, they stopped at the George Inn in Halifax for a late breakfast.

"We need petrol," Charlie announced.

"Couldn't you have thought of that before we left home," asked Susan, "Chas, you had all day yesterday to prepare."

"Sorry Mum," he muttered, determined not to rock the boat any further.

"If you're hoping to be a skipper you'll have to plan ahead better than this."

"I am planning ahead. I've given up my job at Hicks and I'm going to take another refresher course at Riversdale."

"Oh, I see. Well since when? You never mentioned it."

6

"I told Dad. He's opened a business account with Lloyds."

"That's right dear. I'll be topping it up from time to time. We're going to keep proper accounts from now on. Chas will be able to claim expenses."

"Well I suppose it had to happen but I really think we should have discussed it first," Susan replied. "I am a partner in all this."

"More of a sleeping partner, I think," said Chas.

"What do you mean by that? Are you being rude?"

"Well, you won't want to be bothered with every detail of the Ace of Spades Limited will you?"

"I shall want to know how the money's going, where it's being spent and what on. I wait to see if you can repay it. I have my doubts," asserted Susan.

"Mum. Get this. Trawling is profitable, very. Why would so many boats be doing it otherwise?"

"Chas, I'm tired of arguing. All I want is to be kept in the picture."

"OK, From now on I'll do that. When fitting out's complete Saxon and I will sign on a crew. I shall live, eat and sleep aboard. You won't see me for weeks on end, months. That should please you."

"Chas, don't you know anything about families? I'm your mother."

"May I interrupt?" Charlie said quietly, hoping to pour some calming oil onto troubled waters.

"What is it? Haven't you been listening?"

"I'll just see if the porter will get the car filled up. Leave it to me," said Charlie. Half an hour later with a full tank they hit the road again. No more was said until the boatyard was reached. Charlie turned into the main gate and parked in the reception area while Susan applied her make-up, determined to make a formidable impression on the director of the yard.

"Well Mr Holmes, this is our big day," said Chas as he alighted and ran forward to shake the rough hand of the shipbuilder.

"It's a big day for me too, Charles," he replied in a gruff Yorkshire drawl.

"Call me Chas. Everybody else does. Let me introduce my Dad and Mum, Susan. Dad likes to be called Charlie, so you'll have to remember that."

"I've assumed you want a little time to relax after your long journey. There's a sandwich lunch in the Board Room here at the yard and when Stainton arrives we can go through the contract together."

"Stainton?"

"He's our contact with my fitting-out berth down at Princes Dock."

"I see; that's very thoughtful but you're the main contractor. We shall put everything through you."

"That's understood."

"We've got Brian Haslam acting for us on the technical side. I think he's the best naval architect in the profession when it comes to trawlers. Technology is moving so fast these days it must be difficult to keep up."

"Yes indeed. We have our own design team here and we shall be pleased to liaise with Haslam and sort out areas of responsibility. When we've finished with the hull up here at Beverley she'll be floated down the river for fitting out in Princes."

"I'm surprised you can still make it pay," said Susan.

"Yes, for the time being, Mrs Forbes but for how much longer it's hard to say. The ships are getting larger and soon we'll have to close here if things go on as they are. This yard has been building iron ships since the 1880's and most recently as the famous Cook, Welton and Gemmell Company."

"That's a long history."

"It will be a sad day for the town when we have to close. We've had to pay for having the river dredged. Quite an undertaking that was."

"We can have a general chat over lunch," said Charlie, "I've brought a letter of intent which we can sign today. We should be able to sign the contract within two weeks. I'm in charge of finance and we can negotiate stage payments today."

"Excellent," replied Holmes, "I look forward to doing business with you."

"I take it that this is a fixed price," said Charlie as he looked at the Bill of Sale. "It's quite a big uplift from the price you mentioned before."

"It came out at well over five hundred and fifty thousand with the extras you mentioned but we'll hold it to five-twenty if you can sign today," he replied.

"Subject to contract then," said Charlie, as they shook hands."

"As for the technical side, no one can claim to be up to date. Things are moving ahead so fast. We like to think that our craft will not be left behind so we try to second guess the scientists and make provision for updates as they come along. It's good for our business too."

The bird's eye view over the slipways from the Board Room was impressive. On that bright summer day in 1965 they could look down on a picture postcard scene of activity everywhere; cranes swinging their heavy loads over ships in various stages of construction, racks of steel, timber and other raw materials, the hum and grind of steel on steel, the flash of the welders, the hammering and thumping as plates were shaped. Workmen and craftsmen acted together as if in a gigantic ballet of creative effort. At the sharp sound of a hooter, activity slowly came to rest as the ship yard staff started for their homes in the early evening.

Meanwhile, business completed, and with the proposed specifications in Chas's briefcase the Forbes family made for their car.

"Your vessel will be laid down on slip number one, right under my nose. From my office I'll be able to keep an eye on it all."

"We'll be in touch within the next fortnight," said Chas. "I plan to come over at least once every month and we'll bring Haslam next time."

"I'll look forward to that." He raised his arm in a salute as they drove away.

"In spite of everything I liked that man," remarked Susan as Charlie steered the Lagonda through the narrow streets.

"I'm glad you said that Mum. Everybody likes David Holmes."

"Do you really think he's as confident in the industry as he likes to sound?"

"Mum, get real, he sells boats doesn't he. He's got to be confident. He's the best. This yard runs like clockwork. I've been around quite a bit and I've yet to find a trawler skipper who doesn't agree. Contracts finished to time and within budget, that's their aim every time."

"Good, sensible man that Holmes," interjected Charlie.

Chas continued, "I'll be seeing Brian Haslam tomorrow. He's going to hold my hand every step of the way to make sure that C.D.Holmes & Co. gives us, or should I say sells us, what we want. Every detail needs careful study. Especially the net handling winches. Some of the gear will be a first for them. Anyway I'll tell Brian we've got two weeks to approve the spec. Then we'll be going back to the yard."

"I still think the whole things too risky and too expensive. We're not up to it."

"Mum we know what you think. Don't go on." Chas winked at his Dad, who responded with a one sided smile. Susan closed her eyes again, exhausted by the arguments and counter arguments of the day. In her heart she knew that her husband was usually so careful with money. "Why should he be so different with the biggest and most risky adventure they had ever undertaken?" 'Fearless Jack' had salt in his veins but after the war and the loss of their drifters Charlie had not returned to the sea. Although he had a good practice in Bolton, being a GP did not really suit his temperament, she knew that.

2   THE LAUNCH

On a chilly day in March 1967, the Forbes family are there in force to witness the launch. Even Grandmother Eliza, is there and so is Susan's sister, Lucy, and her husband David Brown, the diplomat. They are watching the last minute preparations. The wooden blocks are in place under the hull, put in during the last two weeks of construction ready for the sideways launch into the river Hull. Then the top sliding pieces, well and truly greased with soft soap, have been put under the ship. A cradle will hold the ship upright as it goes down the launch-ways. Six men stand ready with sledge hammers. At a signal from Holmes, Susan steps forward and breaks a bottle of Bollinger on the bow, saying,

"I name this ship the Ace of Spades." The keel blocks are knocked out and the trawler starts to slide slowly sideways into the narrow river, gathering speed as she goes until she hits the water and generates a large wave which surges across the river and up the far bank drenching anyone standing too close. Eliza weeps.

"What's to do Gran? Short of getting married this promises to be the happiest day of my life."

"Oh Chas, I can't expect you to understand. I'm thinking of Jack, your Granddad. I saw the pride on his face when he

12

launched the Ace of Diamonds in 1925. It seems like only yesterday. The Forbes' wheel has turned the full circle hasn't it? Whatever our mistakes in the past, here we are, back at sea again. What a blessing our country's at peace. Let's hope this will be the Perfect Circle."

"What a sentimental old thing you are Mum. I never knew until now," remarked Susan.

"I'm sorry Saxon, our Skipper, couldn't make it to see the launch," said Charlie. "At least Mr Haslam came to see his brainchild take to the water."

"Well Mr Holmes couldn't delay the ceremony and he wants the slip," said Chas. "Saxon's still at sea. He's going to join us in September when his present contract expires. He says the ship he's on at the moment is clapped out, should have been scrapped years ago."

"I want to meet this Saxon," said Susan. "He sounds too good to be true"

"If something sounds too good to be true they used to say 'it probably is'."

"Don't say that Gran. My first trip with him went well. He's a really nice guy. Saxon will teach me a lot. He's forty—eight and very experienced. He was brought up on steam trawlers. It's the only life he's known. I've been into the records. His trawlers bring in full loads almost every trip and that's going to be more important than ever as time goes on. Trust me."

"We do trust you Chas. Don't we Susan?" Susan made no reply, pretending not to have heard.

"Anyway you won't be able to meet him until he signs on with us. He's too busy. Until then I'll be busy here at Holmes's in Beverley or at Princes Dock. There's all the paper work to get through with the Ministry. Then there's the electronics, Decca and the Radar sets, so we'll know where we are. You've heard of Radar, Gran?"

"Yes, of course, it was used to detect German planes in the war but what's Decca?"

"It's a radio system invented at the end of the war. Decca transmissions from three shore stations enable fishermen to plot their position on the special charts. It's a bit complicated to explain in a few words. We had lectures at Riversdale and a spell at sea to learn about it. Iceland has its own transmitters which we can use too."

"I don't want blinding with science; thank you very much. Just give me the gist."

"There's a new American system, called Loran, coming in soon which could be very useful. North of Iceland Decca is not very good you see."

"I don't see but go on."

"Then we've got contacts via ship's radios, ship to shore and ship to ship, Sonar depth sounder and fish finders. I want to see it all installed since I'll have to operate the stuff and mend it when it goes wrong. Everything will be duplicated. There's a mountain of work and its all got to be ready for the first of September. I've got Saxon's list for the actual Granton fishing gear. He says he'll snatch a weekend to come to the yard. There are the nets to sort plus all the attendant warps, floats, bobbins and otterboards."

"You've lost me again. What are otterboards?"

"Each trawl net needs two, port and starboard. They keep the net spread wide. When I get time I'll draw you a sketch.

"Sounds as if you've been into it thoroughly. I suppose you got all that in your year at Riversdale College."

"Yea, right Gran, and Fleetwood. It was a great help and those trips with the trawlers at sea were exciting. I picked up a lot, especially in the hols. I learnt then that if I ever had a boat, safety for the men would be first."

****

Six months later Saxon and Chas drove into the Princes Dock. Mr Holmes and Stainton were there to meet them.

"Good morning David."

"And a very good morning to you and Mr Saxon."

"We'll unload our kit and then come to your office."

"Fine. I've got an engineer from Mirlees on the way. He should be here soon. He said ten. He's going out with you both for the day to hand over the engines. See you later."

Chas and Saxon went over to the Ace and started to unload their belongings and enough food for a week's cruising. Two officials from the yard were assigned to join them. Stainton said they would deal with complaints and answer technical questions. Chas explained to Saxon,

"We have her for a week and then it's the handover. We've got a ten percent retention for a year during which any genuine faults will show. After that it's up to us but from what I know of Holmes, a new vessel from them will always be on their books. As well as Stainton's men we've got the Mirlees engineer for today so it's up to us to get our money's worth out of him. We'll put him ashore tonight and then take off in the morning. I hope we get a bit of dusty weather."

With the engineer aboard they left the harbour, rounded the Spurn Head Light Ship and headed north-east, into the open sea. Saxon at the helm put the Ace through her paces to get the feel of her whilst plotting a graph of engine revs. against speed through the water. About half way through the morning he said,

"Yer know Chas, I feel she's got the power and plenty of it but she doesn't respond. There's no surge. Well there is but not enough. She's built for trawling admittedly. We'll not know for sure until she's under load. Dragging a trawl will make all the difference. We'll know a lot more when we put her on the bollard test. With this engine we should pull about six to seven tons. Flat out I hope she can do 16 knots, and hopefully three to four trawling. If you're going to keep out of the way of those Icelandic coastguards you'll need it"

"Well you've got the experience. I bow to your judgement."

"With the engines at 750 revs she's giving all she's got. I think we should chat it through with Holmes."

"OK we will. At the end of to-day I'll mention it in my report. What does the engineer say?"

"So long as the engines are OK, which they are, he's happy. I can't get any feed back from him on the prop."

The week ended happily. Several of the fishermen from the other trawlers in the harbour came over for a look at C.D.Holmes's newest product. With some satisfaction Chas could see envy in their eyes. Several of the older skippers made some very helpful remarks which he wrote down in the ship's log for future discussion but others were more sceptical about the stern ramp.

"In an Icelandic storm that ramp will be a liability," they said.

The next big task was to sign on a crew. This he decided to leave to Saxon who knew his way around the ports and was in a position to more or less handpick anyone he wanted. He planned one more trip to Belvedere, his parents' home, reconciled to making his new home on board the Ace. Skipper Saxon had a week to sign on the crew. Chas appointed himself as Bosun. He thought he would give himself a year before moving up to Mate and sitting for a master's ticket and after that it would be up to Saxon who, at his age, would probably be looking around for a shore job.

"After all Chas," Saxon had said. "I've been at sea since I was fourteen. I think it's about time I found something else to do with my life. I know Marjory would be pleased. Unlike your Dad I missed Dunkirk, thank God, but I did have 'The Agnes' shot from under me by a bloody U-boat in '43. I reckon I've done my bit."

"You certainly have. Folk like you and your missis are few and far between these days. I'll be ready to take over when you want. Just give me plenty of notice. That's all I ask. I love the sea. My Granddad had three drifters in 1939 but we had none at the end . . . nor my Granddad neither."

"What do you mean?"

"Granddad was killed at Dunkirk. The war did for him. My Dad nearly copped it too but he made it to Switzerland but that's another story."

"Sounds exciting."

"You could say that but I say it must have been nerve wracking. He wouldn't do it again. My Dad said it all happened in another life, risking the mines or German patrols. He said he became inured to it. Lives were cheap. I could never do what he did."

"You don't strike me as a timid person."

"I may seem bold to you but it's partly play-acting. I just hope I'll gain confidence as time goes on."

"You will. I remember how I was when I got my ticket."

"My Dad still takes risks, mainly on the roads. I think he still craves excitement."

"There's plenty of excitement on the trawlers. Perhaps he could have been the fleet's doctor."

"Don't tell him that. He might just take you up on it."

"He'd be fine on our mother ship, the Mirander."

"Mirander?"

"We can't put into any Icelandic ports while a war's on. She carries all sorts of spares, rescue equipment. There's even a good surgery and operating table. Let's hope she gives us cover in '72'."

"Let's hope we never need her then."

"We'll be working out of here a lot of the time. The market here is good and well worth the extra sailing unless the agent says to drop the catch at Scrabster."

"Why would we do that?"

"Well it all depends on the agent and what we've netted. It saves a day's fuel each way."

"If you say so Sax."

"It seems a long way to the banks and a waste of fuel passing the Scottish ports but I know the market here."

"OK. I'm not arguing but I did wonder why you think it's better to come so far south when the banks are almost over the Arctic Circle."

"Not quite but I know what you mean. Anyway, apart from that we can always nip into the yard if any small repair jobs are in the offing. After a local shake down we'll go and steal a catch from the Icelanders. I don't know what all the fuss was about in '58. The 12 mile limit is not doing us any harm. We need some longer warps, that's all. The catches are just as good."

"Well I hope you're right. The deal runs out in 1972. We may not get such a good one next time round. When do I get to meet the chaps?"

"I expect to get them here at the end of the week. I've already got agreements. I should have the seniors here when you get back."

****

The taxi dropped Chas at the end of the quay in the evening twilight. He strolled toward the Ace's mooring thinking about all that had happened to shape his life in the last two years. Self doubt was not his style. He relished the excitement and commitment.

"Thank God there is no woman in my life," he said to himself. "I'm a free man. This is the life I want. Maybe in ten or twenty years I'll think differently. Who knows? I've got all the female company I need right here on the docks. Mum would be horrified if she knew about all my thoughts."

He stepped aboard the Ace and called for Saxon.

"Hi Sax. Are you aboard?"

"Sure thing, come below. I'm just doing a bit of stowing and list making. Victuals will arrive tomorrow, care of Cosalts.

There's still a lot to do before we sail. How are things with you? Your parents?"

"They're fine. A bit tearful but I told them we can always talk on the marine band. It's not as if this is the first time. They're quite used to me leaving but in a way this is a new start for me. What news of the crew?"

"The seniors are due on board at six tomorrow night and I told them to be sober otherwise they won't have a job. The rest are signing on the day after tomorrow. I hope."

They spent the next day stowing and hoisting the heavy fishing gear aboard with the help of Stainton's men. By evening, hot and sweaty, they were relaxing on the bridge deck, wetting their throats. Punctually at six they heard a hail from the quay.

"Hello Ace, can we come aboard?" Saxon slid back the opening port on the bridge and thrust his head out.

"Come on then. Are you all together?"

"Yes Boss. We met by the dock gates."

"Now then let's be seeing you. OK boys, meet Charlie."

Chas interrupted, "I don't want to cut across you Sax. but my Dad's called Charlie and I'm just plain Chas."

"OK, I'll start again." said Saxon with a grin. "Come and shake hands lads. This is Chas, the real Boss. We'll all be working for him although at sea he's bosun under Sean."

"Chas, this is Sean Bowyer, our Mate and Doug Mills, Senior Cook. We've an assistant arriving tomorrow, I hope. I don't know his name, the agency are sending one; then my friend Taffy Picton."

"Slow down a minute Sax. The cook?"

"Trust me Chas, the agency are reliable. They know me well enough not to send a loser."

"OK, but are we taking on any more from the agency?"

"Maybe, but the first trip will sort out any bad apples in the barrel. Good crew are hard to find if we're to have the best crew, happy to work as a team. All our officers are known to me. We've sailed together and they're friends. That's a big big plus, believe me."

"All right then. So we've got Taffy Picton as Chief Engineer. That's brilliant. He's used to working with Mirlees, couldn't be better and another signing?"

"I've to go ashore tomorrow. Another engineer's coming for interview. I'm meeting him in the Harbour Hotel."

"Shall I come?"

"No need, but I'll take Taffy with me. We do need two engineers."

"And that leaves?"

"John Fowler here. He's an old mate from the service. John and I were on minesweepers for a few months in '42. He stayed on and got a wavy-stripe, and Number One on HMS Bangor."

Chas said. "Nice to meet you John. Getting a bit old for this job?"

"I'm not doing it for the money. That's for sure. I want the experience. You can rely on me. I'll not let you down."

"John's our over qualified senior deckhand but he's studying for a ticket. Goodness knows why."

"I'm doing it 'cos I want to," said John. "I've been at sea since I was a cadet. The ship I'm on fills every need."

"Still waiting for the right woman to appear," said Saxon.

"I'm not married either," said Chas. "The Ace is my baby for now but I'll get hitched one day,"

"Meet the other experienced deckhands, Chas. They're all my old buddies. Mike, Scot, Trog and Robbie. I think they've gone below to stow their kit."

The following day Saxon, Sean and John were on the main dock gate to greet the remaining deckhands and the radio op., 'Sparks'. Then Taffy, John and Saxon went into the hotel to interview the second engineer and the second cook/deckhand.

Later as the crew finished their evening meal they were invited to the bridge deck to look around and to sign the ship's log-book.

Saxon said, "Get to know the ship inside out lads. The more questions you ask the better. You never know when you might have to stand in for someone else."

3 DAVID BROWN

David Brown stood in front of the full length mirror. He admired himself. His new clerical grey suit fitted him perfectly in spite of his rather noticeable expanding waist line. The suave young diplomat of yesteryear had long gone but in his place stood a man deeply lined with the experience of war and all that his contacts with MI6 entailed. He no longer dyed his temples believing, not without reason, that dignified grey sideboards gave him some 'gravitas'. Otherwise he was clean shaven, as his wife preferred.

That he was offered the rank of Ambassador and a knighthood to go with it had been a stroke of unexpected good fortune. From being a Second Secretary in Copenhagen he was being sent to Iceland because three other candidates ranking ahead of him had turned the position down. In a private interview at Number Ten, the Prime Minister had said,

"David, we need a steady hand on the tiller in Reykjavik, a man of experience who has the talent to make good friends. We are in a very weak position over the fishing question. Fishing is only a small industry, less than two per cent of our national GDP, nevertheless it is of supreme importance in certain areas. If fishing is banned on the Icelandic shelf thousands of fishermen and workers in dependant industries will suffer. My government will be forced to compensate trawler owners and those thrown out of work. The press will have a hey-day and with an election looming we can't afford to lose those seats, Hull, Grimsby, Fleetwood, Aberdeen. It will be a catastrophe."

"Yes, Prime Minister, I fully appreciate the problems."

"I'm sure you do. Andrew's term of office finishes in three weeks. Do you think you can manage it? I bet you're glad not to be going to Bangkok."

"My wife will be pleased." David had remarked.

****

Susan rang his flat in Esher one afternoon soon after the announcement became public.

"Hello David. Is my sister in?"

"Hello Susan. No she's not. Will I do?"

"Of course, my lovely in-law. Congratulations are in order. David, I'm so glad for you."

"How nice of you to ring. The 'phone's been going all morning. I don't know whether they are genuine or just glad to see the back of me for a spell. The Foreign Secretary was very nice and so was the PM. He said they chose me because I know so much about fishing. That was a joke. All I know about fishing I've learnt on the Spey"

"Out of the frying pan and into the fire, eh, David?"

"I hardly think Iceland can be described as a fire."

"Well it's got a volcano hasn't it? What does my sister think of it?"

"Lucy's cock-a-hoop. Likes the idea of being Lady Lucy. It's got a certain ring about it don't you think? Better than Lady Susan, with all respect to you of course dear."

"Fancy, you of all people, jumping two hoops at one go."

"What do you mean by that?"

"You know what I mean."

"Of all people indeed. Cheek. I've earned it. Anyway Iceland's not a sinecure. There are going to be fireworks for whoever is in post in 1972. By the way, what's going on with the trawler?"

"It is going on. That's what terrifies me. Do you know that deep water fishing is the most dangerous occupation there is? I was against the whole project and it wasn't because of the money. They won't believe me. Do you know that on average, ten fishermen die in home waters every month?"

"That's hard to believe but if true I say 'Thank God for the Mission'".

"Well it's true. I've read it somewhere. It really is true. I went to the docks with Charlie last week to see Chas."

"You mean Charles."

"Yes that's right. He likes to be Chas with his friends. So we call him Chas when we remember. Anyway it's a long drive home from there. Chas came with us for a break. We had an argument in the car. I was trying to dissuade them from going on with it but I failed of course."

David said, "Here am I, being sent to persuade the Icelanders to be reasonable. The FO is bringing some pressure to bear on British trawlers not to antagonise Iceland and your son goes and builds a new ship aimed at precisely what the FO is trying to stop, or at the very least reduce. It doesn't make sense. I can't believe that Charlie is encouraging him. It makes me very angry, so much for family loyalty."

"David, I've tried but they have an answer for everything. They say that the industry has realised that the catches are almost as good outside the twelve mile limit, in fact better since they're not competing with small inshore boats from Iceland itself."

"That's all very well for now but when the agreement expires in seventy-two they may have to fish fifty miles off shore."

"They have an answer to that too."

"Oh, indeed and what is that pray?"

"Chas says that the coastguards can't possibly patrol such a large area."

"Well, the navy can't be expected to shield them and I think he's wrong about their patrols."

"What more can I do?"

"Nothing I suppose but I don't like to see Charlie getting his fingers burnt. Have they produced any figures?"

"They certainly have. They say things are going well and she'll be paid for in three years if the going continues good or five if it isn't. Their big argument is that the capital will earn more than it would have in stocks and shares. I blame Abe for the whole thing."

"Now don't speak ill of the dead."

"Well if it wasn't for Abe we wouldn't have had millions to squander on a lost cause, would we?"

"I must admit it sounds over optimistic."

"They say that even if Iceland is shut down, the Ace and her gear will be adaptable for fishing almost anywhere else. It's not specific to Iceland. There's the Scottish west coast for instance."

"That's ridiculous."

Don't forget it's a freezer. Chas says because they don't need ice, they can land their catch anywhere in the EU."

"I know enough to know that freezers don't go to Iceland. By the time the catch is frozen they could be off-loading in Aberdeen or even Hull."

"Who knows what the market will do? If it does what some say, it will affect everyone. They say the old ships will be driven off, scrapped eventually. Even now there are huge opportunities to purchase good second hand side-winders. Nobody wants them anymore."

"Well then . . ."

"And very large freezers, much larger than the Ace will be, are coming in with distant waters in mind. Charlie makes great claims for efficiency. Freezers can stay at sea for a month or more."

"Well I'm not convinced. It's bound to come out. The Foreign Office won't believe me when I tell them I've had nothing to do with it. I can see my posting here being exchanged for Bangkok after all."

"Oh Lord."

"Sue, I'm sorry to cut you off but I've got a call on the other line," said David untruthfully. He thought chatting with Susan was exhausting.

"Goodbye then David. Do come and see us over a weekend, especially if Charles, I mean Chas, is home. He might listen to you more than he does to me."

"I'll try. Bye Sue."

Putting down the 'phone, he sank back in his chair for a few moments thinking about Charlie's family.

He realised that he felt sorry for his sister-in-law. She nearly always rang him, never vice versa. She seemed to be in need of a confidante. That she was in love with Charlie he didn't doubt for a minute but Charlie's dreadful war wound had left him impotent. Consequently over the years he had become irascible and in many ways feeble. He seemed to have left too many crucial decisions to his erratic son. His niece, Charlene, nearly eighteen, was no comfort. A pretty girl to look at but that's as far as it went. No help from her then. There was no doubt, Chas was going to be a big problem he thought. Headstrong and strong too in wind and limb. Once he had a target there would be no stopping him. No wonder he felt sorry for Susan. He would always remember that he had once been married to her, if only for twelve hours.

4   ZAP and KRAUSE

One of the forgotten corners of the inner city of Manchester is sandwiched between the ancient Cathedral and the bombed out remains of the railway stations of Exchange and Victoria. One day those tottering hovels of small businesses, brothels and doss-houses will be given a final nudge by the demolishers' ball and chain and the whole street will collapse in a large dust cloud. Until then Zap Hoch hobbles to his work every morning, Sundays included, as fast as his crippled legs will carry him.

Zap is one of life's tragedies. Brought up in pre-war Germany his parents intended to flee to Britain in 1939 when he was eight years old and his sister five. But the family got no further than the environs of Ostende. Caught up in the Allied retreat to Dunkirk his parents and sister were killed by a Nazi bomb aimed at the retreating army. Severely wounded in both legs and with no friends and no money in a foreign country, he crawled into a drain under a road and prepared to die. Luckily for his survival, a squad of British soldiers also decided to hide in the same stinking tunnel. Twelve hours later he found himself on a ship bound for England, his bloody legs encased in bandages.

He was brought up in Edgeworth Boys' Orphanage near Bolton in Lancashire. Despite the efforts of surgeons his legs never recovered. Although stunted and bowed, it soon became clear that he had a natural aptitude for drawing and lettering. His neat schoolwork, liberally illustrated with sketches in the margins of his exercise books, became the admiration of his teachers and peers. The Governors eventually found him permanent employment with a firm of solicitors in Manchester. He moved to a new council flat in Rusholm and supplemented his wages with part-time jobs in the area.

His life settled into a quiet routine of employment, turning out beautifully illuminated legal tracts and other documents until one day he had a most unusual assignment. Apart from the fact that he was sworn to secrecy by the smartly dressed young lady who stood before him, it became apparent on reading the documents that this was an illegal contract of a most unusual nature. Here was the stuff of blackmail. He knew the address and the names of the parties to the agreement. All he needed was a means of approaching them at their most vulnerable moment. He decided he could wait. Zap was a timid man. He knew instinctively that he, and he alone, apart from those involved, held a most important secret but he was frightened of perpetrating blackmail which carried a heavy prison sentence.

In the evening and at the weekend he would take the tram to Barlow Moor Road. He disguised himself by growing a wispy beard and tramped up and down past the house named Farmleigh. Slowly he accumulated knowledge of the pattern of life within. Ingratiating himself with the family and their servants, he was able to take post as part-time gardener since the calligraphy work was drying up. Sometimes he could intercept their mail, which the friendly postman left in his care. He overheard unguarded conversations. Soon he had learnt that there were two identical twin ladies and, by their mannerisms, was eventually able to name them independently. He witnessed the departure of one, the young Lady Lucy, in a car emblazoned with CD Plates and the other, Susan, to an unknown address which he knew must be local because she would return with her children every two weeks or so. Occasionally he would take the children for walks to the swings in Withington Park. The permanent occupants of the house, Mr and Mrs Robinson, were elderly and welcomed his attention to the lawns and flowerbeds. Weeks stretched to months and months to years. Slowly, however, his patience wore thin and he decided that, if ever he was to strike lucky, he would have to act.

The matter came to a head when the calligraphy work gradually ended as more modern methods took over. To his surprise he discovered that he was not alone in watching Farmleigh. Eventually the watchers approached him and recruited him to their cause. He learnt that the house was of interest to KGB, for what purpose he could only guess. The copies of the agreement, which he had treasured over the years, changed hands for the handsome sum of ten thousand pounds. A week later Zap was dead. His crippled legs finally gave way and he fell down the concrete steps leading to his flat. He never cashed the cheque. There were two mourners at his funeral, the lady who swept the steps and Oskar Krause.

****

Krause was born in 1923 in Berlin. His father had been a steel worker in the Krupp factory in the Ruhr district of Germany but that finished at the end of the First World War. The family moved to Berlin so that Herr Krause could take up a post with the newly formed Workers Socialist Party. Krause became one of the first members of the Hitler Youth. The rigorous physical training during those early years built a strong blond giant, a blue eyed monster of a man. Despite his intellectual dullness he moved slowly up the ranks of the Nazi Party. During the Second World War he was posted to the Battleship Tirpitz but when that vessel was severely damaged by Allied bombs in 1943, he went to the submarine pens in

Brest. His undercover work was to root out political dissenters amongst the U-Boat crews. He soon discovered that the officers were the worst. As a gauleiter, occasionally sailing with the fleet, he became the most hated man on the station.

With the dissolution of the German forces in 1945 he was recruited to join the Communist Stasi police and was assigned to security at the Harz Missile Factory in Eastern Germany. He worked under a certain Colonel Rostovsky. Apart from guard duties he collected anecdotal stories, gossip and intercepted mail of all the Harz staff, which he fed to Stasi and KGB records. Scientists and engineers as well as more lowly employees of the factory came under his scrutiny.

In 1953 the security of the factory was compromised by the activities of a British spy, named Charlie Forbes, though they could never be certain if that was his real name. The Colonel, desperate to regain his reputation after this, organised a group of agents. Krause and three others were ordered to carry out a foray on mainland Britain. The home of the spy in Cleethorpes, Yorkshire, was raided on the night of 4th July. Forbes was not at the address but Charlie's Aunt Peggy, who tried to obstruct their search of the house, was stabbed to death by Krause's colleague, Bruno Lang.

Later, Charlie was captured in Manchester by Krause and Rostovski's men. He was taken to a rendezvous with the Russian sail training ship, 'Lenin'. Whilst escaping into international waters south of Ireland the ship was illegally boarded by crew from a British destroyer who threatened to sink the Lenin unless the spy was handed back to them. The Captain, Vladimer Maikovitch, of the Lenin shot Rostovski but put it about that it was by the boarding party and subsequently, in Moscow, Krause was put on trial. He was the sole remaining member of the group left alive. As a sop to the British, he was convicted of the murder of Miss Peggy Petrie and sentenced to ten years of hard labour. In the long and lonely night hours in his cell he planned how he would take his revenge on the master spy who put him there.

On his release he applied for a post with the Stasi/KGB having special responsibility for searching out collaborators who could be turned against agents of the Western powers. In 1965 he was appointed in charge of the security of an East German flotilla of trawlers patrolling the whole of the North Sea, the Barent Sea, and Icelandic waters as far out as Greenland, his vessel the 9,000 tonne depot and freezer ship, Kerenski.

5 MORNING DEPARTURE

Saxon rose at first light and went up to the bridge. Looking out over the dock he saw little movement. Across the dock wall he could see the grey waters of the Humber merging with the distant mist. He dialled the cook's berth on the intercom. A sleepy voice answered,

"Wadoeewan."

"Wake up you lazy bastard. We sail in half an hour. Rouse the crew and get some breakfast inside them."

"Aye, aye skipper."

Then he went to the mate's cabin.

"Sean, we said last night we would get away by six. Where are they?"

"Sorry Boss, I over-slept. It won't happen again."

"Get the lads on deck. Get everything stowed away. The gates will open in about fifteen minutes and I want to get the first of the ebb."

"Aye, aye."

"Saxon knew at this time of year that the North Sea would be rough after a week of gales. Nevertheless the fishing on the Icelandic banks would be at its best. Most of the fleet had already departed. He must get going. The Ace of Spades slipped her mooring in Hull fish dock and set a northerly course for the Pentland Firth.

The voyage across the shallow Moray Firth was a shake down exercise for the new crew. Twenty miles out, Saxon ordered the net to be shot for the first time. He throttled back the engine until the Ace was making only three knots. With Sean on the helm he had an all-round view of the action on the deck below the bridge. All hands, bar the engineers and the cooks, were there ready to carry out their assigned tasks. Saxon watched John give every man the detailed orders necessary for the speedy and safe handling of the new equipment.

Chas was there on the deck supervising the men on the winches.

"Make sure the net runs out smoothly Mike, and doesn't snag, he said." The hands operating the winches smiled at each other. One of them gave Chas the V-sign since they knew the routine already. Saxon had explained the gear the previous evening, having taken them all on a conducted tour of the Ace. They knew that the open jaws of the net would entrap anything in its path but the graded mesh size near the mouth allowed small fry and juveniles to escape. The rollers along the foot-rope were designed to ride over any rough seabed and avoid destroying the habitat. John, over anxious for the safety of the crew and far from being a silent observer of all this activity was getting in the way of his own team.

With the stern doors open the men on the winches released first the cod end and then the long conical tube of the main trawl followed by the warps. As soon as the otterboards submerged the neck of the trawl started to open wide. The Granton trawl hit the sea bed after about eight hundred metres of warp had been run out. The helmsman could feel the increased tension and the shock as the engine laboured with the strain. Saxon had said,

"You'll soon get the feel of it, Sean. Listen to the change in the engine note and watch for the increase in tension in the main warps."

That evening, safely anchored in Scapa Flow and with a small catch gutted and in the freezer, they met in the mess over a beef stew to discuss the success of their haul. Saxon went through the operations of their first teamwork together, praising the good points and pointing out the failings where time was wasted or procedures exposed the men to dangers. He said,

"Not bad lads. Not bad at all for a shake down but we've more to learn. This is a new ship built using the latest ideas from the 'Junella' and 'Fairtry'. Some say that stern trawling is a gimmick but it's the future. Mechanical methods are taking over. Without so much manhandling we'll have smaller crews and more money for you all. Get to know your place in the team and then we'll all change places until everyone is familiar with the gear. If there are any shortcomings we'll sort them when we get home. Yes Mike. Did I see your hand up?"

"Skip. We'll have a hell of a job in the fish room, sorting and grading. It's the gutting machine which will let us down if we have a heavy haul. I don't think we'll keep up."

"OK. I'm glad you brought this up. Point number one, you've got to keep up. Two, I can't have a new haul dumped on top of the last one. If that's going to happen I'll slow down or else we'll lengthen the time between hauls. I think you'll get better, too much 'finger' trouble. It's a new machine and it will take some getting used to."

"Can we have two gutters?"

"I'll think about that. It may be the only way. Just for now pick on the best men for the job and see if they can speed it up. A lot depends on it. OK?"

"OK Skip, we'll do our best."

"Do some of it by hand. Use your best men if you have to."

"OK Skip."

"Any more questions?" There were none, only a few yawns.

"Now then get your heads down because we've work to do tomorrow." Saxon grinned with satisfaction at the team of experienced trawler-men he had enlisted. Chas, for his part, realised he had a lot to learn about his vessel and the crew. Early next morning with a cold front forecast from the west, the Ace pulled up her anchor and headed for Iceland.

After three weeks of fishing, homeward bound, when he and Chas were alone together, Saxon said,

"Not bad for the first trip, I reckon we have about ten grand's worth in the fish room, all nicely sorted, graded and frozen solid. You've got a ship to be proud of and the best crew I could muster. Give them time, weeks rather than months, and they'll have it all up there." He tapped his forehead.

****

Twelve months later.

Fourteen days out from Hull one night in November 1968 a force ten storm came down from the Arctic and whipped the waves into a frenzy in the shallow sea north of Iceland. There was no moon and not a star to be seen.

"Bloody damn," Saxon said. "I've never known a night like this, blacker then effin ink." The good fishing had tempted them to linger too long in those unwelcoming waters. The main fleet had heeded the weather warning and sailed south. Now Saxon and Sean had been caught out by a sudden shift in the rising gale. All day the wind had been from the south west but now from the ice fields the bitter wind was building up a layer of ice on rigging and decks. The ship laboured to carry this extra load and the storm threatened to drive them onto the lee shore.

Chas climbed up the companion into the bridge where Saxon and Sean were discussing the best action to take.

"We can nip into Gjogur bay and put down an anchor or two," said Saxon, raising his voice above the howling wind. "It should be sheltered in there. I've done it before. Or we can beat round Hombjarg and keep her head to wind until it dies down."

"It will be calmer nearer the ice." shouted Sean as the first of the really large rollers slammed into the bow. "We're about three miles inside the fishing limit here, more if we put into the bay."

"Surely the coastguards won't arrest us for taking shelter if the trawl is lashed down," Chas said.

"Some of the coastguards won't bother but we can't rely on that. We just don't know. We can't risk losing the catch. It could be an expensive trip. It would be different if the hold was empty."

"Do they know where we are in this shit?"

"Quite likely, they've got radar on the land stations too."

"If you agree then Saxon, I think we should get round the head and when daylight comes try to keep outside the limit."

"OK, I'll rouse Doug for a hot drink and a sandwich. John and I are whacked. Sean, call me if you need help. Get round the headland and keep her head up well offshore out of the breakers."

"Aye aye Skip."

"If we broach we'll be food for the fishes. If you see a light call me. OK?"

"Aye aye," replied Sean.

Three miles off the headland the seaway, kicked up by the underwater rocks and aggravated by the flood tide became the worst Chas had ever experienced. Waves like mountains came roaring out of the night. The Ace was tossed about like a toy. The bridge deck took the full force of the storm as solid green water came crashing against the safety glass. Chas silently thanked Saxon for strapping him tightly into the Mate's chair before he went below. Sean was already firmly strapped to the skipper's. From time to time he could hear the engine screaming as the propeller came out of the water. Twenty minutes later he grabbed the intercom and dialled zero for Saxon. He needn't have bothered. By some miracle Sax was already beside them, standing with one leg firmly braced against the combing below the port light.

"Throttle back to stop that racket when it does that," he shouted above the thunder of yet another wave. Stubbornly the Ace lay in the trough, threatening to yaw with the force of the breakers tumbling down the face of the gigantic waves. The wind howling in the rigging like a pack of wolves blotted out everything bar shouting.

"Give her all you've got on the engine when you can Sean. We've got to push her round to face the weather. Put the helm over," Saxon shouted above the thundering seaway. The Ace slowly responded as the crest tumbled towards them. To the men on the bridge it felt as though the ship was standing on her stern-board. With a roar like an express train, the sea passed under as she upended and plunged her bow once more into the trough.

"Aye aye," Sean responded at the top of his voice and trying not to show his panic. Would she come up or has the wave found its way below?

"Get her head to wind and then she'll come up. I'll call the hands. Get on the intercom for Taffy and find out if all's well in the engine room. I'll take a look to make sure he's still alive."

Slowly the ship responded to the helm. Another sea, almost as big as the first killer wave, came thundering out of the darkness. The white foam of its crest was briefly illuminated by the ships lights. The hurricane sliced off the top and flung it against the bridge deck. The bow reared up as the wave stood her on her stern-doors again for the hundredth time but passed underneath as she tipped forward and took a nose dive into the heart of the next, bringing green water up to the bridge.

"She can't take much more of this," Chas thought to himself. "We're stopped in the water and the helm won't answer." Saxon came back on deck. On and on the unrelenting storm tested crew and vessel to the limits of endurance. Water cascading over the trawl-deck threatened to carry away the nets and other gear.

"The lads are checking the hold. All's well below. There's a lot of water in the bilge. I've started the pump," Saxon shouted.

A wave passed beneath as the Ace took another dive. They heard the impact again as several tons of sea crashed against the safety glass. The whole superstructure shook as the radar housings came crashing down.

"We need to go about Sax. We're heading almost due north," Sean said.

"We can't risk turning in this. We'll be rolled over. Keep her head up for God's sake."

"Are you all right Skip? It's not your watch."

"No, I'm fine. We've got to get off shore, away from this rip. Keep the screw under."

"Have we still got sea room Skip? It feels as though we're being pushed astern."

"The Decca says we're holding our own . . . just. Make more westing. We're too close for comfort. The tide will change soon. We must get more room. It will be easier further out."

"You've got to be joking Sax."

"Just a comparison. The storm is forecast to abate by dawn. We should have gone for the bay after all. Maybe when it gets light we'll turn and run more offshore . . . We'll see."

With the first glints of light shining in the east, Sean was able to put the Ace on a sou'westerly course and run before the remains of the gale. By the evening they set a course for the Pentland Firth and their home port.

****

At Hull the yard straightened out the buckled guard rails and stern doors adding a bit of extra steel for strength without charge. The bill for replacing lost gear, radio antennae and radar was considerable.

"Please don't do it again," said Stainton with a grin but putting on a more serious face he said, "Annabella went down ten nights ago, lost with all hands".

At this shocking news Chas bowed his head in sorrow.

"I knew some of those guys. They were a good bunch."

Sean came bounding into the mess, breaking the solemn tension of the moment. He waved a piece of paper.

"I got it. I got it chaps." There was silence until Mike said, "Got what, old man, the beer ration?"

"No, much more important than that, my masters' ticket." Chas interrupted,

"Congratulations Sean, let's cut into that beer, lads, and wish him many congratulations. I hope you'll stay until the end of the season. With luck I'll get your Mate's ticket."

That year marked the best fishing they ever achieved. Saxon stuck strictly to the twelve mile limit but Chas, when on watch, was not so careful with his navigation. On two occasions the Ace was chased out of the controlled area by 'Thor', a coastguard vessel. Saxon was angry.

"If we get a bad reputation they'll never give us any peace," he said. "You'll be sorry. I'm warning you. I don't want to spend a night in jail and I don't suppose you do."

"Aye aye skipper," he responded in his implacable way.

They enjoyed four more years of good fishing, bringing home big catches and sharing the proceeds. After each voyage Saxon calculated the crew's share, giving double to himself as skipper. All the Ace's overheads were paid, including the heavy bill for fuel.

Chas for his part just took out the interest which he paid to his father. In those years the initial loan had almost been repaid. He was on course to be a rich man.

The British Embassy and Residence.
Reykjavik·Iceland

6 THE LETTER

During his first few months in office, Sir David Brown had worked hard to gain the friendship and trust of all the influential Icelanders. Lucy enjoyed every minute, organising dinners, cocktail parties and reciprocal visits to the homes of members of the Icelandic parliament, visits to Iceland by British MP's and 'Industrial Giants' intent on expanding their exports. In spite of the relentless pressure of the diplomatic round and keeping a permanent welcoming smile on her face, Lucy enjoyed playing up to her new 'Lady' Lucy title but the endless late nights took their toll and at the end of their first year she felt drained.

The winters in Reykjavik, with only about three hours of twilight, are dark, cold and wet but in the spring the city-dwellers, humans and animals alike, wake to the New Year and, suitably dressed, take to the great outdoors. David found himself enjoying the convivial shooting and hunting parties, which his predecessor had done so much to inaugurate. The NATO—American base at Keflavik was the most important issue on the diplomatic horizon.

David would arrange to visit the Base as soon as he could make a date with the NATO Base Commander, General Hank Thorne. He could foresee that the Icelandic Parliament, heavily influenced by the Communists, would use its existence as a bargaining tool to enforce compliance with the fishing limits. While this was no immediate threat to fishing on the continental shelf, any further extension of the limit would spell doom to trawling by British, German and French vessels.

When the Communist Party had been in power its future had seemed to be under threat. Since the election however, and the success of the new Conservative coalition, that problem was shelved for the moment. The continued existence of the Base had been used by the Icelandic Government to great effect in the 1961 settlement of the fishing dispute. The next dispute, which would arise in 1971/2, would bring the whole business out into the open again. He was dreading it.

****

One day in February of 1970, after David had been in office for six months he found a letter on his desk. The envelope had been neatly typed.

"Private and Confidential to
His Excellency, Sir David Brown,
The British Residence,
Reykjavik   *Date 1-02-70*

Your Excellency,
Let me introduce myself. I am the Commodore of the East German fishing fleet at present stationed in Reyoarfjorour at Latitude 64 degrees 55 minutes North and Longitude 13 degrees 50 minutes West. My flag ship is the Kerenski, the mother ship. I have twenty five trawlers under my command.

My primary aim, above the mundane task of feeding my countrymen, is to bring Iceland under the influence of the USSR, to close the NATO base at Keflavik and to deny fishing in these waters to other nations, primarily Britain. I am aware that historically Iceland and Britain are friendly but that relations between your country and theirs are deteriorating over the question of fishing rights.

Although your Foreign Office and my agency have opposing aims, I hope that you will co-operate with me. Between 1950 and 1953 I was employed by the KGB and in that capacity I obtained details of the Forbes and Robinson families. It may come as a surprise to you that I know your marriage is a fraud and the lady now posing as your wife, Lady Lucy Brown, is actually Mrs Susan Forbes.

To assure you of my goodwill I intend to keep this information to myself but I hope you will arrange to meet me as soon as possible in order to discuss our respective positions in more detail. I will be in touch.

Regards,
Oskar Krause, Kapitan.

PS: At the first sign of dangerous weather my fleet will return to shelter in this fjord.

David sat at his desk in a cold sweat. The enormity of what he might be forced to do was unbearable. If his family's secret was out it would wreck his career and probably result in jail sentences. His rise through the departments of the Foreign Service had been slow since returning to England in 1945. He had been in charge of a network of spies in Switzerland during the Second World War but, when he was exposed, declared persona non-grata by the Swiss Department of the Interior. As a result his seniority had been overtaken by other diplomats closer to home.

"These reminiscences will do nothing to help the present," he thought. "I will have to involve Lucy and she will no doubt write to Susan and Charlie. All hell could break loose if this gets out. How on earth does this come to be in the hands of the East German Secret Service? Swapping the twins' identities had seemed such a good idea at the time. Although Charlie's mother and Aunt Edna had rumbled the deception within a week, nobody else had. The two old ladies had kept their council. Lucy (as she was then) had always loved Charlie. Susan, for her part, had set her cap at me and my career. Now she is Lady Lucy and Lucy is Susan."

It had been difficult at first but as soon as they moved to Copenhagen everything had been easy. With a sigh of resignation he pulled a sheet of embassy notepaper from the rack in front of him, took out his Swan fountain pen and started to write, slowly and deliberately, to his erstwhile wife and now sister-in-law. Then he went down to the Residence Assembly room where Lucy was helping the staff prepare the table for the next dinner. David started,

"Lucy dear, do you mind if I interrupt?"

"What is it David? I'm very busy at the moment. This will only take half an hour."

"OK. I've got something to tell you. It's important."

"Will it keep?"

"Come up to the study when you can."

David climbed the stairs back to his desk. Lucy could tell from his demeanour that he had something serious on his mind. She was anxious to find out what it was. As soon as she could she followed him.

"Here, read this," he said as soon as she entered. She sat at his desk and took up the letter. Her hand began to tremble. Having read it, her mind in turmoil, she said,

"Who the hell is Oskar Krause? Do we know him? He's not on any mailing list that . . ."

"I don't know who he is beyond what he says there. He's trying to blackmail me, us."

"Never give in to blackmail darling. You know the rules. The Government will not tolerate it, never has and never will."

"Never's a big word," David replied. "HMG do give in when it suits them but nobody is supposed to know about it, least of all the press. Anyway this is a private matter. We can't tell the government under any circumstances. I, possibly you as well, could be locked up for fraud."

"What about my sister and Charlie?"

"Them too, but it's not so serious in their case. Charlie works for the NHS, it's true, but I hardly think it's in the same category."

"Have you got a plan then?"

"No I haven't. At least the bastard is not asking for money, not yet anyway. There is just the small matter of being a traitor to my country and my calling at stake."

"Are you going to meet him then?"

"Yes, I really think I will. He hasn't got all the counters. He's revealed himself in a most unexpected way. To an extent he trusts me not to wreck my own career."

"If you sup with the devil . . ."

"I know all that and you're right of course. I've written to Belvedere, to Susan. She should get my letter the day after tomorrow. It's gone in the bag."

"Is that wise?"

"I've marked it private."

Three days later David and Lucy waited on the tarmac for Susan's plane to taxi toward them. The embassy car took the trio to the Residence. Susan started to cry.

Lucy said, "Oh dear, things haven't changed much with you then, have they?"

"I'm sorry. I'm sorry, sorry, sorry. I can't help it can I? We're in trouble aren't we? I'm upset. Why were you so vague David? I just had to come, like you said. I didn't tell Charlie much. How could I? You just said that we've been found out by a criminal from the Eastern Block and he's blackmailing us. How much does he want?"

"It's not money he want's. He wants me to be a traitor."

"Oh God. Is the penalty for that still death?"

"I don't think it would come to that."

"Don't be silly Susan," said Lucy. "This is not a time for dramatics. Even Fuchs only got fifteen years."

"Fifteen years. What will my Charlie get then?"

"Now let's be sensible and calm down. David, you tell us. How did this all happen?"

"That's just it. I haven't the foggiest idea. He says he has seen our agreements."

"That's nonsense. Mine's locked away in Charlie's desk. What about yours?"

"Ours is at the bank in London. But he could have seen copies."

"That's got to be it, of course. When I went to that firm I thought the man was a bit spooky. Called himself Zap."

"Well he's zapped us all right. Anyway, it's no use thinking about him. The beans are well and truly spilt now. He could be anywhere. Even if we find him it won't do us any good. Oskar Krause has told us he works for the KGB or at least he used to."

"This is leading nowhere," said Lucy. "Our only remedy is to shut him up."

"What bump him off like 007?"

"For heavens sake Susan, this is serious."

"But how and what does he want from you David?"

"He knows a lot about us. It's scary. I've had another letter. It came through the ordinary Icelandic mail. He must have someone on shore. That doesn't surprise me. You may as well know that the Icelandic Communist party is very active. They call themselves the Labour Union Associates. Their Secretary is Reynir Josefsson, who also happens to be the Minister of Fisheries in the coalition Government."

"Can we see it, the letter?"

"If you like. It just says that bad weather is forecast and I will be able to board the Kerenski tomorrow. I've got a motor boat laid on. It belongs to a friend of mine, Haraldur. I've been less than frank with him, I'm afraid. I just told him it was a goodwill mission prompted by Whitehall. Anyway he's got lobster pots in the bay so he wants to check them while I do my business."

"Do be careful dear," said Lucy.

"Nothing untoward will happen to me at this stage. Meanwhile let's sleep on the problem and talk some more tomorrow evening. Have a look round the capital while you're here Susan. Lucy can get the car."

"I shan't sleep a wink tonight, David."

"I think that goes for the three of us," said David with a laugh. "But if you have any bright ideas in the night then wake me up and share them with us."

****

On the following morning David was by the quay at Reyoarfjorour. His friend Haraldur waved from his launch, moored a short distance offshore. David pulled on his over-trousers and anorak while he waited. The forecast gale had created a severe chop outside but in the fjord the sea was moderately calm. In spite of the shelter provided by the small cabin he anticipated a wet crossing.

"Good morning," he shouted when the launch came alongside. Haraldur shook him firmly by the hand. "Where is she, the Kerenski?"

"Just round the headland. It'll take us about fifteen minutes. It's a bit of luck really. I've got a trot of pots down over there, two miles away. Here's my Aldis. Take it with you and give me a flash when you want collecting. I can be back in twenty minutes or so. If you don't show in an hour I'll call the coastguard and if I haven't finished I can always come back tomorrow."

"It's very good of you, Haraldur."

"No trouble. Nice to have company. I've got several trots up and down the coast and a launch at each bay, not all mine of course."

"What's the Kerenski like? Have you seen her before?"

"Oh yes, she comes back here every summer. Has done for the last few years. She used to be an Argentinian freezer, about 10,000 tons, built primarily for the export of meat. Now she's working for the Huns. She freezes down marketable fish, all the rest she cooks and turns into fishmeal, that's fertiliser. It's a very handy operation. Every six to eight weeks she goes back to Danzig to off load and re-fuel while the fleet get some respite in Bergen or Copenhagen."

Haraldur brought his launch smartly alongside the Kerenski. As David reached the deck from the companion way of the East German factory ship, he was confronted by a tall giant of a man in the prime of life. Obviously fit and athletic in posture and build, his blue eyes and blond hair marked him as an Aryan specimen who had probably been a good member of Hitler's 'Master Race'. Arrogance seemed to seep out of his every pore.

"Herr Krause I presume," said David

"I am pleased to meet you, Excellency." Krause held out his hand in greeting. David did not respond, setting the scene for the interview and fearing perhaps that his fingers would be cracked.

Krause, put slightly off balance by his guest's unfriendly gesture, led the way up to the captain's private cabin.

He said, "It will be quiet in my cabin and we won't be disturbed. The noise you can hear comes from the processing. It's a hive of industry below." Alone with him, David came straight to the point. He had decided that pleasantries, normal in diplomatic circles, would not be appropriate in these circumstances, that cold formality would place him in a stronger position to deal with the blackmailer. He took an instant dislike to this self-assured giant with his false smile.

"What do you want of me Herr Krause?"

"I shall come to that in a minute, Excellency. First would you be so kind as to enlighten me on one or two issues."

"It depends what those issues are," said David guardedly.

"Please call me Oskar and I'll call you David, if you don't mind. It is better to be informal, nicht?"

"Call me what suits you. I shall continue with Herr Krause."

"Can I take it that you have possibly another year, possibly two, in your post."

"You could be right about that. It's unlikely to be more and may be less. Why?"

"My project may stretch over two years and I need continuity."

"What else?"

"Do you deny that your wife's real position is that of wife to Dr Forbes of Bolton?"

"I shall neither confirm nor deny that. If you have evidence of this extraordinary accusation I should like to see it. It may be that I can allay your suspicions. Denying will serve no good purpose since you would then be convinced that I was lying, whatever the truth of the matter. The moment for me to act in refuting this wild idea will come when you make a public pronouncement of the issue. Why not do it? Bring it all out into the light of day. If you have created some kind of evidence, I shall be interested to see it."

"See it you shall. But publicise it no, because I do not want to wreck your career or to disgrace you. I merely want you to offer a little help to me. It may surprise you to know that this new career of mine also hangs on the successful outcome of this project."

"You have already stated in your letter what your objective is. I can assure you that you will stand no chance at all in closing the NATO base at Keflavik. We consider that the base is vital to the security of the Western Allies. Our listening devices, of which you are fully aware, are you not, are able to detect all ship movements in the Denmark Strait. Such intelligence is very important to us."

"I spent ten years in a Russian jail through your actions David. You see I have a personal incentive too."

"You've lost me now Herr Krause. I don't recollect any actions of mine which could possibly have resulted in your jail sentence."

"Think about it David. Think about the day that your navy rescued the spy who is now your brother-in-law."

"I remember the day clearly, but where were you?"

"I was on board the ship you threatened to sink, 'The Lenin'."

"The destroyer didn't sink it. All this is a long time ago. I can't see that it affects the issue."

"Oh but it does as I hope to convince you."

"Let me see this so called evidence then."

"Very well. Here, on the table, and here is a code for your radio at the Embassy. If you activate it I will know that you wish to speak further."

David picked up the heavy paper.

"These are plainly hand written forgeries."

"Forgeries or not, it doesn't matter. We're not in a court now. Even forgeries can tell the truth. Does one of the twins have a scar on her shoulder I wonder?"

"My wife has a faint scar from a riding accident years ago. You seem to be very well informed about my family Krause. I'm truly astonished but nothing you have shown me so far convinces me and I am sure nobody else either. Now I must go. My motor boat will be waiting."

"Good day. I hope you have an easy crossing. The wind is getting up. It always does at this time of day."

David climbed down the companion to the main deck. Across the water, about a mile away he could see Haraldur standing in the stern of his little fishing launch. He switched on the Aldis lamp and pointed it in his direction. After about two minutes he saw his uplifted arm in acknowledgement. Driving to Reykjavik he was deep in thought wondering how much he should tell Lucy and Susan.

****

Back at the Residence David asked the twins to join him in the sitting room. Suitably supported by glasses of sherry he reported the gist of his interview.

"This Krause chap knows me. We may never have met but he knows about me I'm sure. He even knows that you have a scar on your shoulder Lucy. Anyway, whatever his previous contact may have been, he has the evidence all right. I was shocked although I tried not to show it. He has absolutely perfect copies of your agreements, even on the same paper and I'm convinced in the same hand. Zap must have made them and sold them to Krause or a colleague of his. But why did he hang on to them all these years? It's a mystery."

"They wouldn't have been worth very much at the outset. We could have denied it or just swapped back again," retorted Lucy.

"Why don't we just swap now?" said Susan helpfully.

"Don't be silly dear. It's 1970. The years have not been very kind to us. Besides too many people know us as we are."

"I could hold my own in another strip club anywhere."

"Don't kid yourself. You can't wind back the clock. Although it would be rather fun if we could."

"Come on girls. Take this more seriously. We haven't time to reminisce. There's no question of swapping back . . . for personal reasons if for nothing else. No, I think I'll have to have another talk with Krause to find out what he wants me to do. I can't possibly be seen to be acting for the Communists. If that were to be the case, my tenure here would soon finish and probably my diplomatic career as well."

"So what next?" demanded Susan. "I seem to have come on a bit of a wild goose chase. You could have told me all that over the phone David. Just ignore the whole thing. This chap Krause will finish his fishing and go back home."

"I'm not very happy about that. OK, so Krause may go home but he bears a grudge. He had ten years in a Russian prison. It may have been in Siberia for all I know and for some reason he blames it on me. I want to get to the bottom of that but worse, he has collaborators here in Reykjavik. He didn't post that letter to me. Who did?"

"Well the answers may satisfy your tidy mind, David, but they are of no concern to me," said Susan. "I'm going back on the first plane tomorrow. I'll bring Charlie up to date and we'll give you a ring."

"Don't talk on the phone about all this. If you do, don't mention or even hint that any outside agency is forcing me to behave in any way against British and NATO interests. Even a letter could be dangerous. Why do you suppose I asked you to come over?"

"If this chap intends to assassinate you, why didn't he do it?"

"What? You mean on the Kerenski."

"Yes. Of course. He could have killed you there and then and put you over the side. I think you put yourself in danger going on board at all."

"He doesn't want me dead. He's got some sort of a plan for me which he claims will help his career. He's not going to alert the authorities or get his crew involved in an enquiry. We are in a civilised country. Haraldur expected me back within the hour. We agreed what to do if I didn't show."

The following morning Susan took the first flight home.

7 RANSACKED

The catch had just been unloaded in Scrabster harbour. Chas was disappointed at the market prices. He told his agent that they could have got a better result in the Hull Auction.

"Maybe you can Chas but remember I'm saving you a whole day's sailing. Stick with me and I can have you back fishing in two days."

"I'm not sure it's worth it. Direct selling is all very well but the lads do need time off. They want to get back to their homes. We're not going out again until next week. Meanwhile I'm going home too."

"Believe me. You won't get better prices on the spot market. It's all about what comes in on the day."

As the refrigerator trucks drew away Chas watched them grinding slowly up the steep hill from the dockside. It was then that Saxon dropped his bombshell.

"I'm sorry Chas, I really am. That was my last trip."

"What do you mean?"

"I mean that I'm resigning. Now, right now."

"You can't mean that, surely. You've not given me any warning, any notice. We have an agreement, remember?"

"I know that, I'm sorry, I really am sorry. I've made up my mind to give you my share of that catch . . . By way of compensation you understand."

"Come and sail with me as Mate. Keep your share and sail with me once more."

"Now you're tempting me. Marjory will have left home by now. She said she would pick me up today. She'll be livid if she drives all this way for nothing."

"You could say we are short handed until John gets back."

"No, that's not fair. Let me think about it while I pack."

"But if you've packed up that means you've decided but what brought this on."

"I'm too old for this game. I can't stand the tension. It's only a question of time before we get caught inside the limit."

"OK, we are taking a chance but only a small one. We have radar and with a bit of a start we can be outside the line with fourteen knots. There are forty to fifty boats out there, not all British, all doing the same thing. It's long odds that they will pick on us."

"I don't see it that way. There's warp cutting going on, ramming and all sorts of harassment. The tension's too much. They've even opened fire on a couple of occasions. The crew feel it too. We're making good money but that doesn't compensate for our health. Have you thought of that?"

"Well I have to cope with tension too."

"If we lose our gear it will cost you ten thousand pounds at least. If we have to go home with an empty hold it'll cost more. Don't you see? The only thing that bothers me is that if I go, your crew may go too. That will make me feel guilty but then again I feel guilty anyway. I tell you, the tension is too much. I've got to go home. Sorry . . . I won't be signing on again with anyone else. I may do a bit in my own wee boat, just round the bay. You can't expect an old man to do what a youngster can do."

"You're not old."

"Well maybe not in your language Chas, but frankly I want to do something new with my life and that's the truth . . . I think I'll have to go after all; make the break right now. Marge will be here in a couple of hours. I'll go and pack my kit. No hard feelings then?"

"You've been a good friend. You'll always be a good friend. Where shall I get a mate?"

"John's been studying for it. He's got the sea time and only one more paper to write. He's older than the rest and not new to the sea. He'll be ideal and welcome extra money. I happen to know he's getting married and plans to buy a house. You don't really need so many deck hands anyway. You could sail with the crew you have tomorrow if need be."

"Anyway we're having a break. The weather's foul and forecast to be like this for the rest of the month. I'll promise the lads a bonus if they turn in next week. I can't pretend I'm not choked but the Forbes family can cope with challenges. My Dad was clearing Jerry mines on the Swiss border in 1942 and he was only twenty-one. If he can rise to a challenge I know I can. So don't fret about me. I can cope. With one less man aboard everyone will get a bigger share. Anyway I might find a school leaver who wants to go to sea, if only for the experience, an apprentice."

"Not a bad idea that. Make sure he's over eighteen though."

"I shall miss you Sax. Go pack your kit. I'll give you a hundred for your sextant as a souvenir. I may need it one day if we go across the pond. You won't be needing it, that's for sure."

"Done. I'll meet you in the pub whilst we wait for Marge."

"And what about your black book?"

"That's private Chas. You should know by now that skippers don't share their black books with anyone.

Anyway it's all in my shorthand. I think I'll give it to the Hull museum. Your own book is more up to date than mine."

****

Chas arrived at Belvedere to find his home in chaos.

"Hell, Mum. What's going on? Having the place decorated or something?"

"No, we've just had burglars."

"Why us?"

"I don't know. They think we're a posh house I suppose. Your room's OK.

Not been touched. The police think they were disturbed because they did downstairs pretty thoroughly but hardly anything upstairs."

"Gosh, perhaps we were a bit lucky."

"Being burgled is not lucky."

"What's gone then? I can see they rooted through all the drawers and bookcases."

"Nothing much. The police think they were after jewellery or money."

"How strange. In that case you would think they would make a bee-line for the main bedroom."

"I've given up wondering. I just want to get the place straight again."

"I suppose."

"Tell me how it all went."

"Not so well. The catch was light, the agent gave us a rotten price and Saxon has left us. It's not the fish that were gutted, it's me."

"Have you heard about the proposed new fishing limit? Will it make any difference?"

"I'll say. What do you know about it, Mum?"

"Only what David tells us. You know how I felt about it at the start, even before you started building. If only you had listened to me then."

"Mum, The Ace is nearly paid for."

"Yes, that's all very well but I think there will be a glut of boats for sale when it happens. You'll never get back your investment."

"We don't intend to stop fishing, if that's what you think. Maybe the sidewinders . . . could be a disaster for them. They can't go much further without freezing. Most haven't got freezing. We may have to give up Iceland and go further afield. The man from MAFF thinks we should try off the western Hebrides."

"So we won't see much of you then."

"Maybe. I spent most of this trip trying to dodge their coastguard. Several times I hauled the trawl with only half a catch in it. They've got a cutter which they tow and try to get astern of us so they can cut our warps. It's like a giant pair of scissors."

"I'm sorry."

"There must have been about twelve boats that lost their trawl nets, everything. The crews will get no pay out. One vessel was nearly arrested but managed to hide behind a group of us just outside the limit. He was so lucky. The navy are useless. The older men say it's not like last time. They say that in the fifties and early sixties they used to protect the fishing fleet. Now it seems they're terrified of the coastguards."

"Have you read the newspapers?"

"Not yet, why?"

"Some of them think you should stop taking Iceland's fish."

"Well they've got a point I suppose. The fact is we've always fished off the Icelandic coast and a lot of people will be out of work if we stop tomorrow. Twelve miles is OK but fifty miles is a bit much don't you think?"

"I don't think anything. It's really up to the government to sort out what's what but I do think it's all wrong for them to go about barging into other people's trawlers. Someone might get hurt."

"Several have. One coastguard electrocuted himself. It was on the Aegir. She collided with our Apollo and then stopped while the engineer carried out a repair. They said that Statesman, you know, one of our tugs, although actually at least a mile away, had caused a wave which came inboard and swamped his welding set. There's talk of the Icelanders breaking diplomatic relations. That will spoil David's efforts big time."

"Well then. There's enough danger on the sea without all that. Surely the Government can sort something out."

"Too right. The seas are free. Always have been and it's OK so long as we keep the catches within reason. The fact is there are too many trawlers trying to catch too few fish."

"Ha, who are you to talk?"

"The difference is that we are one of the first of a new generation. We're using gear which doesn't scrape the sea bed as much. At least we certainly don't set out to. Anyway if it gets too difficult I'm going to fish further afield and deeper, maybe off the west coast of the Hebrides or even Greenland. Like I said, you just won't see me so often, that's all."

"Dad and I will be sorry about that. What's going to happen about Saxon? How will you manage now?"

"I've taken over as skipper and I'm going to promote John Fowler to be Mate. He's a wonderful guy and he's got his mate's ticket now, well almost. I can't imagine why he hasn't been a skipper long ago. Also I've put an advert in the local press for an apprentice. It's going out next week. So by the time we get back from our next trip I may have some replies."

"When are you going back?"

"Tomorrow. Early."

****

That night in bed Susan wanted a serious discussion.
"Charlie."

"What is it? Have I got too much sheet?"

"Darling. I want to talk about us."

"Can it wait till morning? I'm so tired. It's taken two whole days to sort out the surgery. I had to cancel all my non-urgent appointments. The police were there the whole time. All the medicines had to be accounted for and tied up with my records. It's been hell. Those chaps mean business."

"Oh dear. I suppose they found a lot of innocent mistakes."

"Not a lot but they went over and over everything until they were satisfied. Talk about a grilling. At one stage they had Kay in the waiting room and me in the surgery."

"Kay?"

"The new nurse. I forget. You've not met her yet."

"Why was that?"

"They wanted to see if we contradicted each other. They must have thought they were on to some big drug bust. I could see that the inspector was quite disappointed at the end. He couldn't pin anything on us. All the important stuff was accounted for."

"I can't sleep. I must talk to you."

"Go on then. What's worrying you?"

"Chas goes back in the morning, early. We won't have time for a chat with him before he goes but it's all about our secret . . . the swap. He needs to be told. He wanted to know yesterday what the burglars could have been looking for. It's almost bound to come out in the end and I would rather we told him than anybody else. It's not just the swap anyway. This fellow Krause bears a grudge and he's out to get us."

"All right, so we do tell him. It might not be such a bad idea but when, now?"

"Not now, all three of us are too tired. We may have to drive up to Scrabster to see him when he gets back."

"Well then. Isn't it time we got some sleep?"

"Good night darling. Turn over. I want to give you a cuddle."

****

Two days later David activated Krause's radio code. The next day a note was delivered to the Residence.

Dear David,

Excuse the informality but I am assuming that you prefer I drop your official title and you must do the same for me, understood? I am pleased that we should confer again.

On this occasion I will send my deputy since many know me in Reykjavik. His name is Max and he will be at the Grand Hotel at eleven hours next Tuesday. He will answer all your questions and also inform you of the role we wish you to play in this project. Regards Oskar.

****

David arrived deliberately late for his appointment. He wanted to cultivate the appearance of a busy man who has little time to spare for unimportant matters. Besides which he determined to get a look at Max before deciding how to cope with the interview. He saw a small man standing at the desk, talking to the receptionist. He was dark, brown complexion with black hair going thin on the crown. He coughed and the man turned. It was then that he decided Max, for Max it was, would make up for his lack of inches by being aggressive and rather unpleasant. Abruptly he introduced himself.

"Good morning Ambassador, I am Max from the Kerenski. I am here at the request of Herr Krause. Shall we find somewhere to sit?" He spoke with a thick German accent that reminded David of his long posting to Switzerland during the war.

"Good morning Max. Yes, over there will do nicely, not by the window."

"Sehr gut, I've ordered coffee. I suppose you will be wanting to know more about the details of our project."

"That's correct."

"Please understand. Oskar has not formalised every detail. He is hoping to make good use of your contribution."

"How does he know that I intend to make a contribution?"

"That is an assumption of course but we do have to make full use of every informations we have. He tells me that you have concurred in one particular and that is quite simply that the lady you sleep with is not actually your wife. He says your actual wife lives in the town of Bolton with another man, nicht?"

"I did not confirm that and when Krause spoke to me Bolton was not mentioned."

"Please, David, I have Oskar's permission to call you that, I hope you agree. We are working to collect as much informations to help us. Bolton was not mentioned before because we did not know two days ago. Oskar feels a little bit angry that you yourself did not mention this. He has been to much troubles to find out from public records in your country that the Lady Lucy has a sister called Susan. Our legation in Manchester has been working night and day. From the dates on their birth certificates, we now know what we always suspected, that they are twins, probably identical twins. It was easy to discover that she lives with a Doctor Forbes in Bolton. Now that is very interesting. The pieces of the puzzle are coming together very well."

"If I confirm all this to you now, if confirmation is necessary, then please tell me, who is your postman, your contact, here in Reykjavik?"

"I will tell you; in fact I will write it down for you and give you his telephone number. He is Reynir Josefsson, a very valued member of our party, in fact the secretary of our association here."

"I know Reynir. He's the fisheries minister."

"I will report to Oskar that what we know is correct. We know that Mister, as he was then, now Doctor Forbes married Susan Robinson and that you married Lucy Robinson. It's all there in your records David. Now Forbes is not all that common a name, nicht. So we assume that Charlie Forbes, a spy working for the British Intelligence and Doctor Forbes of Bolton are one and the same person."

"You're very thorough I must say."

"Indeed we are. These astonishing revelations continue. There is a British trawler, well known to the Icelandic coastguard, called the Ace of Spades, which is frequently present in these waters. The Kapitan of this vessel is Saxon MacDonald and the Mate is guess who?"

"You know already so why ask me?"

"Let's not beat the bushes. The Mate is Mr Charles Forbes, nicknamed Chas, nicht, son of Doctor Forbes, nicht. Now we have two documents which Oskar tells me you have seen. These documents, which may not be genuine indicate that sometime in September 1953, the sisters changed places. Why? We do not know why. The answer to that is not in a public record is it?"

"Of course not. Yes I have seen the documents and they are plainly hand written forgeries. There is no substance in that lie. It seems to be some kind of plot or else a joke, maybe a party joke, a bit of fun in someone's eyes."

"We believe they are genuine copies and the originals will be somewhere in your family. Last night, if I am not mistaken, your true wife's home, Belvedere, Chorley New Road, in Bolton was searched. There is much more to this mystery that we could find out but the searches will be totally unnecessary if you will now confirm to me what I said at the beginning." With a sigh of resignation David said,

"All right then, I do confirm it. Just call off your thieves in Bolton. I don't want any more ransacking."

"Very good, I will see to it. Thank you for saving us a lot of work. Now we have established the truth, I want to convey to you our feeling about your help."

"I can't do anything which will prejudice my loyalty to the British Crown. I would sooner die."

"Of course, of course, I understand that completely. We do not wish to learn any state secrets or anything like that. We merely want you to use your influence to close the NATO base at Keflavik."

"I have no influence in that direction. I am astonished that you think I have."

"Well, you may have more influence than you give yourself credit. You are the Ambassador after all."

"It's ridiculous to think that. The base is vital to NATO. They will never give it up."

"That doesn't prevent us from trying and with your help we may even succeed. You see we believe that The Ace of Spades is a spy ship. So this affair takes on a double sinister aspect, nicht? Mark this David. Your career depends on the outcome. We do not ask the impossible. Think out a scheme for us. Maybe your nephew can help us. Nicht? Why don't you speak to him? I believe he's already been listed by the coastguards."

"How do you know that? Have you a contact with them?"

"We nearly had the Base closed down in 1962 didn't we? Now I must go. Our fleet is bound for the Barent Sea where we have a contract with Mother Russia to catch their fish. Oskar will be away from these shores unless you call. He could turn by helicopter if necessary. Just give me ten minutes to get clear of here. Good Day."

With that cold request Max left the hotel. David ordered more coffee and then realised that Max had left him to pay the bill. He sat in a reverie. That Krause was out of the way for a time was a slight relief and would give him some leeway. As he left the hotel, he had made up his mind to make contact with a friend in the Foreign Office who could possibly help him but first he must 'phone the Forbes.

****

Back at the residence David waited patiently for his booked call to come through. At last,

"Susan, is that Susan?"

"Yes David it is. Why should you ring on this day of all days?"

"I want to know how you are."

"Sick, absolutely sick. The house has been turned over, ransacked, looted, raped, need I go on?"

"No, don't go on. I've got the picture. I feared as much but it won't happen again. What about the surgery?"

"What do you know about this? Have you been organising something?"

"Of course not. It was them. I'm sure of it. Krause's henchmen." They were looking for the you-know-what. Where's Charlie?"

"Not here. We got a call from Kay, the nurse. The surgery was broken into as well. Charlie went down there. We never thought to link them together. It's pretty obvious if you think about it."

"Better not phone the police."

"Too late for you to tell us that. We phoned last night and they said they would come as soon as possible this morning."

"Pity."

"The surgery's in chaos. Kay has checked the drugs. Nothing's missing. Everything has been accounted for but unfortunately she phoned the police too."

"OK, I've got the picture. Ring me back when you know the worst."

"Before you go tell me your side of it."

"I met Krause's henchman yesterday and he told me your house would be searched unless I confirmed what he knows about us."

"Yes?"

"So I did, on the understanding that he would prevent any search of your home."

"Don't go on anymore. I'll ring you back as soon as I've checked with Charlie. It should be in his desk in the surgery."

Susan rang back half an hour later.

"It's gone. It's bloody gone David. How they knew where to look I don't know. Charlie was so fussed up about the drugs, he never thought to look."

"Where was it then?"

"One of the desk drawers had a double bottom. They just tore the drawer to pieces. The place has been wrecked. Since Kay called in the police he's got some explaining to do and I don't know what he will do about appointments."

"What about Belvedere?"

"Almost the same as the surgery. Some rooms not touched, our bedroom is OK but the study completely demolished. I can't describe it but to give the bastards their due, apart from the desk, very few actual breakages. The detective inspector put his finger on it. He's no fool that man. Forensics say there were two gangs working separately so the inspector said that the surgery gang must have called off the search at home after they found what they wanted. Otherwise I'm convinced they would have tackled upstairs. They questioned me for ages trying to find out if I knew what they were looking for."

"But you didn't tell them."

"How could I? In any case, even if I had known I wouldn't have told them. What do you take me for? For heavens sake, I'm insulted."

"Have the police gone now?"

"About an hour ago but they are still at the surgery."

"What fools we've been. We didn't need to keep it anyway. If it's any consolation to you, my cleaner rang from Dolphin Square. My flat was broken into but our copy is in the bank as you should know. Incidentally where were you when all that was going on?"

"We went to the Hallé and then for a late dinner with Sheila and Humph so it was after midnight when we got home and discovered the mess. The police got here about an hour ago."

"Are they finished?"

"They're still pretty keen to know what the burglars were after. We can't tell them of course so they think we're holding out on them. They've even had the sniffer dogs round. It's getting nasty."

"It's got nasty Sue. I'm in a fix over here. I'm going to need some help but just at the moment I don't know who to go to."

"I know exactly who to go to."

"Who then? Who do you know?"

"Do you want me to tell you? You'll never guess in a thousand years."

"Go on then, who?"

"Jonny."

"Jonny who? I don't know anyone called Jonny."

"Yes you do. He's the Chief Constable of Kingston upon Hull."

"Good Lord, fancy you thinking of him. He won't be Chief there now. He will have retired by now. I'm pretty sure."

"Even better. He can act ex officio."

"Well, I would never have thought of him."

"You can't trust the FO or the police or even a friend. Come to think of it, who can you trust? Jonny's your man. You'll have to get his address and go after him."

"Tempting, I must say. It's the best thought yet. I've been at my wits end. The trouble has been I know too many people, too well. I can't possibly tell them what this is all about. I could resign from the Diplomatic Corps and let the world go hang. When push comes to shove maybe that's what I will do but Lucy tells me not to be so feeble. She would be heartbroken and quite disgusted with, apart from the disgust that we'll suffer anyway. I'll let you know in due course what I've decided."

"You won't forget that we've got a stake in this too, will you?"

"No, of course not. Leave it with me. OK?"

"You know best. Right now I've got work to do. It could have been worse. By the way, what did you mean when you said it won't happen again?"

"Well it won't will it? They got what they came for."

"No, before we knew that, you said . . ."

"I know what I said. I told them not to do any more digging. I told them they are right about us so there was no need for them to spend oceans of time trying to prove it."

"So how did they react to that?"

"My contact, Max, seemed quite relieved. So now we know where we all stand. He knows, or at least I think he accepts that I will not betray Britain."

"You may have no option."

"I told him I would sooner be dead."

"God David, you didn't mean that surely?"

"No, I don't suppose I did but we'll see if or when the time comes."

"So that's the update. We've been ransacked and the enemy knows all about us."

"That sums it up. Sorry."

"Don't be. Call it force majeur. Call again when something happens. I want to know about Jonny. Bye."

"Bye bye Sue. I hope you get sorted soon."

"Don't worry. We shall. It's not as bad as it looks. It could have been a lot worse. They were thorough but not vandals. Charlie will need a new drawer for his desk. Sad about that being damaged. It belonged to my father. Anyway, Bye. Ring again soon."

8   JONNY

The more David thought about it the more he was inclined to find out if Jonny could help him. Discovery meant more than just being a laughing stock. They were leading a life of dishonesty, if not fraud. Lucy and Susan were each carrying passports which did not belong to them and he was an accessory after that fact. He slept on it, but the following day was no nearer making a decision.

It came to him suddenly. Why shouldn't Susan do the spade work and track down Jonny. After all it was her idea. He could see that he was in no position to devote much of his time to what was essentially a private matter. She had the time and could go away without asking for leave. He knew that Charlie would be fully committed keeping up with patients' demands. He wondered why he had not thought of that before but first he must speak to Lucy. Later that day he had the chance.

"Susan's come up with the best idea yet and I think we should go for it."

"Oh, what's that? Tell me." Lucy was curious because Susan was not normally noted for 'bright' ideas.

"Susan's suggested we track down a man I used to know called Jonny. He would be the ideal man to help us."

"Who is he?"

"She had to remind me and he's probably retired now. He was the Chief Constable of Kingston upon Hull. He played a big part in the Lenin crisis when Peggy was murdered."

"Oh yes, the big square-rigger called the 'Lenin'. Charlie had a narrow escape . . . Another one."

"Yes, and his last, thank God."

"I could do that. Let Susan and me do the tracking. She'll never manage it on her own. We'll start with the police in Hull. They'll probably know where he is."

"That's great, the perfect solution."

"I'll call Susan and tell her."

"And I'll carry on here sorting day to day business and finding out more about the inside working of the Althing."

"The what?"

"The Icelandic Parliament."

"Oh yes, I do remember, sorry."

"They are the ones who call the shots. If they pass an act banishing NATO, then NATO will go and that will let in the Russians. We can blame the British trawlermen for much of what is happening."

"Oh, how come?"

"Well, you know, they banned the landing of Icelandic catches in Hull and Aberdeen, so without a market the Icelanders have gone to Russia to sell their fish. The Russians can't believe their luck, getting a toehold in a NATO country. It's more than they could have dreamed of."

"Gosh, I never knew all this. Since when?"

"It's recent."

"Anyway, what's all this got to do with Susan and me?"

"A threat from Russia will make the Americans really wake up. If Jonny can get a contact in the NATO Base we may be able to hatch a plot and bring this whole business to an end."

"So you're going to get help from 007 after all."

"Don't be funny. This is not a laughing matter."

"Of course I'll help you. I'll be glad to. I'll make a few calls, Susan first."

The following evening after dinner Lucy joined him in his study.

"Do you want to know how I've got on today?"

"Of course I do darling, tell me all."

"Well I spoke to Susan, first. She's very keen, partly because it's her idea and partly because she thinks we can come up with a plan. Then I phoned the Hull police. You were right. Jonny has retired and lives in Majorca."

"Have you got a number?"

"I've got an address but not from Hull. I got it from the Chief Constables' Association in London. They were a bit reluctant at first but I talked them into it. So now Susan and I are going to fly out and see if we can make contact. He lives at 10, Carrer D'Amengual, Terreno in Palma."

"Why don't you write?"

"He might never reply and then we wouldn't know what to do. At least this way we can talk it through with him. I've booked on Iberia from Ringway via Barcelona. I love that name, 'Ringway'. Has a certain panache don't you think? It would be a shame to call it Manchester. We go next Tuesday and I've booked us in at The Belver Hotel."

"You have been busy. Does Jonny know any of this?"

"Not yet. We'll just walk round to his house and ring the bell. Although we've never met he's bound to remember David and rescuing Charlie from the 'Lenin'. What's more he'll know that Oskar Krause is a crook. He met Krause when the 'Lenin' was in the Hull docks and Charlie's aunt was murdered."

"This is no time for a joke."

"No, really. It was Charlie's aunt. Aunt Peggy. Lang did the stabbing aided by Krause and it was Krause who had Peggy's blood on his shoe. I don't think we'll have much trouble getting him to help, if only to advise."

"Yes, at the time Jonny and I kept in touch via our courier. He was very helpful once I had filled him in with what was at stake. Of course Krause has his personal axe to grind. He wants to kill Charlie. He blames Charlie and me, mainly Charlie, for his ten years in prison."

"If we get an interview we'll tell Jonny absolutely everything. We'll hold nothing back. It's just been our bad luck that Krause got his hands on our agreement."

****

Susan stretched across Lucy's lap to get a glimpse of the city below as the plane circled Palma. The white-washed houses and shops sweltered in another Majorcan heat wave. In the centre the tall Gothic Cathedral stood serene, isolated from the teeming commerce by the Arabic buildings of the old city.

They took a taxi to Bellver Hotel on the Paseo Maritimo. The Receptionist told them how to find Carrer D'Amengual. Later, after a light lunch, they set off on foot from the hotel. They rang the bell of number ten. Someone slid back the bolts on the inside of the door which, like many in this old part of the city, opened directly onto the pavement. The silence of the afternoon's siesta was punctuated by the occasional bark of a guard dog and the noisy scooters which rattled up and down the steep hill. The heat in the narrow lanes was oppressive. The twins sweated profusely in the swelter of the late summer stillness after their climb from the sea front. They waited patiently. The door was restrained by a security chain but opened just sufficiently for them to see a grey haired elderly woman.

"Si, ¿que quieren? ¿Quien sois?

"Do you speak English, Madam?"

"Un poco, a little." Lucy spoke slowly hoping the lady would understand.

"I'm Lucy Brown and this is my sister Susan Forbes. We are old friends of Mr Myles-Johnson. He will remember my husband David and I'm sure he will remember Charlie, my sister's husband."

"¿Tienen una cita? ¿Os espera Señor Myles?"

"No, we have no appointment."

"Por favor llamen o envíen una carta para solicitar una cita y entonces decidirá Señor Myles."

"Please tell him we are here. Por favor."

A man's voice came from behind the old lady's shoulder.

"Maria ¿Quien es?"

"Dos Señoras, dicen que te conocen."

Susan raised her voice.

"We've never met Sir but you know our husbands, David Brown and Charlie Forbes."

"Indeed, I do remember them. What brings you to Majorca?"

"To see you Sir."

"Quita la cadena Señora. Esto será interesante. Come in ladies, delighted to meet you."

"So, Sir, you're the famous Jonny. May we call you that?"

"Please do."

"We've heard so much about you, how you managed events which led up to the rescue of Susan's husband. The dark angel."

"You make it sound as if I'm, or rather was, a bit notorious."

"Not at all," exclaimed Susan. "Famous." Jonny smiled.

"In Kingston perhaps. That was my last posting."

"Are you really retired?"

"Really. Have been for a couple of years. Why?"

"Well, I don't know how to say it . . . you look so young."

"Now then young lady. Why dark?"

"You are dark, or rather were until your hair turned white."

It was cooler in the house. They went across a small courtyard, where a fountain was cascading over a bronze water nymph and climbed a short flight of steps into a sumptuous living room, grey tiled floor, white walls liberally spread with a variety of modern oil paintings and with a French window giving a panoramic view over the bay and the ships.

"What a gorgeous room," exclaimed Susan.

"It's lovely," agreed Lucy. Maria brought in a jug of iced water.

"Would you like something stronger?" Jonny said.

"Oh. No thanks," both the twins said together.

They sat in deep armchairs whilst they told Jonny the purpose of their visit and the history leading up to it.

"So you're on a mission."

"You could put it like that," said Lucy.

"We're getting desperate. We had to come. Our husbands are too busy to get away. Mine tied to his practice and Lucy, Lady Lucy, with a direct threat to David but you know about him. Now that we've put you in the picture the question is, can you help us?"

"I see. I'm very glad you came. It's a pleasure to meet you both. You really are identical aren't you? I can't get over it."

"Now that we've put you in the picture, the question is can you help us?"

"I don't know that I can. You say you've put me in the picture and I'm sure you have but I need to know a lot more. I don't mind the idea of getting involved at all but whether I'm the best person to help you is another thing entirely."

Lucy said "There's nobody else we can trust. We've told you our deepest secrets. Only the blackmailers know what we've told you. If you turn us down . . . Knowledge can be bought but not trust. That is beyond price."

"So Krause is out. It doesn't seem like ten years. I wonder how he got the job. Master of the East German fishing fleet is he? He's not a seafarer. There must be a real skipper aboard. It's my guess he's just a gauleiter."

"What's that?"

"The very worst kind of security agent. He's a dangerous man ladies. If he has a personal vendetta against your husbands then beware. I have one or two contacts in the MoD. Give me about a week to mull over your proposition. Anything I do ex officio, I'll do gladly. I can't say I'll be able to take a front line job, but I'll do what I can. My wife died last year. It's left me desolate, so maybe this is what I need to get me going again."

"Jonny, we'll be so grateful. We are sorry to hear of your wife's death. We would have made an appointment to see you but didn't know your telephone number and we wanted to meet you in person."

"My number's ex-directory anyway and how could I refuse two such lovely ladies. Give me time. Like me, my friend the General, ex-Commander of the Yorkshire Light Infantry, retired last year. Has-beens like us need something to do. I'll sound him out for ideas with your permission but not to mention about your unusual marital arrangements."

"Please no," said Susan.

"Another obvious pathway to follow is MI6. David will know someone I'll be bound."

"That's just it. He has lots of contacts there but he doesn't know who to trust. This is hardly a matter of national security but if they thought he had been turned by the KGB it very soon would be." Lucy said.

"I see what you mean. Quite a dilemma," Jonny pondered.

"David thinks Krause is planning to have him assassinated. The business about Keflavik may be a blind or just a secondary plot. The fact is he's got a hold over David and possibly all four of us."

"Assassinated. How would that help him?"

"Closing the Base . . . we think that's just a blind. We believe all Krause wants is revenge."

"News like that can travel faster than light but your secret is safe with me. This kind of thing needs very careful handling. I'll have to go back to Blighty for a spell. I'll be nearer to that front line so to speak."

"That would be wonderful."

"I'll be on the next plane, just as soon as I can get a ticket. This emergency needs action."

"We'd better be going then. It's going dark. We've been here hours."

"Don't worry about that. It's been a pleasure but I'd like to show you a bit of the city if you're both free this evening."

"Mission accomplished; we're free. Our plane leaves to-morrow evening."

"Excellent. So we can paint the town red, as they say."

"But we've nothing to wear," exclaimed Susan.

"Even better."

"Only what we stand up in."

"Everyone's very informal here. Don't worry. We'll go to the Abaco. I'll get you a taxi back to the Belver and join you there in an hour."

"Bye then."

"Hasta luego."

9   KEFLAVIK

The Icelandic General election of 1971, as David Brown had feared, produced a left wing government again, in which Reynir Josefsson was still the Minister for Fishing. Consequently the future of the NATO base at Keflavik came once more on to the national agenda. The new government had campaigned on the question of extending the fishing limits and so the following year, when the old fishing agreement expired, a new bill was passed in the Althing.

This measure had been rumoured for years, the British Foreign Office steadfastly ignoring all reports which David had fed to Whitehall. In spite of the International Tribunal in The Hague pronouncing this unlawful and the negative outcome of the Geneva Conference, the members of the Althing coalition decreed the fifty mile fishing limit.

Without any international agreement the Second Cod War was to come into effect on the 1st September 1972. At first the British Government decided not to provide protection for the trawlers. Naval frigates were sent but ordered to keep watch beyond the new limit. It was not until eight months had passed that the trawler skippers said they would go on strike unless Whitehall authorised close naval protection in the disputed area. The Althing were outraged but consoled by the success of the propaganda war waged by the Icelandic media.

The East German fleet headed back for respite in Denmark while the mother ship, Kerenski, returned to Gydnia, the port for Gdansk, with the frozen catch and the processed fish-meal. Krause, landed on Iceland by the Russian Kamov helicopter, intending to remain until the fleet returned in about three weeks. Meanwhile he assured Reynir in a private interview that the East Germans wished to maintain cordial relations and that they would keep strictly outside 50 miles. Then Krause raised the question of the NATO base.

"You see Reynir; it's going to be in the long term interest of Iceland to be included within the Communist sphere. We can offer you access to more fishing in the Barent Sea and a guaranteed supply of all your material needs in return for which the NATO Base at Keflavik will become entirely yours, with friendly support to our submarines and cargo vessels passing through the Denmark Strait."

Reynir said, "From my point of view, Oskar, your proposition sounds very attractive but I will have great difficulty getting it passed by the Althing."

"Not if you can show that the arrogant British have no intention of abandoning their right to fish close to your shores. I have a plan which will demonstrate quite clearly their intent."

"Oh. Tell me about it."

"I have a great deal of influence with one trawler in particular, the Ace of Spades, a vessel with freezing capacity, the largest vessel in their local fleet. Chas Forbes is her skipper. With a little encouragement from someone you will appoint, he will be persuaded to fish inside the fifty limits. Let him continue until he has a full catch and then strike."

"How?"

"Arrest the vessel, confiscate the catch, and put Forbes on trial. Give him a long sentence and fine him heavily or confiscate his vessel. Perfect don't you think?"

"If it works."

"It will work. Sour relations with the British skippers who will do all in their power to continue fishing in our waters. Meanwhile I have some leverage with the British Ambassador, who incidentally is a complete buffoon and who will not intervene effectively. His main interests are hunting, shooting and fishing and his wife likes parties. Are you going to the British Embassy dinner next month?"

"Probably, why do you ask?"

"Draw the Ambassador out into making some sort of a statement. Ask the question. I'll prepare a brief for him. Make sure he gets it before dinner, the day before if possible and stress that it's very important for our future relationship with him. His attitude must make it plain that Britain has no intention of withdrawing their fleet."

"What will this statement say?"

"It will outline that the British are not so much concerned about Keflavik but that the fishing is more important. It will infuriate the American Ambassador and go some way to convince our Prime Minister that they have little to lose by asking NATO to leave."

"Such a remark will be obviously untrue and if made by David Brown would end his career."

"So? A crisis such as this will tip your Althing over the edge. Your coalition has a majority, nicht?"

"Yes, but it's only a coalition. The Americans at the base are very generous and pay handsomely for all their needs."

"We, the USSR, can match anything they do."

"It sounds like a well thought out plan. How sure are you that Chas Forbes will act as you state and how sure are you that you can arrest the Ace of Spades?"

"Very sure. I have a special reason for wanting this vessel brought in. It is a great coincidence that the opportunity we have to oust the Yanks should also realise my own personal ambitions."

****

Two days after that conversation Charlie met Jonny off the London train. He drove him slowly back to Belvedere, renewing their acquaintance. Only when they sat down with Susan did Jonny start to give an account of his progress.

"I want to see David sometime soon to get the lie of the land. I want to get into MI6," he said.

"Why is that then?" Charlie wanted to know.

"As head of Visa Section in Switzerland, he had a direct line to MI6. He's been trying to find out who is dealing with the Iceland question. There are a few old colleagues who will remember that and wonder what he's doing now without a proper brief. I don't want him to be involved directly but I do need a contact."

"All right. I'll go with that for the moment," said Charlie. "But David's already involved with Krause."

"That's just it. We could be treading on dangerous ground. Don't forget he's a murderer and he was the one involved in torturing you."

"OK, but tell us what you are up to."

"It's early days. Someone must be handling the Iceland problem, if not us then the Americans. I have found out one thing however."

"Tell us."

"A note was passed from the CIA to MI6," said Jonny. "It said that trawling off Iceland by Britain, West Germany and France is a hindrance to negotiations vis-à-vis Keflavik. Apparently the lease will be due for renewal soon. The Icelanders are a canny lot. What they are doing is tantamount to blackmail, trawling on the one hand and the lease on the Base on the other. In the eyes of the Americans, the fish are small beer compared to the needs of NATO. Krause is going to make trouble for us."

"Going to? He is making trouble. He's got the proof he needs to blackmail David and us too. We were mad to keep those agreements. The sooner Krause is out of the way the better," said Charlie.

"Call in James Bond 007," said Susan with a wry smile.

"Oh shut up Sue. This is serious stuff. If you can't be sensible then . . . How about a cuppa?"

"OK then I'll get it but see if I'm not right."

After Susan went to the kitchen Jonny leant forward and said in a low voice.

"Actually, she may be more correct about that than she thinks. Maybe . . . But thinking out loud for a moment, perhaps the best outcome for us would be for the Icelanders to send Krause packing on the grounds that he is a Russian spy. We must try to convince our friends in the Althing that he is acting entirely with Russian interests in mind and his sole purpose is to make trouble between two friendly countries, namely Britain and Iceland. But first we must stop British trawlers fishing inside the new fifty mile limit. Is that likely?"

"The trawler owners won't agree and our Parliament is supporting them. They want naval protection as of now in spite of what the Admiralty thinks. What is happening up there is almost a war," said Charlie. "They think a show of strength by the navy will scare the Icelanders off. They don't know the coastguards. We've lost this war before it even begins."

"How do you come to know so much about it all?"

"Chas has his ear to the ground and I take 'Network', the Mission's monthly mag. Time is not on our side. I don't think we can wait for an amorphous bunch like the trawler owners to have a change of heart. They're just thinking of their own pockets not to mention the livelihoods of thousands in places like Hull and Grimsby."

"Politicians, politicians, always thinking of short term party advantage. Nothing to do with Western Security. There are other places to fish. By the way, how did you get to know the contents of that note?"

"What note?"

"I told you. The note from the CIA."

"Oh yes, sorry."

"It's an open secret in the House. All it has done is to stiffen opinion. The Labour Party has put its trust in the navy but the Admiralty are a bit more realistic."

"What have the Admiralty done then?" asked Charlie.

"They've tied the hands of the OTC, the Officer in Tactical Command, through the RoE."

"Gosh Jonny, you talk in riddles. What's the RoE?"

"Rules old boy, the Rules of Engagement."

"For instance?"

"Well, no live ammunition for a start. The problem is our public image. We have the fire power to sink their fleet tomorrow if we wish but think what that will do on the world stage. It would be seen as a criminal act, which it would be, even worse than the Suez fiasco. Iceland has cast us in the role of the aggressors. That's the line their newspapers are taking."

Susan arrived with the tea tray. Charlie said, "Thanks Sue".

"We need that, thanks Sue—dry work this discussion business," Jonny remarked.

"So is it James Bond or not?" she said.

"It's not that simple. We've no alternative but to bide our time until the other side make a move," said Jonny. "We won't win this war and NATO might lose the Base. So let's be realistic."

"All right then, let's. You seem to have done a lot of work on this in a very short time, Jonny. How do you do it?" said Charlie.

"I've been around a long time and I've been lucky but I can't tell you my source, not yet anyway. Now I know the problem I'm half way to finding the solution. I'm convinced of one thing."

"Which is?"

"We can't do much without help. I've got an idea who to approach."

"Who?"

"Keep this to yourself but my friend, the General who used to command the Yorkshires is related to the local CIA, they're cousins. It would help a lot if I could tell him why we are so keen on getting Krause off our backs."

"Out of the question. I gave David an undertaking."

"We've got to eliminate Krause. It's the only way."

"Eliminate. Is that a euphemism for something really serious, aggressive?"

"Could be, but its early days yet."

"Why don't we just tell Chas to pack it up and fish elsewhere?"

"Why don't you? replied Jonny.

"Chas is his own man. The fishing's too good. Most of the time he trawls outside the twelve mile limit but inside the new fifty. That comes in on the first September."

"And."

"He only strays over the line when he's got a shoal in his sights. He says he knows what he's doing. He's got targets to meet, remember. He doesn't want me on his back for ever."

"So he's bound to be taking the risk."

"Along with about fifty others and with naval protection. He'll have to fish within the limit or go home. There aren't any fish fifty miles offshore. Naval protection will be essential. Chas seems to think the coastguard won't be able to patrol such a large area."

"Would that were true. They've got a Catalina. They can fly over the whole area twice a day and radio the whereabouts of the fleet to the coastguard ships."

"So what's more important, Chas's fishing or Krause's threat or the NATO base at Keflavik?"

"Depends where you're at. In our eyes removing Krause is top priority but I doubt if the Althing see it that way and I don't suppose that Hank does either."

"Who the hell is Hank?" Charlie wanted to know.

"He's General Hank Thorne, the commander of the Keflavik base."

"Yes of course he is, I forgot. Let's get next to Hank and convince him to co-operate with us then."

"I'm working on it. I'll make better progress when I've talked to the General. Leave me to it for a few more days Charlie. I won't waste any time. This whole thing could blow up in our faces at any time. Meanwhile if you want me I'll be at the Cora, near Euston."

"OK. I know it. Stayed there myself, a long time ago."

"I'll leave you with this nasty thought. Krause will remain a threat even if we all pack up and go home. He's got spies out on your family. I'm sure of it. Why don't you send Charlene away for a spell? She will be very welcome at my home for as long as she wants to stay."

"Gosh Jonny, that bad?"

"Take life seriously. They ransacked your home didn't they? When she was a baby they took Charlene as hostage once before when you were in Germany. Get real Charlie boy."

"Put like that, I'll take you up on your offer and book her flight today."

"What about your wife?"

"What about me?" Susan interrupted.

"Why don't you both go and stay in my home for the time being?"

"I don't want to leave Charlie. I'm sure Charlene could make a few friends out there without me. Anyway we can't commit her without asking first," replied Susan. "She won't go anyway. She's got exams to take and she takes them very seriously."

"Well, it's on the record. You can't say you haven't been warned." Jonny shrugged.

****

Back in Reykjavik David's secretary brought him the latest Telex from Whitehall. At dinner that evening he showed it to Lucy. It was from the Foreign Secretary. It said,

1st September 1972

My Dear Brown,

I have been instructed to write to you by the Foreign Secretary since I reminded him that your tour will end on the thirty-first of October. At the moment he is having difficulty finding a suitable replacement for you. Now that the new Icelandic government has taken over, we need someone with experience of affairs and a detailed knowledge of the main players in the Althing. The Cabinet is most apprehensive that the policies of the Communist coalition will be very anti-Western and swing decisively in favour of the USSR. You are the best link we have to monitor the situation and bring pressure to bear on contacts you have cultivated in other parties. Most importantly it is imperative that American and NATO forces maintain good relations with the Icelandic authorities at all levels. My department is doing all it can to maintain friendly contacts with influential officials and politicians of all factions.

Coming now to the nub of this request, he would like you to remain in post until June of next year. By then we expect the present crisis will have been resolved. Needless to say if a settlement is realised, the naval forces will be withdrawn.

Yours truly, Peter Hutchins, PPS.

David exploded,

"The Foreign Secretary's a twit. The war has begun. How can we retain good relations with anyone, NATO, the Americans or the Icelanders? All my good work destroyed and now they want me to carry on until the middle of seventy-three."

"David is this true? I don't believe that you said 'yes'".

"I can't refuse an order. My job depends on it."

"It's not an order. It's a request."

"Same thing."

"Surely it's not the same thing. That's silly."

"Silly or not it's the way things work my dear."

"I don't think I can stand two more of their winters."

"You didn't say that when we first came here. You were delighted and we've made a host of friends."

"I'm not grumbling about friends. They're delightful. It's the weather and the latitude."

"Cheer up. Think of all the parties you can arrange."

"I'll swap parties any time in exchange for peace of mind. Why can't we go home?"

"That would gain nothing. Krause can track us down anywhere in the world. We've got to stand and fight."

"How can we? He's got the edge, firepower, manpower, mobility. We're just sitting ducks."

"Jonny and I are working on it. With the Yanks on our side we'll win in the end."

"I wish I shared your confidence."

"I've every confidence in you. Why can't you trust me?"

"I do darling but . . ."

"No buts. A good part of our security depends on having influence and friendships and that's where you come in."

"Well, there is that but it's all such hard work. No sooner than we finish one party or dinner than I'm planning the next. Then there are all the other Embassy dinners. I'll have to go to

London for some new rig. My dresses are beyond redemption and what about the Annual Dinner?"

"Well, what about it?"

"I'm definitely not going to wear last year's gown. I fancy something in blue, electric blue."

"OK, Its time you had a break. Why don't you have a few days in town with your sister."

"David, that's a wonderful idea. We'll raid the boutiques in Bond Street"

"Leave it to me, darling. I'll ask Dilys to fix it."

"Thanks."

"Say this time next week for two weeks."

"I'll ring Sue to make sure it's OK. By the way, thinking of parties, whose idea was it to sit me next to Vilbert, the Chief of Police last Thursday?"

"Darling, I sat him next to you, not the other way round. I thought he would be flattered, flattered to be at the top of the table that is."

"Well, you might as well know that he's a randy bastard. He spent a good part of the intervals between courses squeezing my thigh. I hope I don't have to sit next to him again."

"Oh dear, I am sorry."

"And what's more he very elaborately kissed my hand when he left and said he hoped to meet me again soon."

"Did he indeed? I don't know when that will be. I've already included him in next week's shooting party but you don't come so that's all right."

"Oh well. I suppose that's just one of the several hazards of being an embassy wife. I expect the secretaries have more to put up with than that. It's something to do with the climate, the long dark winters. Icelandic males seem to have a bit of a reputation."

"Maybe your relationship will blossom. The experience might stand you in good stead next time you park illegally."

"I'll ignore that remark. Anyway I assume the die is cast and we're doomed to two more years of this draughty building."

"OK. If I can't manage the FO at least I can have a shot of curing the draughts. Just for the record I wasn't too overjoyed at staying on but I do enjoy the summer and getting out in the mountains. Maybe you should come with me on a hunting or shooting trip. You'd enjoy it."

"I'll think about it but right now I have a lot to think about and so have you. Five of our trawlers were arrested last week. Their fines come to nearly a hundred grand."

"They know the risks. Why should that concern you?"

"Isn't it obvious? Chas is out there. We know how much notice he takes of limits and what's going to happen now the fifty mile limit is in effect?"

"You worry too much. Chas can take care of himself. He's a rich man. A fine might do him good. Teach him a lesson."

"I'll try but it's not easy."

"Another message came in today."

"Important?"

"It's about Keflavik. Jonny wants to meet the Commander of the Base."

"Is he coming over?"

"Yes he is. Next week. I'm going to put him up here. The outside world will know him as a cousin of mine. Getting Hank to come over here will be difficult so I might have to go to the Base to talk it through with him. I think that this might be what the FO are getting at, getting to know people et cetera."

"What's the point of it? Jonny is supposed to be helping us not the Americans."

"We'll see. Meanwhile I'll ask the staff to fix the spare suite."

"OK, as you say."

With that final comment the Ambassador and his wife went to bed.

10 RESCUE AT SEA

John was on watch. With an hour of slack in the Pentland Firth and a calm sea the crew set about preparing the ship for the next trip. Over the months they had worked out the essential routines. The homeward passage allowed them to catch up on much needed sleep. Then after landing the catch the Ace started the outward passage when cleaning and repairing damages took over. The crew were never idle. The mate and the bosun would oversee the work. On his rounds Chas always gave special attention to the engine room and the fish handling areas, the gutting, washing and sorting rooms. The crew tried to maintain order while fishing but there was always a need for scrubbing and hose jets to ensure the next catches would not be contaminated. Hosing the decks in port was not allowed.

Everything seemed to be in order. In the galley Doug was busy preparing a late lunch, the Sunday roast. Looking at the wash over the stern doors, Chas could just make out the faint smudge of the Orkneys on the horizon to the south. By tomorrow night he would be in the box off the southeast of Iceland.

The navy had already said, in a memorandum to the Trawler Owners, that they would not be patrolling tight boxes or Designated Fishing Areas (DFA's). The trawlers were merely advised to stay in groups and rely on civilian protection provided by the tugs from MAFF, the Ministry. To the fury of the skippers nearly eighty trawlers had had their warps cut by the new coastguard vessels in the last month.

"What's the forecast skipper?" asked Mike, now the senior deckhand.

"It's going to be OK for the time of year. Force three from the west, temperature down to the fifties, almost a full moon."

"What's the fishing going to be like?"

"With this weather it should be good and if the Navy do their bit, as promised, then we should be in for a good time. If this area's no good then we'll sail round to the northwest DFA and try there. We've got a lot of hold to fill haven't we Mike?"

"Aye aye skipper."

After Doug's usual high quality lunch in the mess, Chas did his best to inform the crew what the new conditions would be like.

"If the navy are up to it we should get uninterrupted fishing provided we stay in the group. They've guaranteed coverage from the nineteenth of May."

"At last, thank the Lord for that," exclaimed the Mate. "What does guaranteed mean?"

"It's not the Lord you should thank Mike, it's the skippers. I did my bit. Told the BTF, we were coming home unless something is done."

As Chas climbed to the bridge he called back,

"We'll shoot at about zero four-hundred. Meanwhile get your heads down boys. You'll not be getting much kip until the hold's full."

The Ace of Spades steamed on into the night. At first light a call came in on channel sixteen.

John phoned Chas on the intercom.

"All ships message on the radio skipper," said John, interrupting Chas's sleep. "From the 'Everton'. She's at 63 degrees 35 minutes, Lat. and 15 degrees 42 minutes Long. She's been fired on and holed below the water-line. From what I can gather, she's under arrest by the coastguard. It's the 'Aegir', threatening to sink her if she don't heave to. She's only about twenty miles away. I can see her on the radar. Two vessels close together. I think she's trying to make a run for it."

"OK, John. Maximum revs. I'm coming. Have any navy ships answered?"

"Only HMS Jupiter, and she's 250 miles away. There may be other trawlers in the area but they haven't answered."

"Poor old Everton. I'm surprised she's still out there. An old side-winder, a rust bucket if ever there was one. Maybe it's the insurance they're after. I'll rouse the cook. We'll need hot drinks and dry clothing if there's men in the water."

"Aye aye."

"And get the lashings off the lifeboat. Survival at these temperatures is only about fifteen minutes. Give me another call when you're ten minutes off or if anything changes with the 'Aegir'."

"OK skip."

"I'll be in my cabin." Sleep was denied Chas as he tossed about in his bunk wondering if they could meet the Egerton in time. In the end with about half an hour to go he rejoined John on the bridge.

"I've calculated her speed and course skipper. We should intercept soon. I think the Aegir has given up the chase. Perhaps they've seen us coming and think we are the support vessel."

"Have you spoken to the Everton?"

"I've called her up on Channel sixteen but she doesn't answer, or on eight. We should be in sight now. I'll send up a white flare."

"You do that. I'll go below and get two of the lads up. This is costing us good fishing time but we can't go away now. We're almost half way to the Faeroes."

The flare was answered with a red one, fine on the port bow. John decided the range was about 2 miles. Everton replied to their call on VHF.

"Hello Ace. Going to channel eight, out." A few seconds later Everton came through on Channel eight.

"Hello Ace. We need a bloody pump, fast. Our's can't keep up. There's four feet of water in the effing hold and rising. The engine room is water tight."

"OK skipper. We can lend you a pump. Send your lifeboat over. We'll be alongside in ten minutes. Jupiter is on the way. Should be here in about ten hours. Can you stay afloat? We'll stand bye in case you abandon. OK?"

"Many thanks Ace. We'll stand bye on eight. My lifeboat's on the way over to you."

As soon as the lifeboat was alongside Mike and Trog lowered the auxiliary pump into it. A little while later they heard the noise as their pump started to discharge Egerton's bilge water over the side. Their next message was pessimistic.

"Hello Ace. We've got your pump going but we're not keeping up. I reckon we've got another two hours before we bloody well go down."

"OK skipper. I'll relay that to Jupiter on Medium Wave."

"Hello Everton. Jupiter got my sitrep. They're sending their Wasp with more pumps and a repair party. They'll have to drop the men by wire into your lifeboat. There'll be three men and all the kit. Quite a lift I'd say. I hope for your sake they make it."

"A million thanks Ace. Please stay near until the Wasp arrives."

"That's OK, we'll wait for Jupiter," Chas replied.

"I owe you a pint, Ace. Out."

An hour and a half later the Radar picked up the approaching helicopter. Soon it was overhead and they saw the first of the sailors dangling on the end of the wire. He looked very precarious, swinging backwards and forwards over the

Edgerton's lifeboat. After a minute or so in obedience to the sailor's hand-signals the winch man dropped him into it. The second man was not so lucky and got a ducking. The last load consisted of the repair kit and another petrol driven pump.

Working over the side six feet below the Egerton's waterline one sailor secured a steel plate over the hole. The jagged shards were all pointing inboard. The plate was secured by a threaded rod pre-welded onto it and passed through the six inch diameter hole to a toggle and nut on the inside. The second sailor, working below the flood in the hold, tightened up the nut and soon the level of water in the hold succumbed to the action of the three bilge pumps. Tarred rope was hammered into the assembly until the inflow was, to all intents, stopped. After working like this for eleven hours HMS Jupiter came alongside and the exhausted men were transferred back.

"Yer know Boss. We could have claimed salvage," remarked Mike.

"Maybe we could but we're not going to. We're all in this together. Could be our turn tomorrow. As soon as Jupiter gets here we'll shoot the nets and start fishing. It's a bit deep out here. I'll get us over the ridge to the north. It's about five-hundred meters but we've got the warps, a bit more winding for you that's all. Rouse up the rest and put them on stand-by after the gear's ready. A hot drink from Doug would be a good idea."

"Aye aye, skipper."

Twelve hours later and with three small hauls in the hold, Ace joined the fleet in the south-eastern group. They heard later, during the general chatter on the fleet's VHF's, that the sailors from Jupiter had repaired Egerton's leak and that she had continued fishing, anxious to fill her hold before the long journey back to Hull.

Chas said,

"If the fishing's no good here we'll sail round the coast into the northern DFA. That's where most of the boys are now. We can fish all the way."

"Aye aye."

"You go below John, and get some kip. It's way past time and thanks. I feel safer with that civilian tug on our quarter. So long as he stays there we'll be OK. I think it must be Lloydsman. He's fast, got over twenty knots. Pity we couldn't have him sooner."

"Why was that then?"

"MHQ said they were on charter to some American outfit. If we'd had Lloydsman a month ago I reckon half our warps would have been saved. We've been dead lucky so far. Let's hope it stays that way. See you later."

After the nineteenth of May everything changed when the navy announced the re-instatement of the north-western and south-eastern DFA's. The whole fleet continued to fish inside the fifty mile limit.

****

"Thirty knots on the anemometer Skip."

"Yes. I'm afraid we're in for a blow. At least it will be a warm one. Should last for twenty four hours or so. When it gets dark we'll stop fishing. The bloody coastguards are shadowing us. It's got to be Odinn. She's been with us all day and can do twenty knots flat out. Unless it's my imagination we're getting more than our share of attention. I just hope that 'Scylla' stays put. Haul in twenty minutes."

"Aye, Aye Skip," responded Mike. "I'll call the hands."

Putting the Ace on a westerly course to face the rough sea, the hands manned the main winch. It was then that Chas sounded the alarm. The coastguard Vessel Odinn had started her run in. Although out of sight in the thick mist kicked up by the breeze, Chas could see on the radar that she had set a course to intercept. Constrained by the trawl at three knots he had little room to manoeuvre. Odinn was still two miles away. That meant he had six minutes to act. He throttled back and threw the gear into neutral. The Ace began to lose steerage

94

way. After two minutes she was head to wind and stationary and beginning to fall off to starboard. He gave her a short burst.

"Tell me when the warps are up and down Mike. We can't afford sternway. We might foul our own warps. I'll keep her head to wind as best as I can."

"Aye, aye," said Mike leaving the bridge and running to look over the stern. The warps entered the sea at a sharp angle. He spoke into the intercom.

"We're still trailing Boss but I think we'll be OK if you can hold her at that. We could do with a bit more sternway."

"Thanks."

"Chas gave the Ace a short burst astern as 'Odinn' loomed out of the mist about a cable away doing her twenty knots. She lost way as the skipper put her engines astern to let the warp-cutter sink to the required depth and swept passed Ace's stern at about ten knots. Charlie held his breath. The skipper leant from his bridge as he came level with Chas and waved. Chas waved back, knowing that this time the cutter had failed to make contact. He put the Ace on slow ahead.

HMS Scylla made her move. About time too thought Chas. She put herself between the Ace and Odinn who did a tight circle intending a second try. Chas watched in awe as the Frigate entered a tight circle too.

"Blimey, look at that. I never knew a frigate could turn like that," he exclaimed.

The two ships, like dogs spoiling for a fight passed within a few feet of each other. Odinn sheered away and disappeared into the mist closely followed by Scylla.

"Get the trawl in as soon as you can down there. They'll be back. We'll heave-to overnight. John will you take over? I'll get some kip. Wake me at midnight and I'll do the dawn watch, OK"

"Aye, aye," John replied.

"Make sure every thing is gutted before the hands turn in, and make sure they get fed. We'll shoot at first light, about two o'clock."

The gale, as forecast, had blown all night. Chas tossed and turned in his bunk until dawn. He struggled into his waterproof suit and sea boots. The Ace reared and plunged into the steep waves but by six o'clock the wind subsided leaving behind an oily swell. The welcome sun broke through the scudding clouds and for the first time in almost a week Chas could see most of the British fleet. He guessed that there would be at least fifty ships over the banks.

He spoke into the VHF.

"Hello Scylla, Scylla, Scylla, this is Ace of Spades. Do you read me?"

"Loud and clear, Ace. Channel eight please."

"Going down, Channel 8, Scylla." Chas adjusted the frequency and spoke again.

"Do you read me Scylla?"

"How can I help?"

"We're going to shoot and would be grateful for a sitrep."

"The coastguard ships are away at the moment. The crews will have gone home for a rest and a good breakfast. I'll call all ships on eight when they return. The Nimrod should be keeping an eye open for us."

"Thanks Scylla. I'll listen out."

For the next three days there was uninterrupted fishing for the fleet in the north-western DFA. Chas took the Ace right up to the old twelve mile line. On the fourth day there was renewed activity from the coastguard.

"Pass this round John," said Chas. "We've not a lot of space left in store. I reckon the enemy will be back so we'll steam round to the south over night, fill the hold and then head for home. The forecast is set fair, winds four to five. We'll be low in the water with full holds, top speed about twelve I reckon. Keep a twenty-four-seven radar watch. We don't want to be nabbed just now. Haul in half an hour and then stow for the transit. I'm going below for a spell. Wake me for the first dog watch, OK?"

"Aye, aye Skip."

****

In the early hours the Ace of Spades was about fifteen miles out of Keflavik when she changed to clear the south-western point of Reykjanes and set a south-easterly course. The sea was calm and the morning overcast with a thin layer of alto-stratus cloud. Chas felt a strange brooding sense of foreboding in the air. There were no gulls circling the stern. Charlie thought they must have had their breakfast off another trawler. The rising sun, fine on the starboard bow, cast an eerie sidelight on the sea which changed to the tint of copper. Deep within the seabed below there was a deep rumbling, a sepulchral vibration, which sent a responding shudder through every part of the Ace. In a matter of seconds every man aboard was on deck and looking to the east. The marine band radios crackled into life and the air was rent by voices of alarm. Chas shut down the engine to slow ahead as they watched a plume of black smoke and rock shooting into the air dead ahead. The shadow of the explosion appeared on the radar at a range of sixty-three miles.

"What the bloody hell is that?" exclaimed John as he emerged from below. "Is this the start of World War Three?" said several of the crew. "What do you think Chas? Is that radio active?"

"It's got to be an earthquake or a volcano. It's not radio active. If it was it would be playing hell with the electronics," said John.

"Stand-by for a tidal wave chaps." Chas shouted into the intercom.

The effect of this warning was immediate and with one accord the crew went below in search of life-jackets. About half an hour later the sea became agitated but not dangerously so.

The air was filled with the rumbling of the explosion. Jets of red lava shot up, as if fired from a gigantic cannon. Describing glowing arcs they fell into the sea which then erupted afresh as the quenching sea boiled like Vulcan's cauldron. As they sailed on, the sea now changed to a chocolate colour. It was still steaming as great shoals of fish came to the surface, belly up.

"What a waste Boss," exclaimed Mike. "Pity our freezer is already full."

"Not such a good idea Mike," Chas laughed. "Much as I should like to go and help, we've got a fish room full of contraband. We're better employed getting the hell out of it."

The Helgafell volcano which erupted with such force after being dormant for an estimated five thousand years shocked the small population of Heimaey who were swiftly evacuated by the coastguard vessels. The relief operations lasted for the next few weeks leaving the trawlers free to continue fishing unhindered. As one coastguard remarked, "The Devil came to rescue the British."

The skippers' ultimatum had paid off. HMS Plymouth and HMS Cleopatra returned to guard duties. The trawler fleet made the best use of the interlude afforded by nature to refill their holds.

"We'll give the agent one last chance. After that it's Hull. OK boys," said Chas over dinner.

11 CONFESSION

The Scrabster Harbour Master had told them that the Ace of Spades would be in sight about a mile away.

"She'll be here directly. Dinna fret. It's usually misty over the sea at this time."

They heard the distant roar of the Ace's engine and then all of a sudden she loomed out of the mist throwing up a strong wash like a dog holding a huge bone.

Once inside the breakwater the man at the helm turned her round. Soon she was alongside the quay. Without waiting for the lines to be secured Chas jumped across the six foot gap and ran to meet his parents.

"Hi Mum, Dad it's good to see you but what are you doing here?"

"Great to see you Chas and bang on time too."

"We've got to meet the transport. They'll be here in half an hour and they won't be kept waiting. There's got to be a story to this. Why the visit?"

"It's true we've come on a special errand. We've booked in at the Park Hotel, Thurso. Come and have dinner with us and we'll tell you all about it."

"Sounds great. I'll look forward to that. Give me a couple of hours to sign off the catch. It's a good one too, plenty of halibut, we struck lucky, and then I'll be up. I'll change and have a scrub. John can take over until tomorrow. We'll be away in the morning to catch the tide at about six."

As Chas watched his parents drive up the hill he thought to himself,

"I wonder what's brought all this on. It's a long drive from Bolton. I was there four weeks ago, why didn't they mention anything then? It must be important to bring them all this way. Oh well. Strange couple my Mum and Dad."

Later, showered and spruce, not looking in the least like a trawler-man, Chas pushed through the swing doors of the hotel to where his parents were waiting in the bar.

"What's yours?" said Charlie.

"I'll have a Newcastle Brown, thanks Dad. I can't afford to get a skin-full with an early start but a pint will serve me fine. If you get down to the quay in the morning I'll introduce you to the crew."

"That would be nice. I'll be there," replied Charlie "but I can't speak for your Mum."

"Please give the men my best and just tell them I can't get out of bed in the morning. I'm sure they'll understand." said Susan.

"Let's go in shall we?"

After dinner they sat in a quiet corner of the hotel lounge. Luckily they had it more or less to themselves.

"You might find this all a bit upsetting Chas, but let me assure you that you've no need to be worried. I'll do the talking or most of it. Mum will interrupt as necessary. Won't you dear?"

"Rely on me."

"It's quite a long story. When you were little we were living in a flat on the military base in Germany, Osnabruck to be precise. You were born in 1945, the same year the war ended. After I got my medical degree I should have stayed on in Manchester."

"Why didn't you then?"

"Well, we were short of money and I got offered the job in Germany on what was, in those days, a very high salary provided I did some undercover work for MI6. I was working at that time for David, Uncle David. Well to cut a long story short, Auntie Lucy who was living with us . . ."

"Yes, I think I remember that. She left rather suddenly to marry a man in East Germany and then she came back after she had Charlene, my sister but she's not really my sister, because she's Auntie Lucy's and the German. Was he called Carl?"

"Yes, that's right but Carl was killed by an East German border guard and Lucy with Charlene made her escape back to us."

"Gosh. Stop there Dad. This is rather a lot to take in all at once. I'm for another." Raising his glass. "Do you want one?"

"I'm all right, thanks."

"Mum?"

"Sherry?"

"That would be nice, thanks." There was a brief interval while Chas gathered his thoughts.

"So that's a nice story. Lucy got married to David and Charlene came to live with us. Why was that?"

"Well, David didn't really want a baby, someone else's baby. I think he wanted one of his own. Anyway it hasn't happened that way and now we're too old for that."

"So is that all? It all seems straight forward to me. Not worth a journey to tell me that."

"No, it's not quite all. You see, we grown ups got into a love tangle. We were only about 25. I fell in love with Lucy and David fell in love with Susan."

"I thought Susan loved you Dad. Mum you do love Dad don't you? Hell!"

"No, it's not a very nice story but it has a happy ending which is all that matters. Let me continue."

"Can I say a bit now?" Susan interrupted.

"Go on then darling."

"Well Chas, there's being in love and being really in love. Puppy love is not the same as grown up love, as you will find out one day. Your Dad, got a terrible wound while he was working for David, which meant he couldn't have anymore children but neither could he make love to . . . Golly Charlie, I'm getting myself in a mess. You take over the story again."

"Well, you see my boy, I was in love with Lucy and she with me. Then it turned out that David worshipped your Mum, Susan."

"So you got divorced. Is that it?"

"No it's not, we swapped. We just swapped. Lucy came to live with me and called herself Susan and Susan, the real Susan, went to live with David and called herself Lucy, now Lady Lucy. She rather enjoys that."

"Hang on a minute. So Mum, you're not my real Mum at all?"

Chas hung his head in silence for a while and then he said,

"Are you my real Dad?"

"Of course I am and your Mum's genes are the same as your real Mum's. Identical twins have the same, you see. It was the obvious thing to do. We never told anybody. Only Granny and Aunt Edna could tell the difference. Uncle Frank never knew and Edna never told him. The whole thing was perfect. I believe it was meant to turn out that way. We were saved the stress of a divorce and two marriages. Getting divorced in those days was very different from now. You've no idea how things have changed."

Chas leapt to his feet, horrified, knocking over his beer. He almost ran out of the room. Charlie put his arm round Susan who was crying. He watched Chas pacing the car park at the front of the hotel.

"He'll come back darling in his own good time."

Later, when a rather subdued Chas returned, Charlie continued.

"Now you may like to know this as well. Charlene is really your half-sister. I'm her real Dad, not the German at all but she doesn't know that. If you want us to tell her we will but later, when she's a bit older. Now we can't afford to let anybody else know about this, outside the family. I think we are on dangerous ground and if it came out we could be charged with something unpleasant like perjury."

"I see why you've come but did you have to tell me now. I've got enough to think about at the moment and it's a lot to take in. You could have told me all this on my next visit to see you. Why the urgency? Why are you pestering me now? I'll be home in six months."

"It's urgent Chas because the cat is out of the bag. Someone who bears a long standing grudge against me and Uncle David knows our secret and he has the proof. That's what the burglary was all about. Very stupidly I kept our copy of the agreement. It was not so much an agreement as a promise. A bit like the promise we had to make at our wedding. That's what the burglars came for and that's what they got. We didn't need to keep it but I was very sentimental about the whole thing and it was a precious document in my eyes. It was in my desk at the surgery in a kind of secret drawer."

"Who are these burglars?

"I suppose they are East German agents, possibly from the Consulate in Manchester. We'll never know but the agent who bears the grudge says he spent ten years in a Russian jail, all because of David and me. He's a guy called Oskar Krause and as far as we know at the moment he's up to no good in Iceland."

"What's he doing there? He's not trying to interfere with our fishing fleet I hope."

"Not that we know at the moment. David is trying his best to find out what they want him to do. I may as well tell you. He's being blackmailed by Krause who wants him to do something to upset the Iceland Government, really upset them, so that they will close the NATO base. I think Krause is a little crazy actually but with him on the loose anything can happen. David could be in danger and so could I and, come to think of it, so could you."

"So it's urgent. I see. Are you telling me to get out of Iceland, Icelandic waters?"

"No, I don't think so but keep your nose clean. Don't get arrested."

"Dad, we've had over eighty trawlers fishing inside the fifty mile line. They can't arrest us all. Why should they pick on me? I think I know what I'm doing."

"I sincerely hope so Chas."

"It's getting late Dad, Mum. I'd better go and get some kip, I need it." Chas gave his Mum a big bear-hug. Holding her close he whispered, "I wouldn't have any other Mum than you."

"I'll walk down with you to the Ace. Won't be long Sue."

The following morning Charlie was on the quay-side to meet the crew. He was very favourably impressed. They showed him all over the Ace."

"Just let me know when you're short handed. I'll come and sign on myself," he said.

"Not a bad thought that, you could be the fleet's doctor."

Taking his Dad's right hand in his he said,

"Well, goodbye and thanks for the warning. I'll get used to the idea. Don't worry about me. I'm carrying a lot of responsibility already, looking after my chaps. A bit more won't hurt." The two men stood face to face for a moment then with a smile Chas moved towards his father and wrapped his arms around him. Charlie went to the end of the breakwater to watch the Ace fade into the morning mist and then he walked back to the Park Hotel deep in thought about the future.

12 RIOT

"Now Max, let's see what we have," said Krause. "Our suspicions have been proved, all along, nicht? I shall not be satisfied until His Excellency, Ambassador Brown and his brother—in-law have been eliminated. Ten years of my life, wasted because of them."

"So the question of the NATO base is of secondary importance to you. Is that right then Kapitan?"

"Absolutely right. KGB Command has posted me here to do a job, to close down the NATO base. But you and I, Max, know that comes second to my personal ambition, to kill my enemies."

"How do you propose we set about your plan then, Comrade Oskar."

"The first target will undoubtedly be David Brown. That task I delegate to you Max. Summer will soon be upon us, the time when the Ambassador organises his shooting days with his friend, Harald Gunnarsson. They normally go out in parties of five or six. It would be a pity if there was an accident and a member of the group was shot but it must seem like an accident. That is absolutely essential. I do not want a murder enquiry to get in the way of my next move."

"If it appears to be an accident, will not that deprive you of your greatest satisfaction?"

"Time for that later. In due course a letter will appear in the British press. Need I say more?"

"I understand Comrade but how do you intend to proceed with the elimination of Doctor Charlie Forbes."

"That's somewhat more complex and may well involve the elimination of some of Forbes' collaborators as well. I have not yet decided the best, and when I say 'best', I mean the most spectacular way of orchestrating the affray. I need to involve the forces at my disposal in the closure of the NATO Base."

"Surely a daunting task."

"Daunting indeed but one I shall enjoy planning. We shall have my friend Reynir to assist us. We need him to put a proposal in the Althing soon and in the meantime there is little we can do except to advise the coastguard not to interfere with fishing for a time. I have been informed that the Ace of Spades is fishing almost up to the old twelve mile limit. They have even taken shelter in Hyamms Fjord from the weather to enable them to catch up with their gutting and packing. They will be allowed to sail back to Britain unmolested. Their catch, worth probably as much as fifty thousand pounds, will be a small amount compared to the value of the ship, which will be arrested as soon as they return. Nicht?"

"So what do you want me to do when I to return to Reykjavik?"

"Your primary task my dear Max is to liaise with Reynir. Everything must be done through him. I want him to advise Commander Gudmundur Kjaernested who is in charge of the coastguard. First to institute a lull in the hunt for poachers and then, after about three weeks, attack them with all the coastguard fleet. I want the Ace of Spades arrested above all else. Contrary to their normal practice, I want them to co-ordinate their attacks."

"And Ambassador Brown?"

"That is a task for you, as I said."

A week later Krause arranged another meeting with Max.

"My dear Max, now is the time to act."

"My plans are well advanced Kapitan. I have made contact with Reynir and he is in favour of the idea. Anti-British feeling is running very high with the general population at the moment. There are several members of the Communist party who have already promised to support us. We have a long article in Morgunbladid which should do the trick. We have to be careful at this stage not to alarm the Ambassador otherwise he may take avoiding action."

"I admire your thoroughness. You will still have to reckon with a lot of feeling sympathetic to Britain. Historically Iceland and Britain, especially Scotland, have always been good friends."

"Have no worries on that score. Everyone is more patriotic than political. The Cod War reaches across every party. Now we have a substantial representation in the Althing we shall make sure there is no undue police presence on the night."

"And when is the night."

"My ad hoc committee are undecided at the moment. I expect to get some advice from our sleeper in the Residence. A month from now there is to be an important dinner there. Maybe that will be the best time."

"Unless Reynir is there."

"I don't see that should matter. If he is there it should be a good alibi for him, nicht?"

"Well I leave it to you. Keep me informed please."

"Certainly Kapitan."

****

The British Residence in Reykjavik stands above the road and about the length of a cricket pitch from the iron gates which are situated on the edge of the pavement. The tall windows of the main dining room face the road. Lucy was busy preparing for an informal evening with a few friendly influential 'nobs'. Invited guests included Jon Petursson, the Chairman of the Trawler Company, Albert Gudmundsson, a famous footballer and coach and David's shooting pal, his great friend, Haraldur Gunnarsson. From the embassy itself the First Secretary, Robert Cecil and the Head of Chancery Brian Holt, were also expected, all with their wives of course. It took most of the afternoon to lay the long beautifully polished table. At about three o'clock Lucy's attention was drawn to a small crowd gathered in the road. This was not unusual since the embassy building always attracted its fair share of tourists. By four o'clock the crowd had noticeably become larger. A lorry was tipping what appeared to be a pile of stones on the opposite side of the road. Half an hour later another lorry came and tipped a similar pile some yards away from the first.

Lucy stopped what she was doing, polishing glassware and walked upstairs to David's office.

"Darling, I suppose you will think I'm being a bit silly but I want you to come with me to the dining room or better still, our bedroom and watch what is going on outside. I don't know what to make of it but it doesn't look good."

"I'm very busy at the moment. Can it wait?"

"Darling I'm worried, come . . . Come now."

"All right then, I'm coming. Just a minute."

David followed his wife to their bedroom which is situated directly over the dining room. When he saw the size of the crowd now assembled in the road he became alarmed.

"I see what you mean," he said. "You should have come sooner. Has anyone else noticed? Nobody has told me."

"Brian and Robert haven't come from town yet and the kitchen staff are all in the basement."

"Phone the police. Ask to speak to your friend, Vilbert Agnarsson. He's invited to-night isn't he?"

"He's no friend of mine, darling . . . the best knee stroker in town."

"He likes you."

"Huh."

Some time later Lucy said,

"Agnarsson's not there. I spoke to the duty sergeant. He said he had no one available at the moment but he would send a constable as soon as possible. It doesn't seem as though they rate us as a very high priority."

At that moment there was a crash and the sound of falling glass, followed by a cheer from the crowd on the road. David went to the bedroom window. He estimated the crowd had now grown to about two hundred, mostly young men with a few young women amongst them. No elderly were to be seen. He 'phoned the embassy's offices in town. Brian Holt was still there but on the point of leaving for the Residence.

"Brian," said David. "We're under siege here. Are there any hooligans attacking the office?"

"Not as yet. I'll get to you as soon as possible."

"Go to the police station first and get the law and hurry. It looks as though we'll have to buy a lot of glass tomorrow."

"OK. I'll give you another call from there. Good luck."

With that there was another crash from the dining room. David could see the lawn littered with stones which had fallen short. Lucy rang the guests who had been invited to dinner and cancelled everything. She rang Robert Cecil.

"Is that Margaret?"

"Yes, Lucy, it is. Brian just phoned. He said the Residence is being stoned, not you personally, I mean the Residence. Robert says he's coming to see you. You had to cancel dinner?"

"Has he left yet? If not tell him to go round the back. There must be two hundred hooligans at the front. The gates are not locked. It's only a matter of time before they push their way in."

"I'll phone the police."

"I've already done that, several times, and Brian's there. The noise here is deafening. Every time they score a hit, break a window I mean, they send up a huge cheer."

"I can hear them in the background. Aren't you frightened?"

"Funnily, I'm not actually. We've had worse. Not here I mean but in Egypt over the Suez problem.

They've been at it since five o'clock. The lawn is covered in their ammunition. There are a few with catapults. Pretty accurate too. The stones from those come right through the curtains too."

"My dear, I should be terrified."

"I must go Margaret. Your husband's just arrived. Robert, how nice of you to come over. There's nothing much to do I'm afraid except sit it out."

"I can help clear up."

"Not yet you can't. The whole thing was organised. The stones were delivered this afternoon by lorry, two loads."

"I might guess who that was and he got rent-a-crowd too."

The crashes from broken windows were getting much more frequent. A small gang of boys were on the lawn recovering stones which had fallen short. Someone came with fireworks, probably marine rockets.

After a few minutes of bombardment with these, the dining room curtains were set alight. The crowd suddenly went silent except for a few wolf-whistles and jeers. David and the butler used the fire-extinguishers and when these were exhausted the staff, now organised by David, started a chain of water buckets. David used a recently purchased radiogram to play 'Land of Hope and Glory' on maximum volume. In the silence which followed the fire, the strains of the 'British Anthem' served to galvanise the crowd to renewed fury. He turned it off.

"I'm going outside to speak to them," he said.

"No . . . no, darling you mustn't. You'll be stoned to death."

They all heard the sharp crack of something more lethal than a stone.

110

"That was a gun."

"You're right Robert. That was indeed a gun shot. I've heard enough in my time," said David.

"This is not a joke any more."

"As if it ever was. How can you say that Robert?" said Lucy.

"Everyone move into the back room, please. As for the blaze, let it burn. Come on," said David

The crowd was suddenly subdued. As if the rifle shot had been a signal to terminate the proceedings, people began to drift away.

"Are you still going to talk to them?" asked Lucy.

"No. Definitely not. Not now."

"It was you they were gunning for darling. There's no one here worth hitting, only you."

"I think I may have had a narrow escape."

"What were you going to say? What could you possibly say? Their newspapers have said it all. It would have been a crazy gesture. In any case they are beginning to drift away now and I think someone has called the fire brigade."

"The fire's under control. I hope they don't make it worse."

"The police are here. Took their time didn't they."

"At last."

"I don't think we can expect much from them. When all comes to all we shall only need some new curtains and glass. I'll see to it in the morning. Robert."

"Yes."

"We'll keep a vigil if you don't mind. You do from now until four and then wake me and we'll have breakfast at eight in the morning room, OK?"

"Fine, that's fine. I'll try to get a constable posted on the gate too."

By the evening of the following day the Residence had new windows along the frontage, paid for by the Althing. Later it turned out that there were three lorry loads of ammunition but the third driver lost his way and tipped his load outside the Danish Embassy. The negative publicity which followed the 'hooliganism' of the Icelandic Kristal Nacht lasted several months and did much to take pressure off the Royal Naval escorts at sea. Furthermore David noticed an easing of the tension with the American forces in Keflavik.

"It turned out to be a good night for us," he remarked. "Well worth a few windows which their Government paid for anyway."

The following week David had to revise his thinking. A British trawler, Northern Wave, from Hull was seized and a prize crew put aboard. A frigate went alongside and the Captain demanded that they withdraw. On meeting with a refusal he put a party aboard the trawler and captured the Icelanders, removing them to Her Majesty's ship. The coastguard refused to have his crew back so a stalemate ensued. It seemed that the nine members of his prize crew would be guests of the Navy until the frigate returned to a British port. At first David was rather amused by this impasse but messages back from the Foreign Office took a more sombre attitude. In the end David solved the problem. The nine were embarked onto the motor-lifeboat in the night near the coast; cost to the Admiralty was about £3000. As the weeks wore on, the four Icelandic gunboats gained the advantage. They arrested a score of trawlers allegedly poaching. The offending ship would be escorted to Reykjavik, his catch confiscated and the skipper fined or put on trial. Coastguard vessels could return to their home base only to set out on patrol the next day, refuelled and refreshed. Meanwhile the naval escorts patrolled the disputed area in all weathers along with the fleet auxiliaries, a tanker, the Mirander and several civilian tugs on charter to MAFF, the Ministry. The Mirander supplied food and medical aid having a full operating theatre. The Icelandic Catalina Flying Boat kept the coastguards up to date with the position of the fleet and, more importantly, if any trawlers were fishing outside the 'box' where they could be easily arrested. Ships resisting arrest were often fired on. Solid shot delivered to the bow below the waterline could sink a trawler unless repairs were carried out within a few hours.

****

Krause and Max met the following morning to talk over the result of the previous night's attempt to inflame anti-British feeling.

"Now Max, what news?"

"We failed."

"I know you failed. I'm astonished that you ever attempted such a mad scheme and without consulting me first."

"My marksman, Schlinkler, was incompetent. He was stationed on the first floor of an office on the opposite side of the road. He had five rounds of ammunition in a sporting rifle. His shots were drowned out by the angry crowd but he claimed a hit on the Ambassador. Our target could not be properly identified behind curtains. When the curtains caught fire he thought he saw Brown passing buckets and he fired off three more rounds only to be stopped by a posse who came up inside the building. I don't know how they got in but there were four of them. They took his gun and escorted my man back to the pavement. They said the protest was to be peaceful and he was lucky not to be arrested for attempted murder."

"That was a stupid plot. It could have been a disaster. As things are the whole fracas has been a waste. The world's press is against us. We have handed the enemy a propaganda coup of value to them which could last for months. If you had consulted me I would never have sanctioned it. I see in the paper this morning that the police have identified one of your bullets. They dug it out of the dining room plaster. All we need now is for your vigilantes to shop you. You could be locked up for a long time. Forget the shooting party option. You'll have to think of some other way. The co-incidence could be too much for credibility. I need to know every move in future. On no account attempt anything like that again."

13   ARREST

The Ace had been at sea for three weeks. The crew were worn out. At the end of the summer season the catches had been more than disappointing. "Catastrophic," John said,

"If we don't turn for home tomorrow or the day after we'll have a mutiny on our hands."

"If we do go home with only three quarters of a catch, if that, there'll be a pretty poor payout for everyone," retorted Chas.

On board the Ace two men had been injured and were no longer able to carry out their duties putting more strain on the other men. Chas knew that to put into Reykjavik for them to be hospitalised would result in the arrest of his ship and himself.

"Skipper, this is not funny. I think Tim has broken his arm. He's in terrible pain or he would be if I hadn't dosed him with morphine. We really should go home."

"OK, we will. As soon as we finish this trawl, we'll stow and set off for Hull. We could put him aboard Miranda. He would get treatment for his arm. If it is broken the quack would set it."

"No skipper. It'll be almost impossible to transfer him in this weather, too risky. The rubber dinghy will be swamped. Better to take him home and then his family can visit him."

"OK. Pass the word. Let this be our last haul and then homeward. Sparks."

"Yes Skipper."

"Tell Eastbourne we're off home."

"Aye, aye."

The weather had been unrelenting, day after day of winds in excess of gale force, sometimes severe gales. The Ace had circumnavigated Iceland twice in search of the shoals. The constant westerlies had forced the bulk of the fleet round to the east of the island. In the west three trawlers had been driven ashore and lost. The coastguard vessels in the area had risked their own lives to rescue the crews. Two trawlers had gone down with gunshot holes below the water line. The Navy frigates had attempted the impossible in protecting the fleet. There had been several instances of ramming with blame allocated to each side of the dispute in equal measure. The Admiralty was getting short of frigates to send on Icelandic patrols.

"Skip, there's a hell of a lot of talk on channel twelve. It sounds as though HMS Diomede has had a serious collision with Baldur, one of their gunboats . . . converted trawler . . . sturdy little beast."

"Yes John, but the coastguards have been a lot more aggressive recently, especially Baldur."

"This is something special. They've worked out a tactic to deal with us; steam alongside and then use their duel-screws to rotate their stern into the frigate's mid-ship plates. It's a bit like an aggressive pony lashing out with hind legs."

"How bad was the damage?"

"I didn't catch all that but she has a gash in her port side and is to be sent home to Chatham for repair."

"If she can make Chatham the damage must be containable."

"Not so apparently. The crew are doing a massive job keeping her sea worthy."

"Skip, there's a vessel coming up fast on our starboard quarter. Could be the enemy. Viz is less than two miles."

"About three miles and two cables. Soddin hell he can move."

"Where's the navy?"

"Leopard, ten miles, dead ahead and Eastbourne, bearing about forty-five, starboard, in sight about a mile."

"Right then, rouse the crew, steer for Eastbourne as soon as you can and start hauling."

"Aye, aye."

"If it's Thor I think we can outrun her as soon as the net's in and get behind the Eastbourne. It's going to take ten minutes to winch in the net at this depth. It will take Thor about three minutes to realise we've changed course. He's relying on his radar, same as us. Sparks, radio Eastbourne and ask for cover."

"Eastbourne's replied Skip, says he's shadowing three of ours, fishing, out of sight at a range of about five miles. They can't help us. They're steering east northeast doing three knots."

"Cod end aboard, skipper."

"We'll never do it, now. Damn Eastbourne. Here comes Thor. It's not Thor. It's Aegir. Hell, no wonder he can move."

"In sight now. Skipper, he's changed course to intercept us. I think he's going to hoist a signal flag. Yes, there it goes. K over L, 'stop instantly'. I think he wants us to stop."

"Oh really. I would never have guessed."

At a range of a mile Aegir opened fire with live shells. The shot landed about a cable off the Ace's bow. Two minutes later another shot landed alongside, so close as to splash the bridge deck. Chas stopped the engines while the Icelandic vessel came alongside.

"They know how to shoot," remarked John.

Captain Kjaernested put the loud hailer to his lips and spoke across the narrow gap between the coastguard vessel and the Ace.

"Unless you follow us into Reykjavik, Captain we will sink your vessel."

"We've stowed our gear and intend to head for home Captain. We have been informed by our Ministry that we are entitled to fish in these waters," Chas spoke into the radio more in hope than anger.

With that another shot rang out at point blank range. Using solid shot the coastguard vessel punched a hole in the starboard bow of the Ace six feet above the water line.

"Follow me," came from the Aegir.

"He means it," said John. "Better do as he says Skip."

"Send someone below John. Find out if anyone's been hit and have a look at the damage. Mike, take the helm. Follow the Aegir."

Four hours later the Ace entered Reykjavik harbour. A launch came alongside with ten men aboard. They took over the navigation of the Ace which was moored to the main quay. The Ace's crew were instructed to go ashore where a bus waited to take them to the police cells. Chas and John were detained on board to answer questions put to them by the harbour master, Captain Georg Baldursson who said,

"Please complete these forms and handover your seamen's papers and those of your crew."

Chas said,

"Two of my crew members are hospital cases. Both are severely injured. Please will you attend to their needs as a matter of priority? We were on passage to England when arrested, in order to get those men properly treated."

"We will attend to their needs Captain, rest assured. We in Iceland are not barbarians but first, the forms please." Formalities completed Chas was then asked to sign away ownership of the fish in the cold room. Next, an elderly seaman came aboard who introduced himself as Captain Bjorn Liefsson.

"Hello, Captain Forbes. Who are your owners?"

"This is my ship. The legal owner is Ace of Spades Ltd. Registered in Hull, England. My father and I are the sole shareholders."

"You and your ship and your Mate are under formal arrest. Your case will be heard in court tomorrow. There will be a fine according to the size of the vessel. Your fishing gear will be confiscated. On receipt of the money, paid into Landsbankinn, your ship will be discharged. Under the command of your Mate, your ship and crew will be escorted to the edge of Icelandic waters, fifty miles offshore. They will then be free to sail back to their home port. You, Captain Forbes, may well have to serve a term in our prison."

The following morning Chas found himself in the courtroom after a sleepless night, his mood alternating between anger, frustration and self pity. Though furious he swallowed his pride and listened patiently to the arraignment delivered by the prosecutor. The magistrate asked Chas to plead and if he had anything to say. Chas pleaded 'guilty' to fishing within fifty miles of the coast of Iceland, stating that he had been assured by the British Ministry that the sovereignty of the waters within fifty miles but outside twelve miles was still 'sub judice' and that he was entitled to fish there with the protection of the British Navy.

The Magistrate stated that the Navy offered no such protection, which was illegal anyway. He sentenced Chas to two years in prison with the possibility of remission after one, subject to good behaviour. There was a fine of ten thousand pounds in addition to the fishing gear and the catch, which was also confiscated. The case took less than ten minutes. Chas' advocate sought leave to appeal which was granted. John was released but cautioned not to fish again in Icelandic waters.

Chas was led below to the police cells. He asked for permission to 'phone the British Embassy.

****

"Uncle David. Is that Uncle David?"

"Yes it is Charles but are you speaking as my nephew or are you speaking as a British citizen asking for the protection of the British Government?"

"Come off it Uncle. Don't sound so bloody pompous. You know, I suppose, that I've been thrown into jail by the bloody Icelandics."

"Yes Charles . . ."

"I'm Chas. I can't abide Charles. Why couldn't I have been Jack or something? My Grandfather was Jack."

"You're in jail Chas because, whatever my Government thinks, you have offended their laws on their home patch."

"Hang on a minute Uncle. I offended no one. Their home patch does not extend fifty miles off shore. They threatened to kill the lot of us. I was shelled with live ammo. That's got to be piracy by anybody's bloody laws."

"I'm sorry. This is not getting either of us anywhere. I'll try to get to see you tomorrow. It's highly irregular for me to go round Iceland's prisons. That's normally a job for the first or second secretary."

"God Uncle. You sound like some almighty monarch. I'm your nephew for heaven's sake."

"I'll see you tomorrow. Bye now."

"Good bye and thanks a million," came the sarcastic riposte.

Chas spent a miserable night brooding on his predicament. He didn't relish his stay in a police cell. He came to the conclusion, rightly, that the level of comfort, or rather discomfort, was aimed at drunken Saturday night revellers. In the morning, unwashed and unshaven, he felt like a vagrant picked out of the gutter instead of the skipper of an important trawler. Breakfast, instead of his customary egg, bacon, sausage and chips, had consisted of a thin mixture of milk and sawdust or so it seemed.

At two o'clock the cell door yielded Uncle David.

"John, Uncle, where's John. He's my Mate, the Mate of the Ace. He needs to be with us."

"Patience Chas. Here's what I've done so far. It may not seem much to you but I've done everything possible in the time available. I've paid your fine, all ten thousand pounds of it."

"How are the crew?"

"I'm trying to get the authorities to repatriate them by air. Meanwhile they're sleeping in the seamens' hostel."

"What about Mike and Tim. I would like to see them in hospital but I don't suppose they will let me do that."

"They're both out. Tim's had his arm put in plaster. Mike's been bandaged up. I'll give them your best wishes. The rest of the crew are well."

"That's good news. I hope they get sent home but not John."

"If that's what you want."

"What's happening to the Ace?"

"The harbour master is looking after her pending your appeal if there is to be one."

"I object. It's my ship. Don't I get any say in what happens to my ship?"

"Well what do you want to happen to your ship?"

"I should be aboard for one thing."

"That's impossible. You know that. If the Ace stays here, waiting your release, what will it look like in two years? It will be a wreck with barnacles and weed growing like a garden on its hull and not a scrap of paint on the top-sides. Be realistic. Issue instructions to your Dad to sell her."

"Over my dead body. I'll be out of here soon. Just you see."

"You won't get out unless they let you out. I'll do what I can but we may have to sell the boat to pay lawyers."

"That's nonsense. I've got money in the bank."

"Anyway, relax and know that we are doing everything possible. If my despatches to the FO ever get read this stupid war may finish quite soon. Escape from the State prison is impossible so they run the place on a loose rein. The Icelandic Government is a lot more humane that ours. They believe in rehabilitation."

"I don't care about that. I just want to know when my appeal will come up."

"Like I said, escape is impossible so just be patient, relax. Make use of the library and other facilities."

"Relax, how can I relax? Uncle, whose side are you on? Now you sound like an Icelandic travel agent."

"You don't really have much choice. You can't stay here. The weekend's coming up and they need all the cells every Saturday night . . . You really want to appeal?"

"Too bloody right I do."

"You realise that if it goes to a higher court they may increase your sentence."

"I'll take that risk. What I want is an English lawyer. My advocate was useless. The Governor of the State Prison has been to see me."

"You're privileged. How did you manage that one?"

"He just came. Said he was trying to help. He suggested that I should appeal to the higher court. I told him my advocate had already asked."

"What did he say to that?"

"He just nodded so I told him I wanted an English lawyer."

"OK Chas. I'll see what I can do. It'll cost."

"I'll pay. Another thing. When can you get Dad over here?"

"Why? He's working."

"Just for a spell. I know how busy you are."

"All right then. I know when I'm not wanted but believe me, no one but no one, not even your Dad, could have done more than I have."

"He's got a majority share in the Ace. I don't want her to be sold. Keep the Ace on a mooring until Dad gets here. Keep John on full pay and ask him to keep an eye on the Ace. As soon as Dad lands I want to talk to him."

"I'll see what I can do. Is that all?"

"That's all Uncle. Sorry I was rude but I'm under stress."

"I understand that Chas but don't be rude to the prison staff. By the way, you did right pleading guilty. Otherwise it could have been four years."

"See me tomorrow?"

"I doubt it. You'll probably get transferred tomorrow. Maybe you'll be in the State Prison at Grundarfjordur. There are some other skippers there too you know. You'll have company. All I can do now is to ensure reasonable treatment for you. It's a bit like a hotel, very comfortable only you can't go out, that's all."

"Where the hell is it?"

"It's on the peninsula, about a hundred and sixty kilometers north of here. That's about a hundred miles, too far to walk. In the winter it's virtually inaccessible. It's built on the side of a mountain about half a mile from the road."

"You seem to know a lot about it."

"There's good hunting in the region. It's very isolated."

"How am I going to get out? It sounds like Dartmoor."

"Now I really must go. I'll do what I can. Bye."

"My God uncle, are you not even coming to see me again?"

"I haven't the time to spend a whole day visiting you."

"Well then send my Mum, my real Mum."

"I'm not sending anyone. Lucy may wish to see you but that's her decision. You can run up a bill with telephone calls and I'll pay. If your Dad come's over he will wish to see you straight away. When you get visitors don't alienate them by being bad tempered or angry. What you are going through is largely your own fault. Now I really must go. It's going to get dark and the roads might be icy. Don't forget we shall be doing our best for you.

"Bye Uncle."

****

In Bolton Charlie is busy making some hasty plans.

"Kay, I've got to fly out to Iceland, today or tomorrow."

"What's happened? Why the rush?"

"Susan's just opened a telegram from David. It was delivered by hand. It's bad news. Chas has been arrested. He's in the lock-up at the moment and says he wants to see me. Cancel everything today. I'm going home to pack."

"What's he done?"

"Nothing much except fishing. Fishing in a prohibited area apparently. Can you get me on a flight later today or tomorrow?"

"I'll try."

"And then fix up a locum. Dick can usually manage it at short notice. That's if he's not in a four-ball at the Old Links. Phone me at home. Allow me twenty minutes to get there."

Charlie reversed the Lagonda out of its parking niche at the front of the surgery. Once clear of the town he broke the speed limit up the Chorley Road and twenty minutes later walked into Belvedere.

"I'm home," he called from the front porch. Susan came out of the kitchen wiping her hands.

"Darling. What are we going to do?"

"I don't know what we can do but if he wants to see me I'm going. It must be serious. Maybe he thinks I can do something to help. I suppose the coastguard arrested him for trawling in a prohibited area. Let's see the telegram."

"Here". Susan passed the telegram and then overcome with emotion she sat at the table, put her hands over her face and started to cry.

"It happened two days ago but he only came before their court this morning apparently. David must have sent this as soon as the case closed. He got two years. Here, have my hankie." Susan spoke through her tears

"I'd just finished speaking to Kay and put the phone down as you drove in. She says there are no more Icelandic flights this week. You could go tomorrow via Copenhagen and catch a connection the day after that. Cooks have shopped around apparently and that's the best option, apart from flying out on Monday. In any event Dick is already doing a locum but he could start on Monday."

"Well, it seems Chas will have to wait. It's only two days. Going via Copenhagen won't help."

"I'd like to come too."

"Why on earth Sue?"

"You never know. I've no special reason but the authorities might yield to an impassioned plea from the parents and the promise not to do it again."

"That's ridiculous. Chas is not a child. He knew what he was doing. Frankly I don't really know why I'm going out there. I'm sure there's nothing to be done."

"Charlie, don't be like that. He could get some remission. Maybe we could plead to get him out on bail pending the appeal. I'm worried. If Chas does something stupid they might extend his sentence."

"There's no chance of bail. Unsupervised he could jump bail on to a cargo vessel or the ferry. If he did that he could cause a diplomatic incident with profound repercussions. No forget it. You're wasting your breath."

"No need to be sharp. It was only an idea."

"Sorry darling. I'm all on edge. I must get through to David. I'll book a call, person to person."

"I tried. The exchange said there's an hours waiting list."

After the forecast delay the phone rang. It was David. He said,

"I've paid his fine pro tem. I'll be sending you the bill Charlie. It's ten grand."

"What's to become of the Ace?"

"So long as we pay the mooring fee she'll be OK for the moment. I've found a retired skipper, by the name of Liefsson, to keep an eye on her. He's sleeping aboard and running up the engines every day."

"How much is that costing?"

"I don't know yet but I'll be picking up the bill for that too. When Chas gives the OK I'll put the Ace up for sale if you like. There'll be a lot of trawlers for sale soon. The best ones will probably find themselves in the Pacific eventually."

"I'm flying out on Monday. It's the best I can do."

"There's no hurry. Chas is quite safe inside and the Mate, John, is staying on for a while in case he is needed. Chas has some idea about getting out soon. If there is a settlement I'm sure all the skippers in jail will be released and their vessels too, as part of it."

"Well we're coming,"

"We."

"Yes Susan wants to come with me. Is that OK?"

"Of course. It will be nice to see you both even if the circumstances are unfortunate."

When Charlie came off the phone Susan said,

"We'll never get our money back, Charlie. I didn't want all this to happen right from the start.

I think Chas should have let John bring her home."

"I agree with that but he didn't, did he? Anyway, unless something comes along soon we'll have to let John go home too. We can always get him back with a scratch crew. He's one hundred per cent reliable"

"Amen to that."

14   CONTACT

The East German fishing fleet had returned. Kapitan Oskar Krause planned to fly out to rejoin the Kerenski in the Barent Sea. His job demanded that the activities of the trawlers should be closely supervised since it was not unknown for crews to defect to the west but before he departed he wanted a full report from Max on the progress of a certain court case, namely Iceland versus Captain Forbes.

Max reported, "So far so good Comrade Oskar. Things are beginning to take a shape at last. Aegir had one hundred percent success. Captain Kjaernested is a wily old bird. He stalked the Ace with the benefit of a thick mist, keeping well within the group of Icelandic trawlers. Then when he knew he was within striking distance he put on his twenty knots. Ace's only option was to reach 'Eastbourne' but she was fully occupied by the manoeuvres of Thor and Tyr. Our plan could not have worked better. One of their most important vessels is in the bag and going nowhere for the moment. Captain Forbes has been sentenced to two years in the State Prison. Reynir has suggested to the Governor that Forbes might use his father's and uncle's influence to get his sentence reduced by appealing to a higher court. Now, as I understand it, Forbes has already been visited by Ambassador Brown. I am hoping that the good Doctor, Doctor Charlie Forbes will be visiting Iceland before long, your old enemy, nicht?"

"Is that reliable?"

"My information is 'yes'. The Legation in Manchester has sent a telex. Forbes Senior has booked a flight with SAS. I shall watch all incoming flights from England. Stage two of our plan is to demonstrate to the Althing that Britain has no intention of ever relinquishing fishing rights beyond the twelve mile limit and will not submit to what they call 'blackmail' over the NATO Base. Iceland's agreement with NATO can be terminated at any time with twelve month's notice. All we need is a resolution by the Althing to bring this about and then NATO will have to bring pressure on the British."

"We need to do more. The British Embassy's dinner will be crucial but so far we have done nothing to persuade Ambassador Brown. He regards his duty to his Foreign Office as paramount. He can easily call our bluff. Once his secret is out he has nothing more to lose and we shall be disarmed."

"What do you propose to do then Comrade Oskar?"

"I propose to leave the detail to you. As for me, my work is on the Kerenski."

"The time will come when we shall have the perfect opportunity for a strike, a strike when we can eliminate your enemy, Charlie Forbes, but we lack the means. I can provide the opportunity but you must provide the means."

"Their trawler is now in the old harbour, nicht?"

"That is correct, Comrade."

"We must persuade the authorities to release the ship in such a way that Doctor Charlie Forbes is on board when the skipper, who will be Chas, the doctor's son, takes it to sea. A remote activated bomb perhaps? I will make enquiries but whatever we do it must not be connected to this Legation, understood?"

"I understand completely Comrade. I will provide the opportunity if you will provide the means, agreed?"

"Perfect. I will keep you informed."

****

Jonny flew in from London. On his arrival he telephoned David at the Residence knowing that he would not be still at the offices in the city. Nevertheless he hoped David would be prepared to meet him at the late hour.

"David, can we meet?"

"Here or in town?"

"At your offices."

"Sure, I'll be there in twenty minutes."

Jonny walked from the hotel to the embassy office. David drove his personal car.

"Hello Jonny, it's good to see you again. When did you arrive?"

"I was lucky to get a seat on the afternoon flight. I'm staying at The Grand for the moment. It's impossible to be invisible so I'm just a tourist doing a bit of bird watching, hence this camera."

"I thought you could stay with me at the Residence."

"No way. I need to fade into the undergrowth."

"OK then. Fill me in."

"Charlie's planning to fly out on Monday."

"So I believe."

"You realise this was a set up?"

"What do you mean, Jonny?"

"Krause and Captain Kjaernested planned it very cleverly and Reynir sent a message to the prison. Chas fell into their trap. He's asked his father to fly over."

"What good will that do?"

"None at all that I can see, as yet, but I think you should get Charlie to stay on for the dinner."

"What about you?"

"I'm incognito remember, but I think it will look a bit funny if he flies back beforehand."

"I think he only plans to stay for a week. Hard luck about you though. It's one of Iceland's big events. We have to invite the Althing en-bloc and nearly all the Ambassadors as well as personal friends and other dignitaries."

"I'm surprised there's a room big enough."

"It's always held in the ballroom of the Grand."

"In view of what's going on at the moment I'll be surprised if anyone will turn up."

"Yes, that will be interesting. Most of the invited Embassies will come, I'm sure. So will friends and most of the 'also-rans'. As for the Althing, I'm not sure. 'Iceland first, politics second' that's their unofficial motto. They are totally nationalistic to a man."

"I've got a contact in the Base," said Jonny.

"That's quick work. You've done well. What's his name?"

"My friend the General got it via MI6. He's CIA and stationed there. He's expecting me to send him a wire from your secure Visa Section and then he'll come back with a point of contact."

"I see. There's something you should know. Krause has a gofer called Max. I've met him. With the German trawlers away he'll be holed up somewhere here, probably in the East German Legation. He'll be party to all their plans. It's vital we find out what they are up to. We may get all the evidence we need to see them off."

"I think we may be too late for that. The Kerenski is back from Gydnia"

"Oh, I see." David's brow wrinkled in thought for a moment. "Well then never mind. We've other fish to fry," he said, more in hope than conviction. "We may be lucky. Max has a mistress who is working for us."

"Ok. I'll see what the CIA know about that. Have you a name?"

"Not yet. See what you can find out. The CIA may be a good place to start."

"I've got to say this. Krause is not going away just because we see him off this time. What's Charlie done about his daughter?"

"Nothing that I know of. Term starts next week. She'll not want to go abroad now. Anyway she'll be OK with Kay there."

"David, that's madness. I told Charlie to fly her out. I offered him my place. Maria would make her very welcome."

"That's good advice Jonny and kind of you but I don't think we can do much just now. Thanks all the same. It's better if you leave by the side door. There's no bird watching in the dark."

****

Lady Lucy stood just inside the visitor's lounge at Keflavik Airport. On the tarmac outside, David, wearing a heavy service overcoat and a Balaclava helmet, stood with his eyes watering in the stiff north easterly wind. The plane was still out of sight in the mist although the waiting crowd had heard the announcement of its imminent arrival. Minutes later the SAS Viscount Turbo Prop taxied up to the terminal building. The hydraulic steps lowered and passengers started to descend.

"Susan, Susan." Lucy's shrill voice was carried away by the breeze. Soon they were in each others arms. "Sue, it's lovely to see you. We're in terrible trouble here. They've locked up Chas."

"I know that's why we've come but I don't know if we can help."

Lucy said, "I've got the germ of an idea. I'll tell you about it later." After exchanging a long hug with Susan, David escorted them to the waiting embassy car. He returned to see Charlie standing in the immigration line with his arm round Lucy.

"Over here old man. Special clearance. The luggage will be put in the other car. No waiting."

Charlie said, "Hello David, great to see you in spite of the circumstances."

They shook hands and embraced. In the car on the short journey to Reykjavik, David gave them a brief résumé of recent events leading up to their decision to visit Chas in prison.

"So, he applied for bail?" queried Charlie.

"Turned down old man. Turned down out of hand. They'll be thinking he can do a bunk. It's too easy down at the docks. They're not as tight as the police are."

"It's terrible," said Susan. "Who do they think they are?"

"Don't for heavens sake try that one here Susan," said David. "It may work in the Bolton market but not here."

"You've no need to be insulting, David. I'll just have to shut up."

"Good idea," muttered Lucy.

The embassy car drew up outside the Residence. The driver walked round the car and opened the door for the twins and Charlie. The other car stopped behind them. David thanked the drivers who helped with the luggage.

As Lucy helped Susan unpack her large suitcase she remarked,

"Gosh Sue, are you planning to stay a year? You've brought more stuff than I have in my wardrobe."

"I really don't know. It's up to Charlie. We've only booked the locum for a week. I'd no idea what it would be like, weather and such and Charlie mentioned a big dinner so we don't expect to stay for more than that."

"So you might miss the dinner. Anyway, I'm glad Charlie didn't stop you from coming."

"After I got your wire nothing could stop me. My only worry is Charlene."

"Kay will keep in touch with her I'm sure."

"True. Now what's the big idea?"

"Too soon to say at the moment but I've got ideas and it all depends on you. Do you think you could keep out of sight, I mean really out of sight, in this room?"

"What's this all about Lucy? In this room? For how long? What are you on about?"

"My plan, no, my idea depends entirely on you and it's to do with getting Chas out of jail."

"I fail to see . . ."

"Don't ask questions. Trust me. We now know who the enemy are."

"Who then? The same gang that broke into Belvedere presumably."

"Yes, but they were acting under orders. Orders from here, Iceland."

Just then the internal phone rang. Lucy answered it.

"Tea's in the drawing room. David says to go down. I'll tell him you wanted a rest after the journey. I'll tell you all about my idea later. Trust me."

After tea Lucy made her way back to the bedroom while David telephoned the Grand and asked for Mr Myles-Johnson. When he was through he said,

"Jonny, The CIA man is coming to the Grand. His name is Felix. I don't think that's his real name for a minute. He's our contact on the Base. Be in the lounge at eight tonight."

"Wilco David and thanks." Jonny rang off.

****

Promptly at eight Jonny was to be found propping up the American Bar in the Grand Hotel. At half past eight the bar was getting more crowded but still no Felix. He was on the point of leaving when the barman asked him if he was Jonny.

"Certainly. I'm waiting for a friend."

"Here, this call is for you," the man said as he passed the receiver.

"Hello."

"Felix here. Cross the road and two blocks down towards the harbour on the right is Dick's Disco. I'm just inside on the left nearest the doorway."

"I'm a bit old for a disco."

"Never mind that. Just do it. OK?"

"OK. Just as you say."

Ten minutes later Jonny stood in the dimly lit foyer letting his eyes adjust to the smoky air and the dull red lighting within. At a table on the edge of the dance floor he spotted a young man seated and talking to an attractive blond wearing a wrap which covered her vital parts but little else. The man looked up. Jonny was taken aback. Felix looked as if he was just out of college.

"Hi, Jonny, meet Celia."

Jonny walked up to the table and shook hands with Felix and then took the limp paw of the blond who just smiled, got up and walked off with an exaggerated hip roll. Five minutes later Jonny saw her dancing.

"Who was that?"

"Just a hostess, that's all. She's an air hostess by day. So you're Jonny, the mysterious Jonny."

"Nothing mysterious about me, I assure you. You must be Felix."

"The same. Let's take our drinks upstairs where they have some private booths. It will be quieter and we can talk without shouting."

Moments later and with the curtain of the booth drawn across, Felix said,

"Now what's this all about?"

"It's about your future. I'll put you in the picture as much as I can. Do you think this place is bugged?"

"Not unless the whole place is. Why should it be?"

"The seeds of this were sown over ten years ago. Dr Forbes, Charlie, was engaged by David Brown to work behind the iron curtain. You've met David haven't you? This was in 1953, or thereabouts."

"Not yet. I have that pleasure to come."

"In the course of his work Charlie fell foul of Oskar Krause. Today Krause is the political Kapitan of the 'Kerenski'.

"The what?"

"My God Felix. What do you do all day, read trash mags?"

"The Kerenski. Is that a ship?"

"It most certainly is. The East German mother ship to a fleet of trawlers out of Gydnia, used to be called Danzig on my school atlas. They are selling their catches from the Barent Sea to the Eastern Bloc. This guy, Krause is the ship's gauleiter. Krause was, at that time, a member of the party which arrested Charlie and took him in bonds and unconscious, aboard the sail training ship Lenin. There was a shoot out in which five members of the Stasi/KGB were killed. The sixth member, Krause, survived. Charlie was rescued by David Brown, his MI6 controller, and taken on board HMS Bangor. Krause was arrested by the Captain of the Lenin, put on trial in East Berlin and sentenced, under pressure from the British Foreign Service, to ten years in prison for the murder of Miss Peggy, Charlie's elderly aunt in Cleethorpes. Krause has served his sentence and is now assigned to the Kerenski. His main aim is to persuade the Icelandic Government to close down your Base but he has another aim which is to kill both Charlie and David and any one else in their family who gets in the way. So you see this is a vendetta which will continue long after the present minor skirmish over fishing rights has been settled."

"OK. But I don't see how this Krause can affect us, the Base. Main aim or not?"

"The Iceland Government, The Althing, is dominated by the Communists. They want to force a Bill through parliament terminating NATO's lease on Keflavik."

"I've heard all this before. All I can say is 'Fat chance'."

"My information is that with a Communist coalition in power the Communists may succeed this time. I have three good reasons for saying that. Firstly, since Icelandic Trawlers have been banned from landing their catches in England, the trade has gone largely to Russia. The Russians can hardly believe their luck. Their trade in hard goods has broken into

Iceland's market. Even your chaps at the Base are buying Skodas."

"We're not sentimental. They're half the price of a Mini."

"OK. But second, you have to realise that Britain and Iceland are locked into a dispute over fishing rights. There's going to be blood on the carpet before a conclusion is reached and the Brits come to their senses."

"And what's the third reason?"

"It's a bit more complex since it rests on public opinion. Icelanders are very nationalistic. It took a war, World War Two, to give them independence from Denmark. Although only a small country with a population about the same as Hull in England, they are determined to pay their way in the world and remain independent. They print more newspapers per head of population than any other country in the world. If their pattern was repeated in England we would have over a thousand newspapers every day. Can you believe that?"

"Go on. I hear what you say."

"It's generally felt that your Base is a manifestation of western colonialism and could result in Iceland being a target in an atomic war." Jonny was warming to his subject.

"And so it could, even if the Russians took over the Base."

"Just so. Most Icelanders don't want the Russians either."

"What you're saying is that this chap, Krause, is out to make trouble between the western powers and the Althing and that the best way to suck up to them is to get rid of British trawlers and settle the war."

"That's about the long and short of it. Unfortunately it comes down to personalities in the end."

"Oh really. Who are these personalities? Do you know them?"

"I know some of them."

"What's your role in this? I'm intrigued."

"I'm ex-officio but that doesn't mean to say that I'm . . ."

"I get it. You're the private dick who wants to push his fingers in someone else's pie hoping some of the gravy will stick to them."

"It's in your interest, believe me, to know that I'm a white hat. This crisis is only just boiling up.

The Russians have planted their agent on the Kerenski. He has a Kamov KA27 helicopter, we believe armed."

"So?"

"Violence is only just around the corner. If things get out of hand the Althing will almost certainly ask NATO to leave. That way the Government will be doing something which will get support from most of the population and will stay in power, whatever the Conservatives, the so called Independence Party, do. The Russians will move in. Your Base will be taken over by Icelandic personnel and they will offer the facilities to the Russian navy, who will then effectively command the gateway to the Atlantic. In case you don't know, the British Embassy was stoned by an angry mob last month. Someone took a pot shot with a powerful hunting rifle, probably at the Ambassador, David Brown."

"So where do I come into all this"

"That's up to you but if your people want my advice we need to meet your Boss, General Thorne."

"Who's we?"

"I think the Ambassador and me."

"Maybe we can fix something but I'm not sure that my boss will relish you settling a private dispute with this Krause at our expense under the pretext that you are some sort of ex officio NATO agent. It just won't wash. We'd better keep that between you and me."

"Thanks. I won't wrap it up. My cards will be on the table."

"What precisely do you want to do?"

"The next time their helicopter threatens our fleet, I want to shoot it down."

"And start a war?"

"That's a topic open for discussion another time, I think."

"Well, I'm just the bag carrier. I will look forward to our next meeting. Meanwhile I'll report all this upwards. They probably know it already, even if I didn't."

As Jonny left the disco he stood for a few minutes on the sidelines and watched Felix dancing with the girl in the wrap. Secretly he wished he was younger and wondered if she too fitted into the picture.

15   DOUBLE OR QUITS

"What's all this about? If you think I'm going to be a prisoner here then you're mistaken."

"Listen, Sue. It's only for a short time. I'll see you have everything you need. You do want him out, don't you?"

"Of course I want him out but how am I to know you have a plan which will work. For all I know you might be in cloud cuckoo land. As of now I won't do it. Persuade me."

"I can't if you won't be . . ."

"And what am I to say to Charlie?"

"Tell him you're ill. Tell him you can't drink that horrible tap water."

"Nor can I. It tastes of sulphur."

"And I'll tell David the same."

"We'll never do it. It's ridiculous. What about room service and the chambermaid?"

Lucy paused and thought about this for a moment. Then,

"OK . . . You win. I'll think of something else. I promise you. Just give me time."

"I can't keep it a secret from Charlie, whatever it is. He's bound to suspect that we're up to something. Besides, if you do get Chas out of jail we'll need a follow up plan. So, now tell me. What is the great plan and why did you want me to be a virtual prisoner? I can't believe that. We're only booked for a week."

"I know that but the Annual Dinner's in two weeks time and I want you to double for me. I'll be getting Chas out of prison and you can be my alibi. You won't have to do anything, anything much that is. I'll lend you my rig and make up. Even David won't know the difference."

"A dinner, you mean I'll be on show?" She exclaimed.

"In a way you will be but no one's going to raise even one little eyebrow. I doubt if anyone will know I even have a twin. A good proportion of the country's top brass, including the prison governor will be at the dinner."

"And what will you be doing?"

"Getting Chas out of prison, like I said."

"How will you do that?"

"I have a plan, believe me and even if it doesn't work we'll be no worse off."

"We will be if they catch you."

"They won't. I'll see to that. They know me at the prison. I'm an official visitor. David finds it convenient to use me to keep contact with any Brits they've locked up."

"It all sounds very far fetched to me. I hope you know what you're doing."

"Don't worry about me. Keeping a low profile here will be more difficult, knowing you."

"Just now you said it would be easy. So what's next?"

"Stay here for today at least and I'll get somewhere else for you to stay. There's no reason why you shouldn't go out, so long as we're not seen together. I'll find somewhere for you to stay and we'll need Charlie to think of some way to get Chas out of the country."

"That's not going to be easy."

"Charlie and Jonny will come up with something. Jonny is our best bet. He's trying to get the NATO Base to co-operate.

"And how are we going to explain it to David?"

"You think of something and I'll be thinking too. Now I've got to go. They're waiting. David and Charlie were going to take us on a trip today to see the geysers."

"Stop. I have had a better idea. Listen."

"I'm listening."

"I'll say the water's made me ill. So that will give me an alibi for today. Then because I'm getting anxious about Charlene and anyway I can't stand the water and I'm not doing any good here, tomorrow, in spite of any objections, I'll fly back home. Then in about ten days, just before the dinner, I'll return incognito. No one need know I'm here except you and Charlie."

"Sue, you're a genius. Why didn't I think of that? It'll cost but I've got some savings in my account. I'll go out and buy the tickets today. Now I must be off. I'll send up room service with some dinner for you. Bye for now."

"Bye, enjoy the geysers."

But by the time Susan had said this, Lucy had gone.

****

The helicopter circled the town, losing height and touched down on the lawn of the East German Legation except that it was more a mud-patch at that time of year. It was late afternoon but it was already very dark. After the long flight Krause climbed stiffly down the short ladder. Max was there to meet him. Their conversation was brief and to the point. He believed he had no time for politeness in spite of Max's outstretched hand and welcoming smile.

"Well Max?"

"A good flight?"

"As usual. Have my bag brought in. I'll be here for a week. The fleet needs fuel and the Kerenski is heading back to Gydnia. I'm tired and slightly ill."

"I'm sorry."

"Even more sorry when I tell you that 'Beowulf' lost their skipper overboard. He was trying to help a deckhand caught in the net as they were shooting. Both men were lost. It makes me sick to think of it. There's bound to be an enquiry. I hope it won't affect my posting. I've work to do here."

"I'm sure you will not be blamed, Comrade Kapitan, not in any way."

"The net had been run out. The crew could have jettisoned it and turned the trawler round. As it was they decided to sail on as if nothing had happened. Another deckhand told me all this. He was slightly injured also and came on board the Kerenski for treatment. Nobody can survive in water at that temperature in the time it takes to turn round. He told me the crew, especially the mate, were more concerned about the loss of the gear than those lives."

"So what happens now, Comrade?" Max asked.

"I need to send a report to the Minister. Another job for tomorrow, Max. They should have turned round. I'm convinced of it. Let's get inside. It's cold out here."

"Your room is on the first floor, Comrade Kapitan. We are overcrowded at the moment. The financial inspector is here. He expressed some surprise that you did not stay with the fleet."

"Kapitan Kohl, The Kapitan of the Kerenski, knows the routine. He's arranged fuel for delivery to Trondheim two weeks from now. Anyone who deserts from there is braver than I am. Now business, what news?"

"As you know Kapitan Forbes has been arrested and is in prison. His ship is impounded and likely to be confiscated. The good news is that Doctor Forbes has flown over and is staying in the British Residence."

"What does he intend?"

"He seems to think that the combined pleas of himself and his brother-in-law, the Ambassador Brown, may secure his son's release."

"He's wasting his time of course."

"Not so fast Comrade. It may work to our advantage if he were to be released."

"How so?"

"Where the fisherman is, there will be the doctor. In prison he is secure. Out of prison he is vulnerable, nicht?"

"It was a good day when I hired you. Let's work on it. What do you propose?"

"A bribe maybe?"

"Who, for instance."

"The Governor?"

"Impossible, you can't bribe Icelanders."

"Have you ever tried, Comrade."

"Actually no but all Icelanders have a reputation for honesty, devious maybe, but of the highest integrity."

"How about Vilbert, the Chief of Police?"

"Improbable, I would say, although we can try. Perhaps we can approach the problem through our friend on the Althing."

"You mean Reynir, the Minister of Fishing?"

"The same. He has our interests at heart because they are the same as his, on the surface at least. I'll leave it to you Max to make the first approach."

****

The next morning, before sunrise, Susan stood in the waiting room at Keflavik, expecting to be called forward for the Manchester flight to Ringway Airport. Through the frosted windows she could see the Viscount, with engines running, throwing up clouds of powdered snow which covered the pathway only recently cleared by the airport's sweeping machine. The short walk to the foot of the aircraft's steps was quite perilous but once airborne the plane soon rose above the layer of alto-stratus. The passengers were greeted by the most beautiful sun-rise. The dark blue sky overhead, at that altitude, provided a fitting back drop to the red and white clouds below and the piercing rays. Susan decided that the flight was worth it just for the spectacle. From Ringway she took a taxi to Belvedere.

At that time in the morning she expected Charlene to be still in bed. She would not be expecting her mother to have returned so soon.

"Charlene, Charlene, darling," Susan called. The house was as silent as the proverbial tomb. In the background she could hear the quiet hum of traffic on the main Chorley road. This was a novelty since normally Charlene played the Light Programme incessantly. She climbed the stairs and called again. She opened the door of Charlene's room. Although it was in its typical mess the bed was tidy and obviously had not been slept in that night. The cleaner, she remembered, would have been in yesterday. A quick search of every room told her that Charlene was not at home. She even checked the garage. Then she phoned Charlene's close friends with no result, although one friend admitted to having had lunch with her in Manchester two days ago. Susan rang the college to discover that Charlene had not attended lectures for the last two days. By now she was beginning to panic. Then she remembered that David and Charlie had discussed taking up Jonny's offer to send Charlene to Palma. She phoned Kay at the surgery.

"Kay, is that Kay?"

"Yes, Mrs Forbes. It's a good line."

"I'm not in Iceland. I'm at Belvedere. I was expecting Charlene to be here. Have you any idea where she is?"

"Yes. All is in order. I got her ticket to Iceland, as instructed by Sir David's secretary. She would have flown out last evening. I rang the embassy to confirm the flight."

Susan thought that Charlene would have flown out on the same plane she had arrived on. Kay had confused her. They had planned to send her to Mallorca. Why had David wanted her in Iceland? Should she stay at Belvedere, as she had arranged

144

with Lucy or fly back? If Charlene landed late yesterday, had she asked David to arrange someone to meet her? She couldn't find the answers to these questions without disclosing Lucy's secret plan. She had almost decided to do nothing for the moment when she thought of Kay and rang her again.

"Kay, sorry to trouble you again. Could you do me a favour and find out if Charlene got there safely. I'm so tired. I'll be up again about lunch time. Ring back at two but don't under any circumstances let David or Charlie know that I am here. I don't want them getting anxious just yet. Bye."

****

Charlene waited patiently in the Ringway First Class departure lounge. An air-hostess brought her a cup of tea.

"Are you the young lady who is travelling to Iceland."

"Yes I am. I'm supposed to be on the flight which leaves at five."

"Your escort has just checked in. He should be with you in a few minutes. I'll bring him over."

"Thank you . . . but."

"There he is, the man in the brown suit carrying a soft bag."

"I didn't know . . ."

But the air-hostess had gone. Charlene looked across the room. The young man with the soft bag was looking round the news stand. She decided that she was going to enjoy having his companionship on the flight. He was tall but fair. She guessed he would have blue eyes. As he turned she made eye-to-eye contact and realised she had been staring at him for some time. She looked away and blushed in confusion. The man raised a hand in salute and then came over and without waiting to be invited sat beside her.

"Hello, I'm Emil and you are Miss Charlene Forbes. I am to escort you to the Embassy in Reykjavik." He held out his hand.

"Yes, Emil, I'm Charlene Forbes. I wasn't expecting anyone to meet me."

"A last minute arrangement when the Ambassador, your uncle, discovered you were to travel on the same flight as me. I live in Leipzig and travelling for a holiday in Iceland. My uncle also works in the diplomatic corps. I shall be going to our Legation, I think."

After a pleasant three hour flight they went through passport control. Emil quickly ushered Charlene through a side door into an ante room. Beyond she saw the blades of a helicopter turning slowly almost in time with her excited heart beat.

"There, bang on time. Give me your bag. There's our air taxi, better than a car in these conditions." They ducked under the slowly rotating blades.

"Sitzen Sie sich bitte beim Piloten, Miss Charlene. You'll get a wonderful view from there, wunderbar."

Charlie and Lucy, at the normal passenger exit, looked up as the helicopter passed close overhead on its way to the cabin in the mountains.

****

"Oskar, I've got Charlie's daughter in the bag."

"Max, what are you talking about?"

"Her name is Charlene. I got Emil to escort her to the Lodge. It was easy."

"In other words you kidnapped her?"

"Leave the detail to me. You said it."

"Maybe I did but not to get our Legation involved in anything illegal. How did you get her there?"

"Claus took me to the airport in your chopper. She climbed aboard without raising an eyebrow. In fact the idea of an airlift appealed to her sense of adventure. It was only when we set down at the Lodge that she had any misgiving. She expected to meet her Dad."

"Of course she expected to meet her Dad. What now?"

"We send our terms to David. I've taken the liberty of setting it out in a dossier, all subject to your scrutiny and approval."

"This is madness. We'll have the police on our backs."

"I think not. Emil will stay with her. She will be quite safe, I promise. Emil has agreed to look after her in the Lodge. She has no way of escape from there. To walk out, in the hope of reaching a road, would be suicide in this weather and you know how early it gets dark. Like I said, leave it to me. I shall need the helicopter. No harm will come to her, I promise but if this doesn't move them nothing will."

"How will you break the news?"

"I think we can safely assume he knows who is responsible. All I have to do is to reassure the Ambassador that no harm will come to her unless . . ."

"You are mad. If the newspapers got hold of this we would be thrown out of the country. The adverse publicity will be ten times more than your bungled attempt at the riot."

"We have the lever now. I have informed the Ambassador that the consequences will be dire should this become public."

"How did you arrange it?"

"Not difficult. When Celia, the hostess at the airport, told me that Doctor Charles and his wife had arrived, it didn't need a genius to work out that the daughter would be living on her own at home. She couldn't leave because she has some important examinations to sit. The rest was straight forward. Manchester sent a man round to confirm this was the case and then I arranged a bogus phone call to the good doctor's secretary."

"So what do you plan now?"

"When the time is ripe I plan to restore Charlene to her family. But first Chas Forbes will have to fulfil a little task I will set."

"How will you convey the details of your plan?"

"It should not be difficult. The young Forbes is in prison, nicht? This is the position. One, Reynir wants to get rid of NATO. Two, the Althing want to close Iceland's waters to foreign trawlers. Three, the Forbes family want Chas and Charlene to regain their freedom. I will secure the release of Chas providing he is willing to take his trawler to sea. I will also arrange Doctor Charlie, to be on board."

"How will you do that?"

"Within the time I shall set there will be no one else who can crew the vessel. The regular crew have been flown home."

"There is John, the mate. He is available."

"Indeed there is and I intend to make use of him also. A crew of three is the absolute minimum for a ship the size of the Ace of Spades. There will be no alternative at short notice to get crew. Besides the Doctor has a vested interest in the vessel. As soon as they leave we will set the coastguard on to them."

"What good will that do?"

"In the ensuing encounter the Ace and crew will be sunk. Your enemy will be annihilated. I have a promise from Reynir. With the exception of the Forbes family the result should be satisfactory for all concerned. I will of course release the young lady into the care of Ambassador Brown in due course."

"And the Althing?"

"Will be delighted. They will have no alternative but to terminate the NATO lease as they have always threatened to do unless Britain and the other nations cease fishing in our waters. The British Foreign office will break diplomatic relations as a result of the sinking of the Ace. Although I cannot predict the eventual outcome it is possible that gunfire will be exchanged between our coastguards and their frigates. A real war should place Iceland in our camp for a long time to come. The trawlers will soon depart without their naval escorts."

"Rejoin the real world. You think all this will be the outcome of kidnapping the girl?"

"It will, as night follows day."

"And I am to sanction all this when you have exposed our Legation to prosecution?"

"The deed is done now. I have laid it all out in detail in my report. What do you want me to do? Restore her to her family and apologise? We shall not only be branded as criminals but stupid criminals. I shall resign and you, I expect, will be forced into obscurity or worse."

"Your attitude borders on insubordination. However I will overlook it providing you can bring this fracas to a successful conclusion."

"You may like to know, although it's in my report, that Reynir has arranged with the prison governor to release Chas on parole for twenty four hours. The governor tells me that he has grabbed the chance to co-operate. Reynir tells me that secret negotiations are in progress between his department and the British Ministry. The Althing will consider Chas's action, in breaking his parole, a betrayal. Meanwhile Ambassador Brown will make a statement to the news media, which will infuriate both the Althing and the Americans, if not NATO itself. He may well get recalled by his Foreign Office. The Althing will break off diplomatic relations and the door will be left wide open for our Politburo to move into the vacuum.

"One way or the other Comrade Oskar, we shall get the trawlers to withdraw. The landings in Britain will cease and we shall have a ready supply of Icelandic fish to Mother Russia."

"I can't believe the outcome you are suggesting."

"Oskar, in this the devious Ambassador will be our collaborator. He will no more want the truth to be revealed than we do. To get his niece back he will submit to our plan."

"Very well Max. Nobody must know about this, not even Claus."

"Claus knows I am holding two young adults at the lodge but he is ignorant of the reason. You have my assurance Comrade Oskar. Nobody knows the import of this except the Forbes family and their collaborators and they will keep their own council."

16   THE BAG

The old hunting lodge had been constructed in 1890, partly for summer use by the privileged guests of the King of Denmark, and partly as a refuge for intrepid travellers in the winter. It lay well above the snow line on a rocky plateau out of the prevailing wind. Having been purchased by the Communist party in 1948 it was used mainly for entertaining and occasionally by visiting political luminaries keeping out of the public eye. There was no winter access by road. The location suited Max's designs perfectly.

The pilot tossed their bags on to the snow. Charlene stood clear and put up her hands to cover her ears. She saw and felt the draught of the blades, turning slowly at first, the whine of the starter and then the staccato cracking as their tips broke the sound barrier, drowning the noise of the biting wind. Claus, the pilot, raised a hand of farewell as the skids of the helicopter left the ground. The machine soared away into the twilight. They stood watching the navigation lights fading into the low cloud.

She looked around at the desolate landscape of snow piled rocks but the view was limited to a few hundred metres. She walked a few paces to pick up her bag and turned towards Emil. Already holding his he said,

"Come on, quickly or we'll freeze." Charlene's stomach muscles griped with fear. She managed to subdue her misgivings in spite of the weird turn of events. She ran past him to the shelter of the lodge. He took a key from his anorak while she watched in astonishment as he opened the door. They stepped over the sill. To their surprise the rooms were beautifully warm but this did nothing to allay her fear.

"Emil, what's going on? What is this place and where's my Dad?

"Let's get the door barred and bolted. It's too cold out here. I'll tell you everything I know which isn't much."

A sudden gust from the mountain hurried them inside the lodge. Rent with anxiety, she sat on a stool near a smouldering log fire.

"Go on then, tell me everything. Why are we here, on the top of a mountain, miles from anywhere?"

"Let's see what's here." He opened the envelope addressed to him which he found lying on the dining table. In it he found all the instructions for maintaining the heating and the kitchen. Finally there was a schedule for the return of the helicopter. He looked at her, smiled and then said,

"Come on let's look around." She followed him as he explored the lodge in detail. He discovered the source of heat which came from a large gas tank in a separate shed connected to the main building. Electricity came from an overland cable which appeared to be going to some distant lights, dimly seen in the valley below. He found a large store of canned food supplemented by some fresh in a small refrigerator. There were two separate double bedrooms and two more singles in a small loft. The shower rooms were well provided and, to his surprise, a small door led to a sauna. He returned to the main living room which was luxurious almost to opulence, sheepskin rugs, bulky soft sofas, hunting trophies and dominating this lavish scene there was the large stone-built log fire with embers still smouldering. He judged that the most recent attention must have been no more than three or four hours ago.

Charlene could contain her anxiety no longer."

"Do you know about this? Why we've been dumped here and where did you get that key?"

"The pilot had the key. I've been told to look after you. They said we would be given a large log cabin until your father returns."

"That's bullshit. My father is in Reykjavik, staying at the British Embassy."

"I can't tell you any more. This envelope just tells me how to run the heating and the kitchen. We should get away on the next helicopter trip."

"When?"

"In about a week."

"A week. I'm your prisoner for a week. That outrageous. I've been kidnapped haven't I?"

"Let's just say that you are a guest of The East German Legation for a few days."

"You're a bloody Hun, aren't you?"

He did nothing to pacify her assuming quite rightly that he could do nothing to comfort her acute distress.

"I am a bloody Hun, a bloody hungry Hun. I've hardly eaten anything since I left my home in Leipzig." "Come on then. If you're looking after me let's have a meal."

"Let's raid the larder and then I must get some sleep."

Later she said,

"You're going to tell me . . ."

"I can't stay awake any longer. I've got to sleep. I'm going to bed. I've nothing much to tell. I'm a prisoner just as you are. My instructions are to see that you don't come to any harm. We'll talk in the morning."

After their meal of bread and cold ham washed down with a bottle of beer he said,

"If you will excuse me, I must go. The doors are not locked but it is almost a gale outside and the outside temperature is well below freezing. We are warm and safe here and tomorrow we will talk about our situation. Neither of us can leave here until someone comes for us. Goodnight."

"Goodnight," Charlene replied in a whisper. She turned to see which room he took then curled up in one of the deep armchairs and fell asleep. After a few hours she woke feeling stiff in every joint and with a mouth like a farmyard. She thought there was nothing more to be gained by her dumb insolence and decided to go to bed also.

When she awoke it was nearly lunch time on the following day. Emil was standing beside her bed with a steaming mug of coffee. She reached up and took it gratefully.

"Drink that and freshen up. Your bag's on your chair. You'll feel better after a shower. You have your own rooms which I won't enter, except with your good morning drink. I'll get a snack for us from the kitchen. Someone has prepared everything. We have enough for a week at least but we may be on powdered milk in a day or two. There's a mountain of logs outside covered in snow. I'll spend this morning getting some in and stacking them beside the fireplace."

Charlene turned her head slightly to listen to him but she didn't answer as Emil went away. After some minutes she put the empty mug on the floor, rose rather unsteadily and made for her shower. After a while Emil smiled to himself as he heard water running and resumed piling the damp logs against the chimney-piece. Then he laid out a mid-day meal on the large dining table, more cold ham, cheese, buttered toast and preserve. After that he took a notebook from his case and started to write a resumé of events since he left Leipzig the day before.

When the daylight started to fade Emil lit the fire and sat reading a paperback. He heard her door opening and turned.

"I'm hungry." He stood up and pointed to the table. "More tea or coffee?"

"I suppose you realise that this is an outrage. When I'm free I'll have you locked up for a very long time. My uncle is the British Ambassador to Iceland."

"I'm a prisoner like you. There's no way out for either of us. My only instructions were to escort you to the helicopter and to see that no harm came to you."

"If that's true, which I doubt, who arranged all this, the food, the fire, everything? Who told you to meet me at Manchester Airport?"

"A man phoned my father in Leipzig the day before yesterday and offered me this job . . . without consulting me. My father said 'yes'. He said I would do it."

"What, kidnap me. That's outrageous. We don't even know each other. You must know this is criminal. I can't believe you agreed to do anything so . . ."

"I didn't agree. My father is a policeman. He obeys orders. That's how thing are where I come from. I was going to the Legation in Reykjavik anyway for the experience. I was told that you needed an escort. That's all, honestly. I was told to meet you in the lounge."

"How did you find me? The lounge was full of passengers."

"That's was easy. I was told you are very pretty, aged nineteen, blond. Actually you were staring at me, almost as if we were making a rendez-vous." Huddled in one of the soft arm chairs, all she could mutter was,

"I want my Dad".

Emil found it impossible to cast himself in the role of jailer. He felt himself to be in equal danger. Outside it was pitch black again. At this time of year there were only four hours of daylight.

For the next hour Emil sat and watched Charlene huddled in the deep chair close to the fire. From time to time he stoked it with another log. Eventually he said,

"I'll tell you everything I know about this situation but believe me there is nothing to be gained by crying. We cannot communicate until you stop and realise that you are in no danger. None whatsoever. I'm still tired. I haven't had any proper sleep since I left my home. So if you will excuse me I will go to bed again very early."

"Alright by me. Goodnight," she replied in a whisper. She couldn't think of any way of discovering more about her capture and slowly she came to the thought that she had been very naïve, being so ready to climb into a helicopter when she knew she was expected by her father. She didn't even know how much blame attached to the pilot. Large tears rolled down her anxious face as she subsided into the sofa.

"Go away. Go away Emil. I hate you. Go to bed. You knew what you were doing. Do you expect me to believe you didn't know? What sort of a man is your father anyway?"

"If you think I'm enjoying this then you're mistaken. You hate me. OK. So do you think that makes me feel good?"

"Go away. I don't care how you feel. I'm getting out of here and don't try to stop me."

"You can't go now, not in the dark. Tomorrow maybe we can try together. Look. Over there. See. There's plenty of books, mostly in English. I'm reading an English book called 'Hell Bay'."

"Alright then. Tomorrow we'll move out. Tomorrow. Maybe you'll help me get a meal."

In the following morning twilight Charlene started to look around the lodge for some outdoor weather proof clothing. At the third attempt she found a small closet off the kitchen. Here were snow boots and ski suits of varying sizes. There were several sets of skis propped against the wall. She tried on the snow boots all of which were too large. She turned and saw him watching.

"I've already looked for some outdoor gear. Can you ski?"

"No, I've never tried."

"Even if you can I can't recommend it. We've absolutely no idea of the terrain and if we came off halfway down the mountain we should perish. It would be impossible for us to climb back here and the nearest shelter is at least five miles away. I've looked at the map."

"There are snow boots."

"I can't imagine anyone using those up here. It's much too steep and the snow has to be just right."

"You're trying to put me off."

"I am indeed. Unless you're very fit you'll never make it. Do you think you'll get to a village before nightfall?"

"What about you then? Yesterday you said you would come too"

"I'll have to if you go."

Half an hour later Charlene was ready to leave. The smallest ski suit was several sizes too large, as were the snow boots. She was carrying a small haversack with a hot drink and some sandwiches. Now fully daylight she stood outside on the helicopter pad looking down into the valley below. There was no sign of the village. The sharp wind, cutting her cheeks like ice, blew clouds of powdered ice crystals off the rocks behind the lodge reducing visibility to a mere one hundred meters. She started down hill with Emil close behind. After falling on the uneven surface several times she collapsed on the deep snow and started to cry again. Emil was having equal difficulty remaining upright. Without the shelter of the building they felt the full force of the arctic wind. Charlene's snow boots came apart as Emil pulled her out of the deep drift. It took them an hour to climb to the shelter of the lodge again.

"It didn't work, did it?" she screamed.

"I knew it wouldn't."

"And yet you were prepared to let me . . . us have a go. That surely was stupid or maybe just plain evil."

"I wanted you to find out for yourself."

"My feet are dead. I must have frost bite."

"Here, I'll rub them back to life. Take off your socks."

"I didn't know the snow would be so deep and up to my waist. It's impossible. If any more comes down we'll be here for months."

"The helicopter will be back with supplies before the end of the week. The pilot told me."

"Anyway those trousers are much too big for me and so is the Parka. It's quite hopeless. I can't believe what's happening. Surely my Dad will come looking."

"It will be like, how do you put it, looking for a grain of sand on a beach?"

"We say, 'a needle in a haystack'."

"Ha! Very apt. A new English expression for my collection."

"Look. If we are to stay here, together for a whole week or longer, we must have some rules, some understanding."

"Alright then. So long as you realise that to go outside would be suicide; you can make the rules."

"I'll do the cooking if you do everything else and no coming into my room. I'll look after that. I don't know what we are to do all day. Read I suppose. I've never read very much. Maybe it's my chance to catch up."

"There's chess and some other games."

"I don't know how to play chess."

"If you let me teach you, by the time we leave you'll be expert."

"I'll think about it. Now, I want you to tell me your part in all this. I want the truth. If we are to live here for a while I need to know what part you played."

"This is the truth. I was told to escort you. That you were travelling alone to see your folks in Iceland and that you would be met at our Legation. I was told to help you and that there would be a helicopter to take us to the Legation where you would be met by your father. Apparently the East German Legation is in the same street as the British Embassy, a short walk. So I was puzzled by the pilot's navigation."

Charlene exploded with anger.

"Puzzled? Are you telling me you knew nothing about this?"

"I have been tricked, used. Here, read this." Emil produced a letter.

"It was on the dining table as we entered. You didn't see me pick it up. It explains the whole ghastly plot. It doesn't pull any punches. It is the truth."

She took the letter and sank into her chair by the fire.

****

David and Charlie sat in grim silence in David's office. They had been sipping brandy for a long time. Neither had spoken. Presently Charlie broke the long silence of resentment and said,

"How are the girls taking it?"

"Susan's devastated. She called me for news this morning. Lucy thinks I should do more."

"Why don't you just do as the bastards say David?"

"There's more to this than that. For one thing they won't release Charlene in exchange for a promise and for another it's you and me that they want. 'They' meaning Krause. They won't admit to having Charlene but you and I know that is certain. What must the poor mite be going through?"

"It doesn't bear thinking about," retorted Charlie. "Susan flew home a week ago at the same time Charlene was flying out. If only I had taken advantage of Jonny's offer. What possessed Kay to put her on a flight here when she knew we planned to send her to Majorca? She never checked with you?"

"If she had, I would have known immediately it was a bogus call. I hate to think where they have got her now. She could be in a cell in the basement of their Legation. Does anyone know where that helicopter landed?" said David.

"The pilot."

"We need to get at him. We know that he didn't land in the Legation grounds until an hour after Charlene's plane landed. We got that from one of our neighbours so it's my guess she's not in the Legation at all."

"Where then, for heavens sake?"

"With a helicopter at their bidding, it could be anywhere in Iceland."

"Do you suppose she has anyone with her?"

"Doubtful. My guess is that they've boarded her with someone they know very well."

"That's not likely. Too risky for them. Charlene would merely tell her host who she is and the whole plot would unravel. No David, we can expect Krause to play this one very close to his chest. The consequences for him will be very serious if the Legation is seen to be involved in a kidnap, never mind who she is."

"And the consequences for us too, don't forget."

"There's more to this. There must be an angle we haven't spotted yet. They must know that we'll do anything to get her back."

"Anything?"

"They need her as a guarantee of our good behaviour."

"Meaning?"

"By their definition that means no retaliation. That gives them a free hand."

"The bastards."

"We need help," said Charlie. "I think this is where Jonny comes on stage. He has an entrée with the Yanks and they have a contact in the German Legation."

"Indeed. What sort of a contact?

159

"Something to do with the CIA. Very hush-hush. But it may help us make a contact with the pilot of the helicopter."

"Where is Jonny?"

"He's in London at the moment, due back any day. He's trying for a high level link with the Yanks, Washington no less. He's got his friend in MI6 working on it. We need a meeting with General Thorne, the Commander of the NATO Base.

"It will have to be a secret meeting."

"Why secret?"

"If I go up to the gates of the Base in the Rolly with flags flying the whole island will know about it within the hour. After dark in unmarked cars on a lonely road well out of town. That will be my plan."

"So be it. You know these things better then I do. Can Jonny be there?"

"I don't see why not. Hank will have his bodyguard, Felix."

****

Provisions in the shooting lodge were getting low. They were existing on canned food. Emil was miserable. Charlene hardly spoke to him. The chess games had ended in a quarrel since she accused him of moving the Queen while she was out of the room. Emil couldn't prevent his dreams of seduction tormenting him while he lay awake through the long dark nights. For her part Charlene added to his agony. One moment she was playing the part of a classical seductress and the next lapsing into the role of an innocent iceberg, which Emil knew she wasn't. He dreamt of forcing himself on her but realised he would get no satisfaction from that. His upbringing by strict Lutheran parents had instilled in him a desire to cherish and protect all 'women-kind'. Charlene relished his discomfort. Gradually she felt that she was in the ascendant. Her hope was to escape and to force Emil to help her.

At night she could hear him groan with masturbation and in the morning he failed to appear until nearly time for some lunch. One day she broke her long silence to find out about his life and family. It was over morning coffee, which contrary to custom she had made. She now realised that his story was indeed true, that he had known nothing of the plot to kidnap her. She exploited her power over him to find out his most carefully kept secrets. She discovered that he had a girl whom he met in church every Sunday. The girl, Gerda, was compliant to his boyish urges. Their meetings were easy to arrange since they were both in the church choir. She taunted him with this knowledge and teased him without mercy by knocking on the thin wall between their rooms.

One day she discovered a powerful pair of binoculars and the stand which matched them. A new world opened before her eyes. She saw all sorts of wild life, a snow fox, countless birds, a stag. Then she picked out a man who she took to be a farmer mounted on a snow mobile. She estimated he was about a mile away down the steep valley. Beyond him was a road.

"Emil, come and see. Here quickly." By this time he was compliant with her every command and whim. He came and stood beside her. They peered into the eyepieces together, he with one side and Charlene with the other. They studied the antics of the farmer in the valley, taking fodder to an enclosure in which there was a small flock of sheep. He felt her close presence keenly and hoped to prolong the joint use of the binoculars. Suddenly Charlene straightened and said,

"That's our escape route. He will be working to a routine. He'll be back tomorrow. We'll plant a message on the hillside in black lava stones. 'HELP' should start something." At her urging they spent the rest of the day collecting lumps of lava from the edge of the helipad, where the snow covering was thin. By the time it went dark Charlene pronounced they had enough.

"Suppose he doesn't understand English?"

"They all do and even if he doesn't he'll be very curious about the activity up here at this time of year. Don't be so pessimistic."

"No, sorry."

On the following day they spelt out the message in four large letters on the white snow. Charlene thought they would be visible even to the village which they could dimly see at a range of about two miles.

But this was the day of the helicopter. They heard the sharp staccato note of the engine and the blades as Claus manoeuvred the craft up the valley to land on the helipad with a supply of news, food and fuel.

"What are you doing out here?" he said as he climbed out of the cab. "I shall report that you have been sending messages. It is most likely that I will be instructed to take Herr Emil away and leave Miss Charlene alone."

"No, no. Please don't do that."

"For my own protection I have to send in reports of every flight. Her Krause will be angry if you attempt to leave here. When he has a satisfactory understanding in place with the Ambassador you will be released. We are most anxious that no harm will come to either of you, especially you Miss Charlene. I will say in my report that you have been trying to attract the people in Kjolur. They already know that they must not trespass on the mountain for fear of disturbing the game."

After unloading the new supplies Claus took to the air. The machine hovered over their letters. The powerful downdraught covered them with powdered snow and dislodged many of the stones. When he flew away none of the original message remained. Charlene started to cry once more and ran into Emil's outstretched arms.

17   IN THE DARK

The Commander of the NATO base at Keflavik, General Hank Thorne was a tall wiry fifty-five year old. Every morning, except Sundays, he reached his office in the Head Quarters building promptly at seven-thirty. At that time he expected all incoming letters, messages and important news to be on his desk. On this particular day there was a telex from NATO Head Quarters at Northwood, England, asking for a 'hot-line' conversation with the President of the United States. Some time later there was a ring on the Base telephone. Hank reached for the receiver,

"Thorne here," he said.

"There's a call coming in now Sir. We have a hot secure line to the White House for you, Sir.

"Thank you Adjutant. I'm picking up the phone now." He reached for the red instrument reserved for secure calls.

"Hello General, are you well?"

"Very well thank you Mr President and you."

"As well as one can be at my age Hank. I'll be brief. I'm speaking to you personally because we are dealing with a very serious situation which affects you and our Base in Iceland. Most details may be known to you but nothing is lost by spelling it out as we see it in Washington. My briefing will arrive on your desk today. You must give this whole damned business top priority, top priority. Every facility must be extended to the British to help them sort this out in their own way. Give them every facility and this includes training in the latest weaponry. I leave it to your discretion how you handle this at your end but we need a successful outcome whatever the means. Do I make myself clear?"

"Yes, Mr President, as crystal. I am due to meet the British Ambassador at a secret location this evening. I will report the outcome to Brussels."

"Leave Brussels out of it Hank. This is strictly between Northwood and the Pentagon and is to be top secret and please call me Ron."

"Sure Ron, and thanks for your confidence."

"If I can't trust you then who in hell can I trust? I have every confidence in you. See it through, OK."

As he replaced the special red phone Hank realised he was sweating inside his shirt. "What now," he wondered. He picked up the other phone,

"Get me Felix,"

"Yes sir,"

"And soon." He hung up.

****

Max checked out of the East German Legation in the late evening. The Skoda was standing in the driveway with the engine ticking over and the windows wiped clean of frost. He nodded to the porter as he reversed into the road and drove slowly into the old city. He parked close to the night club where she would be working. Presently he leant across the car and opened the passenger door for the hostess. She got in and shut the door quickly to preserve the heat against the cold night air.

"Darling Max, we can't meet tonight."

"Why not? This was to be our special night."

"I know but I'll tell you all about it tomorrow. There's something new in train and Felix is being very cagey about it."

"Make sure you do, Celia, otherwise . . ."

"You and your threats. You're all the same. You don't frighten me. Felix is just like you. Always watching his back. One of these days you'll walk into each other while you're looking behind. I'm meeting him here, at Dick's, as usual. He wants to know when Krause is back. He wants to trade."

"He does does he? Well I don't think Oskar's into trading at the moment. Felix may have the Ace of Spades but we have No-trumps. That's better than a suit. We have Charlene in the bag."

"I don't know what you're talking about."

"I'm telling you that Charlene is in the bag and until we get what we want she'll be there, maybe for a long long time. Tell that to Felix. Tell him that if he wants to know where the girl is we must be witnesses to an attack on the coastguards by the British fleet."

"What will be the purpose of that?"

"You'll see if it happens."

"Who's Charlene anyway?"

"Felix will know. Now scram. Off with you and be round at my place tomorrow, same time, but before you go I want a kiss."

"Where?"

"The usual, of course."

****

It was a disappointed Max who drove slowly back to the Legation and to another bad tempered interview with Oskar.

"Max, you told me that you have the situation under control. You said that with the girl, Charlene, in captivity the Ambassador would make statements to the newspapers deliberately aimed to antagonise the Althing. So far there has been no statement and no sign that the Icelandic Government

165

intends to escalate their war against Britain and the other western powers. All that has been achieved so far is to arrange for the good doctor's son to escape jail."

"Patience Comrade. Everything is going to plan. The Forbes family are hoping to repossess their vessel which is anchored in the old harbour. I shall do everything I can to assist them. When their plans reach fruition, I shall arrange for the guards to be withdrawn at the crucial moment. Vilbert and Reynir are collaborating with me to ensure that the Ace of Spades puts to sea with Doctor Forbes on board."

"How can you possibly ensure that?"

"Chas Forbes will be short of crew and short of time. I shall organise his escape with the co-operation of the Chief of Police, Vilbert. The situation will be critical for the Forbes. The doctor is a man of great resource and will willingly take a risk to save his son."

"What about Captain Liefsson?"

"I expect that he will be sleeping ashore."

"And NATO."

"If we can establish that the escape of the Ace has been helped by the American staff on the Base, then we will have a winning hand. I am sure that the Althing will support Reynir Josefsson's proposal to close the Base by terminating the lease."

"And what about the girl?"

"She is there to ensure the good behaviour of our enemies. However she is a very small pawn in our plan, Oscar. You should be more concerned about Emil. He's one of us. His father is in the Stasi."

"I am concerned for them both. You have entangled these innocent children in your plan to no avail. When they are released the newspapers will make capital of their story. We shall be utterly discredited and all your work will have been a waste."

"They're not children and I doubt if they are innocent, as you put it."

"The press will paint them as such; you can be sure."

"Maybe it would be better for us if they are not released."

"Maybe."

****

The tiny settlement of Krysuvikurberg lies on the south coast of the Keflavik peninsular. It is totally exposed to the weather from the south-west and is served by a dirt road which ends amongst a small number of charming wooden houses. In the summer it becomes a tourist trap but in the dark and stormy days of winter few live there or go there even to tend their fishing boats. The road is deserted. It was on such a night that two black cars were parked well off the track and concealed by a small hillock of rock and sand. In the rear seat of one car sat the British Ambassador beside the Commander of the NATO forces stationed on Iceland. Jonny was seated in the front passenger seat. They talked in low voices even though this was entirely unnecessary. Outside, standing a few paces away from the cars in the icy blast, were four men. The meeting place had been chosen because it was an isolated spot equidistant from Reykjavik and Keflavik.

"See here Your Excellency, I've been given extraordinary powers by the White House. I am under orders to give you all the help I can, even though I may be breaking NATO protocol and even the law. For this reason this meeting is strictly off the record. Nothing I say this evening must be recorded, no minutes taken, understood?"

"In that case General can we revert to first names? Please call me David."

"Very well, and please call me Hank."

"Thank you for your vote of confidence. Jonny here is my undercover man but he will not be taking any notes. I assure you that everything we do will be aimed at securing the continuing presence of NATO forces in Iceland. Frankly we are in a jam. On the one hand British fishermen persist in breaking Icelandic law and on the other we want to cement friendly relationships with the Icelanders and their Government. As things stand at the moment, there is a real danger that the new Government will resign from NATO and terminate the lease. Control of the facility will almost certainly be handed to the USSR."

"I've had no word from home about this. My man, Felix, is either ignorant or else holding back something of which I should be aware."

"Jonny, you had a meeting with Felix. What did you tell him?"

"I put him in the total picture, starting with Krause."

"I'm astonished. Felix should have briefed you. You know about our riot, I suppose."

"Oh, I know all about that and your cod fleet. I just assumed that was a spat being dealt with by the coastguards supported by your own Foreign Office."

"Well, I have to say that it is a deal more serious than that. The whole business has gone political. The Labour Government is supporting their members in the fishing ports and the trawler men have organised a boycott of Icelandic vessels"

"Boycott?"

"Yes. There is a ban on landings from Icelandic ships in British ports. They won't handle their catches. That's a serious matter for Iceland's exports, so they have taken their business elsewhere, mainly Russia. I am due to make a statement at the embassy dinner next week supporting the action of the Trawlers' Federation and stating that the Royal Navy will continue to support the fishing fleet off Iceland's coast until the matter is settled by the International Court at the Hague and, hopefully, at the Geneva Conference."

"This is madness, Unthinkable."

"At the same time I intend to cosy up to the Althing privately and I shall tell them I'm working behind the scenes to get our navy withdrawn."

"You're playing a dangerous game David. Saying one thing and doing another is not the way diplomats are supposed to behave."

"What alternative have I?"

"Stand up. Be a man. Tell the trawler-men and the navy to bugger off."

"I can't. That's OK by NATO I'm sure. Put into 'dip lingo', it will cut clean across my own Foreign Office, throw thousands out of work in Hull, Grimsby, Aberdeen and Fleetwood and make the entire fleet of trawlers redundant. Our fleet off Iceland catches nearly a hundred thousand tonnes of cod every year. That's how it has been for the last half century. That's the true position."

"I'm grateful for your frankness but I have to say that NATO and the USA will not stand by and see the Base shut down by a bunch of commies."

"The situation is made a thousand times worse by the activities of the East German Legation."

"How's that?"

"They have an agent of the KGB on station. He is masquerading as the master of their fishing fleet on the Kerenski. They have an armed helicopter on board. We believe they will sink several of our trawlers. This would start a shooting war between us and the Icelandic coastguards. The repercussions don't bear thinking about."

"These allegations are dramatic to say the least. Have you any evidence?"

"We have our ears to the deck and Felix is up to date I'm sure. My niece flew out to see me and her family a few days ago. She has disappeared. I believe as a hostage. They're bribing me to inflame relations twixt Iceland and ourselves. Not only am I worried sick about her well-being but about the way this whole scene is developing into a major incident. The end result will terminate the NATO lease on these islands."

"True or false, I don't know, but let me assure you that you have my full support in any action which you decide will be in the best interests of NATO."

"We must ground that Russian helicopter somehow. You have the means. We haven't."

"I'm not prepared to start a shooting war with Russia, the East Germans or anyone on the other side of the Iron Curtain."

"Not even if your instructions come from the Pentagon. You told me a minute ago that the President has promised us full co-operation."

"We will help you to the limit of our ability but the President has given us no instructions about taking overt action ourselves."

"That's a fine distinction."

"That's how it is. We're not going to be the ones to start the third world war."

"Even though we might?"

"The Kremlin knows it has nothing to fear from little old England. When you have your requirements worked out please deal with my Adjutant."

"Jonny knows what we want. Can I suggest he camps out with you at the Base. We are working to get Chas out of prison. If we do, our first port will be your Base to pick up some arms and fuel. Is that OK by you Jonny?"

"Sure is. We need to work closely with General Thorne at this stage."

"That's settled then. I'll be briefing the Adjutant."

"Thanks again. We'll be in touch. I'll settle with the hotel, Jonny, and send your kit down. Do you mind giving me the keys to your room?"

"No problem, here they are. See you sometime. Let's hope something positive comes out of this."

"Please tell Felix to pass this on; we'll do nothing to either hinder or assist the Communist party providing the girl is safe from harm. I'm sure this will be resolved but you'll have to trust us. My family are taking a big risk. Let's hope they get it right".

"They will. I'm sure, with your help. I'll say good night then. Jonny, you're welcome to share my car."

With that, David returned to his own car. The bodyguards used their dim torches to guide them back onto the paved road where they went their separate ways. The sleepers in the hamlet by the shore knew nothing of the momentous meeting which had just taken place. Both David and Hank knew that their actions placed them on the very edges of legality. If discovered, neither of their governments would accept responsibility for them. For his part David had refrained from telling Hank his true motives.

18 A DANGEROUS GAME

Susan checked in at Ringway airport promptly at ten in the morning. The flight to Iceland was to take about three hours. Lucy would be the only one to know of her arrival at about two o'clock. Before leaving home she had rung her to confirm the plan.

"Any news of Charlene?"

"Nothing definite. David has a contact with the Russians. They've got her safe, so they say. Listen. I'll be in the ladies' room after immigration. As you leave the plane tuck your hair under a beret. I'll wear some dark glasses. Cut out the elaborate greetings and follow me to a taxi. I've got a room at a B&B not far from the Embassy for us to use. Tomorrow we will swap places. There will be plenty of opportunities. David will be spending most of the day at The Grand making sure everything is tick-ity-boo."

The staff at the Grand Hotel was, once again, in its notorious annual flutter. The maitre-dom was in a panic because most of the damask table cloths had been ruined the week before by a German delegation and nobody had taken action to renew them. Replacements would be flown in from Harrods of London but it was more than likely that they would be late arriving. Meanwhile he vented his wrath on every member of staff below him. Even the chambermaids, doing their best to spruce up the rather faded décor in the bedrooms, found themselves at the receiving end of his abuse.

This was to be, on the following evening, the most important function of the year, the annual banquet of the British embassy. David was in an even worse state of mind. The Foreign Office had sent a telex informing him that the Althing were on the point of breaking diplomatic relations. It was obvious from the tenor of the message that the Prime Minister held him largely responsible. The Foreign Secretary said he had no business giving instructions to the Captain of HMS Eastbourne 'to cast ten Icelandic coastguards adrift' in an open boat three miles from shore. It was useless for David to protest that the boat in question was the motorised pinnace from the Eastbourne and that the men involved had been removed from a trawler, 'Northern Foam'. David felt that he had been dealt an unplayable hand, first by the skipper of the Eastbourne and then by his nephew and niece, who were both in some sort of confinement and with their father breathing down his neck to get them out. Chas had plainly broken the Law, Icelandic law at least. Nobody seemed to know where Charlene had got to. Gradually the realisation had sunk in that she was the victim of a kidnap.

He spared little sympathy for Chas who he believed had behaved very foolishly. He had already paid his fine and was not intending to do anything more. As for that silly girl Charlene, she should have known better than to get on a plane to Iceland after she had been told that she was going to Majorca. Her abduction was the most worrying aspect of the whole crisis. As things stood he had no alternative but to yield to the demands of Krause.

The bogus phone call could not possibly have come from his secretary, who spoke with a strong Yorkshire accent.

At five o'clock David telephoned the Residence and asked to be put through to his wife. Susan took the call.

"Darling, I've booked us in for the night here, Room 10. It's a suite and very well appointed, much better than last year. Please come down. Get a taxi and bring all your stuff for the dinner and for the night as well. It will be much more convenient and we can have a few friends in the room at six for an aperitif before the rabble start to arrive."

"Very good, give me half an hour and I'll be with you." This was to be Susan's first test. She wondered if she was going to get away with it. At the hotel she picked up the duplicate key of the room and walked up the single flight of stairs to the first floor. She was trembling and out of breath as she opened the door slightly, hoping to get a preview of the suite and to see David before he saw her. To her relief she heard him having a shower.

"Darling. I'm here." She called. Hanging by the door were two warm looking bathrobes. Selecting one she quickly stripped and put it on, folding her day clothes into a drawer. The twin's plan had gone awry already. Susan had imagined she would have more time to change in the comfort and privacy of their bedroom at the Residence. David came into the bedroom. He was naked but still towelling himself.

"You look lovely darling. Give us a kiss. What a smashing hair-do."

"You do like it, don't you?"

"Yes, it suits you very well. Don't spoil it in the shower."

She came towards him and he enfolded her in his arms kissing the side of her neck. She felt him grow tense, his arms tightened around her. He slid his hand under the robe and placed his fingers on her shoulder. She almost fainted in terror and slumped against him. They stood like this for a full minute.

"Well, aren't you going to say something?" he uttered.

"What can I say? You've found me out haven't you?"

"What the bloody hell do you two think you are playing at? Is this meant to be a joke? Where is Lucy? If you think you're coming to the dinner then you're badly mistaken. I must have Lucy at my side. It's the most important occasion of a very tricky year for me. Where the hell is she? Explain."

"There's no time to explain now David."

"Yes there is. There's got to be. I demand an explanation."

He raised his hand as if to strike her. She shrank back and then ran to the bathroom and locked the door. She heard David ask room service for a call to the Residence. She heard him ask someone to check their room, saying he thought his wife had been taken ill. When she emerged he was slumped in the armchair, looking both puzzled and dejected. Presently he took out a paper and started to read his speech. She dressed. Lucy's gown was lovely and fitted her perfectly. It was a full skirted electric blue silk trimmed with handmade lace. The low cut bodice showed off her voluptuous curves to perfection. Susan wondered where her sister could buy such a beautiful garment in Iceland.

Going to him she said, "David, zip me up please. Look." She stood before him smiling. "Cheer up. No ones going to be any the wiser." David's eyes lit up with admiration in spite of the tension between them.

"It will be a miracle if you can carry it off but you look so desirable the men at any rate won't notice you're not really Lucy. Remember, I'm not 'Darling'; It's either 'Dave' or 'Honey'.

The meal was supposed to start at half past seven although many were arriving at six. David with Susan beside him was first in the line-up to greet the guests. Lucy had been good value on these occasions; her repartee was brilliant, so witty and sharp. She had a mind like a telephone directory, remembering all the names and faces from the previous year and adding new ones into her fabulous memory without effort. David had instituted name badges to be worn, ostensibly to enable the company to get to know each other, but in reality for himself. He was so preoccupied with his own worries that he failed to notice the lacklustre performance of Lucy's sister. Knowing nobody, she was reliant on the name badges also and to anyone with effusive comments such as, "how nice to see you again my lady," she could only smile.

Meanwhile Lucy, using the embassy Landrover, drove north to her fateful meeting with Vilbert Agnarsson, the Chief of Police.

At a quarter to seven David tried to circulate round the room but was waylaid by the Deputy Prime Minister who happened to be the Reykjavik Harbour Master, Georg Baldursson.

"Tell me David, did you know that your nephew Charles Forbes Junior is one of our guests?"

"Yes Captain, as a matter of fact it was reported to me last week. As a gesture of goodwill to your government I have paid his fine and arranged for an advocate from England to represent him at his hearing in two weeks time."

"And what do you think the outcome of that will be?"

"It's not for me to say Georg but I hope he can be repatriated and that he will have learnt a serious lesson. He is only a young man and somewhat inexperienced in the law, although a good seaman."

"I'm sorry to tell you that he will be used as an example to other skippers in your fleet."

"My primary objective is to bring this war, if we can call it that, to an end as soon as possible but, and it's a big BUT, we can't withdraw without negotiation. In equity we need time set against tapering quotas. Surely that's not unreasonable. Now, please pardon me Georg. Our guests are taking their seats. I must attend to my more pressing duties. Let's talk some more about this later this week."

"As you say, Your Excellency."

The dinner passed without incident. David was able to make an entirely neutral speech which satisfied no one but had the merit that it offended no one either. He merely pointed out the unfortunate circumstances which had brought two friendly countries into violent dispute and his urgent wish to see it ended honourably to both sides. As an exercise in complacency it was a masterpiece. He said everything and nothing, neither supportive or judgemental. As he sat down he overheard Reynir Josefsson mutter in Icelandic to Gudmundur Kjaernested,

"I always thought the man is a buffoon. Now I know it." David, having sharp ears and more than a smattering of Scandinavian languages was able to grin and raise a knowing glass to his guests. He was so overcome with the importance and the difficulties of the evening, combined with the liberal helping of wine which he took to steady his nerves, that he almost forgot that the woman sitting next to him was not his sparkling wife but her sister.

Later, after the guests had gone, David and Susan retired to their room in the hotel. As Susan nonchalantly prepared herself for bed, he saw her naked shoulders. She was indeed devoid of the scar inflicted by the Vopos on the bridge at Vacha in 1953. For the second time that evening he had to come to terms with Susan's deception. The excitement of the evening, combined with large doses of excellent wine, sharpened his anticipation of the evening still to come. She went into the bathroom. His mind went back to the night in the family home in Manchester, when Susan and Lucy swapped identities. It was hard to remember that the woman, with whom he was about to go to bed was legally still his wife. As Susan emerged he was struck by the thought that time had been kind. Without the trappings of make-up and with only a thin night gown to cover her nakedness she was just as he remembered her. He was determined to enjoy the night before him whatever her objections might be. The twins had cheated him and he was bent on finding out why. Before he joined her in bed he took a shower and another stiff whisky.

****

Lucy drove through the night to her rendez-vous with Vilbert Agnarsson, the Chief of the Icelandic Police. Her determination overcame her fears. Could she persuade him to an illegal act? In the intervening weeks since they had first met, Lucy had seen Vilbert on several informal occasions, the day when she took her driving test, the opening of the Womens' Guild bazaar, the cutting of tape at the entrance to the Botnsheioi Tunnels, a new primary school in Selfoss. She almost felt that he was stalking her. But without David she was glad of Vilbert's company. She had had lunch with him occasionally and helped to entertain him on his visits to the embassy when David was away. He was always pleasant and they had many humorous conversations about Iceland and its history. He had told her of the illness of his wife, who had died three years previously. Although several opportunities had occurred for him he had not fallen in love again.

On this night she had acted rashly, arranging for Susan to take her place at the annual dinner so that she could keep a secret assignation. She dreaded what was in store and had little doubt about what he desired of her. She had only one objective and Vilbert had promised to do everything in his power to secure it for her, the release of Chas from prison.

She had never been to his house and was anxious that she should not miss the junction off the main road. But Vilbert was waiting. He had parked his car in a lay-bye near the turning. As soon as she stopped Chas was there. As she got out he hugged her in a bear-like grip showering her with kisses. She handed him the car keys and said,

"Look after the car Chas. I've left your instructions on the seat—how to find Uncle's Residence etcetera. Tomorrow the police will be scouring the city for you, so stay indoors. We'll be in touch."

"Aren't you coming with me?"

"No, now get moving, hurry."

"But how are you getting back."

"Vilbert will take me. Now don't worry. Just read my note. Lucy turned away and got into Vilbert's car beside him. He leant across and delivered a lingering kiss on Lucy's lips. Chas saw this and his stomach churned at this exhibition of blatant unfaithfulness. He got into her car and drove away tears in his eyes.

"You didn't have to do that," said Lucy.

"It won't do him any harm to grow up a bit. I hope he gives you the credit for getting him out of jail."

The car drew up at the front of the chalet residence. He doused the car's lights. An electric door opened automatically. The house-lights came on and he drove inside. A lift took them up to the second floor. They entered a large room with windows overlooking the valley and the city beyond. Near one end was a table furnished with a meal.

Lucy said, "I've already eaten."

"That's not for now. First the sauna and then a swim. Here."

Vilbert picked up a towelling wrap and gave it to her. "It's a natural hot spring. The house is built on it; perfect don't you think?"

"It is rather splendid," Lucy agreed.

"My wife planned the whole thing. She was an architect. Had great talent."

Vilbert picked up another towel-robe and said, "I don't want to embarrass you. I'll go ahead and see you in the sauna. You can change here and follow down in the lift. Press zero."

"You won't embarrass me but I'll do as you say. I'm yours for the night."

"So let's enjoy ourselves."

"Before you go, tell me. How did you manage it"?

"I asked the Governor for a twenty four hour release. I told him we needed Chas for further questioning and that he would be 'on parole'—he would never leave my sight."

"Now he has."

"Yes. I haven't worked out how I'll overcome that problem. Maybe you can help."

"It may cause an international incident if I do. What would be the penalty if Chas is caught again?"

"They would double his sentence and anybody helping him would also be put in prison. That wouldn't apply to me since I am the other party to the parole but it would to you and anybody else who conspired against the State".

"Not me. I have diplomatic immunity."

"We can't rely on that."

"So I'll just have to ensure his safety."

"Your Embassy may not offer any protection."

Lucy was shocked to realise what a dangerous position she had placed herself in.

"This is not what I came for. Let's go," she said.

"You asked the question."

"I know, silly of me."

He went down in the lift. She followed some minutes later but paused at the entrance to the sauna. Did she have the courage to go through with this? It was an adventure after all and she had what she thought would be a full explanation to offer David. He was sure to find out. Her stomach contracted into a hard knot with a frisson. Was it fear or merely bestial excitement. She was about to find out. Letting the robe slip from her shoulders she opened the sauna door. He was waiting. It was not until well after midnight and a swim that they went to the penthouse and made love. In the early hours of the following day Vilbert took her to the gate of the Residence and kissed her. As she opened the car door he said, "Till next time."

"Don't hold your breath Vilbert."

****

Chas drove down the hill toward Reykjavik. After about two kilometers he parked beside the road. He let his head slump forward on to the steering wheel, his mind in a turmoil. His mother's action seemed to contradict everything he had thought about her. Now he had to come to terms with something so out of character, so blatantly dishonest but nevertheless leading to his release from jail. Was it a gallant act of supreme self sacrifice or cold blooded and self indulgent lust? The realisation that he would never truly know the answer made him feel physically sick. That he had been the prime cause of his mother's abasement was a burden he would carry forever.

Eventually he drove on into the city and followed the instructions to the Residence.

****

Susan lay in the bed at the hotel. At first she had been resigned to play her part to its logical conclusion. But then fear and common sense intervened. She had hoped that Lucy would have returned by now but the fact that David had reserved a room in the hotel had taken her by surprise. She had expected to return to the Residence where she and Lucy could have done the 'reverse swap' without David finding out their deception. She knew that David was the worse for drink, having delivered just about the worst possible speech of his career. It would be like a man, she thought, to use her to assuage his anger. She had been discovered and had still not offered him an explanation.

David remembered his short marriage to Lucy, who used to be called Susan. Then came the swap. Now, by cruel irony he was about to get into bed with his legal wife. He intended to use this unexpected opportunity to discover if she really was averse to the attentions of men but he was undecided how to approach her. Should he continue with the charade? He had almost persuaded himself that he was entitled to enjoy her. The thought gave some stimulus to his natural desire. He removed his pyjamas and slid into the bed beside her. Her courage failed. She turned away whispering, "Not tonight Honey. I'm terribly tired and I have a headache."

He laughed and stroked her back as he said, "That's the classic excuse, darling. I had other plans."

"I'm sorry but no means no." With that Susan threw back the sheet grabbed her night-gown and made for the door but he was there before her blocking her exit. He smiled.

"Am I so horrible then? Have you forgotten that once we were married and in the eyes of the law we still are?"

"That was just a matter of convenience."

"Has anyone ever told you how beautiful you are, even at the age of, let me see, fifty is it?"

"That's what they all say. Out of my way, please David."

"All right then, I'll behave but tell me. What precisely is going on between you two?"

"Which two?"

"Don't pretend you don't know what I mean? How do you come to be here at all and what do you mean by coming to my dinner in place of Lucy? Where is Lucy?"

"I don't know where she is but I do know what she is trying to do."

"This gets hard to believe. What is she trying to do?"

"Something you failed to do."

"Oh. And what is that?"

"It's cold standing here. I'm getting back into the bed."

"So am I."

"Well no funny business then and please put your pyjamas on again. You look ridiculous without them." He complied.

"So tell me. What is she trying to do that I couldn't do?"

"She's trying to get Chas out of jail. That's what."

"At this time of night. Don't be silly."

"Her method requires that this transaction is carried out at this time of night."

When he heard his legal wife say this a cold shiver went down his spine. He lay beside her dreading her next revelation but wanting to hear it all the same. Susan was quiet, taking her time and savouring the exquisite torture she was inflicting on him. Eventually she said,

"Use your imagination. What do you think my brilliant sister is good at?"

"I refuse to go down this pathway. I know perfectly well what she's good at."

"Well then. I've told you what she was about. Don't you want Chas released?"

"Not illegally and certainly I don't want him at the Residence."

"There was a chap mentioned in the Bible just like you. Called Pontius I think."

"I'm not going to lie here to be insulted. I'm going back to the Residence but first I'm going to claim my legal right."

"Indeed, you are not." Susan sprang out of the bed and made for the door once again but without her knowing, David had locked it. He came up behind her and gripped her tiny waist with both hands.

"Don't cry out. Think of the newspapers."

"Let go of me, you beast. I'm not your wife any more."

"But you are. That's just it. Come back to bed. I won't hurt. Promise."

"And let you rape me?"

"There's no such thing as rape between husband and wife, darling."

"Let go." David turned her to face him. He kissed her on her lips and then lifted her off her feet and carried her back to the bed. He forced her down and then lay on her. She did not resist but turned her face to one side. David made no further moves. He involuntarily ejaculated and his erection subsided. Feeling very stupid and full of remorse he drew back. Giving her a smile he got dressed and left the room. As sleep overwhelmed her she heard a taxi draw up outside the hotel. Her last thought was, "I've made an enemy of our David. Will he ever forgive me?"

****

It was early in the morning when Chas found the embassy at last and walked up the narrow path to the main door. He rang the night-bell. To his consternation and surprise the door opened almost immediately. It was restrained by the security chain but nevertheless he could see enough of the figure behind it to know that it was David standing there.

"Uncle, what are you doing at this time in the morning?"

"Good God Chas. I could ask you the same question. Have you escaped?"

"Sort of. I have."

"If you think you are coming here for my protection then you can think again."

"Come off it. We're family."

"You're an escaped prisoner . . ."

"I'm no such thing. How do you imagine I got out? Overpowered the warders?"

"I know enough to know that my wife had a hand in it."

"Let me in. There's enough ammunition out here, left over from your last little riot, to start another one. How many windows shall I break?"

"If I do let you in I may have to report your presence in the morning."

"Good idea, report it to the Chief Superintendent Vilbert Agnarsson. He'll be thrilled."

"What do you mean?"

"Vilbert was the upright citizen of Iceland who slept with your beloved wife last night."

"How do you know all this?"

"Let me in and I might be able to add something to your great store of knowledge."

David opened the door to admit Chas and led the way into his office.

"All right continue."

"Well actually I can't add much. You may know already that Vilbert and Aunt Lucy are the best of friends. Not that anything out of the way has ever taken place. Two days ago Vilbert came to the jail to interview me. It was a sham. All I got to know was that he was intending to take me to his headquarters on the following day since he was anxious to tie up some details about the trawler fleet and our arrest."

"That sounds pretty unlikely."

"That's what I thought. He told me that I would be on parole, in other words, on my honour not to try to escape. I don't have any honour so I don't feel too bad about that. The following day, just after lunch he drove up in his posh car and he took me to the main police station. Then in the evening, when I was due to go back to Grundarfjordur, we set off but to my amazement we met Aunt Lucy on the main road nearby where he lives. She gave me the keys to her car and told me to go. She said my instructions were in a letter on the passenger seat as indeed they were. She got in Vilbert's car and he gave her what I can only describe as a lover's kiss. That was for my benefit I'm sure. He then drove off up a by-road. I stayed to watch and in the distance I saw the light come on as his car entered a garage."

"Go on."

"So you see Uncle. She wasn't unfaithful at all, just renting out her body for a night to get me off the hook."

"Well I'll be damned . . . I can't believe she would do that to us. I can't . . . Let me sit for a minute."

He slumped into his chair by the desk and held his head. Chas was silent, waiting for his uncle to take this 'hammer blow' on board.

"So where is the bitch now?" David hissed.

"Steady. She did it for me, not for herself. It's my bet she's upstairs sleeping it off. Haven't you been up to look?"

"Hell no! I only just got here from the hotel when you showed. Your mother's at the hotel. They did another swap."

"That's wrong. My mother's upstairs, my real mother. My dad's told me everything. Susan's my real mother, except that she calls herself Lucy. She wouldn't have done what she did for anybody else, only me, so that's why I feel as guilty as hell."

"That's got to be a first for you. Since when did you ever feel guilty about anything?"

"I've got plenty to feel guilty about. You don't need to worry about my fine. I'll pay you back with interest just as soon as I can get my cheque book."

"OK. Let's not argue."

"What now? I've got to get away on the Ace."

"Word will go out today about your escape. You can be sure. Vilbert will have to have a convincing story. This embassy is probably the first place they'll come looking."

"Get me down to the harbour then."

"When?"

"Now, right now, before the all stations alarm goes out. Is Captain Liefsson still aboard?"

"As far as I know he is, although he does spend the odd night ashore with his family."

"Good, that's what I expected. Now where's Dad?"

"He was at the dinner last evening. I expect he's sleeping."

"I need to talk to him, urgently."

"Yes, I expect you do. I'll tell you where we're at. We've got a hot line to the Base, that's the NATO Base at Keflavik. The commander there has promised us full co-operation. They don't know our side of it; the entire story I mean. The Yanks think we are working towards an amicable settlement with the Althing over the fishing question. We are of course but second to Charlene, my aim is to get Krause off our backs and possibly his sidekick, Max."

"What about Charlene?"

"You won't have heard will you?"

"I haven't heard what? What haven't I heard? I've been in clink, remember."

"Charlene took a wrong flight out of Manchester. We were in the process of persuading her to stay in Majorca for a spell. Anyway, to cut a long story, she got on a flight to Iceland and now she's disappeared. I think she's been kidnapped."

"Good God, who would do a thing like that? Has anyone been in touch?"

"Not yet but we know; at least it's certain to be Krause. You know about him, don't you?"

"This puts everything else in the shade. I can't believe that . . .

"Believe it Chas. We know she got a flight to Iceland. Your Dad's secretary got the ticket following a false phone call. There was a helicopter at Reykjavik waiting for someone. I think that's how she was taken from us. Krause has a helicopter. Now it's ten-to-one she's locked up somewhere."

"What's going to happen now then?"

"This is all very recent. So far we've done nothing. I've been half expecting Krause or someone will contact us."

"Hell, we've got to do something."

"There's nothing we can do at he moment. The immediate problem is to get you away, out of Iceland."

"Can't I help?"

"Definitely not. You'll be in the way. I can only deal with one thing at a time."

"Haven't you told the police?"

"Think about it. We haven't told the police because that will start all sorts of investigations. That's something we can't afford. They won't murder her or harm her in anyway. The fact is they want the Icelandic government to get rid of the NATO Base and they want me to make trouble."

"What sort of trouble."

"Look Chas, trust me. I'm still the Ambassador although I might not be if this gets out. My problem is to get rid of you, your Dad and the Ace. Let me clear the field and then I can tackle the main problem.

"You make it sound as if I was just a side issue, an also ran."

"Now then. You are in my thoughts all the time."

"I want my Dad to be in on this conversation."

At that moment Charlie appeared wearing a dressing gown and rubbing the sleep out of his eyes.

"Great heavens Chas. So you made it."

He strode across the room and embraced his son.

"This is fantastic. I can't believe it. Tell me all," said Charlie.

"Not now Dad. I don't know the full story. Uncle's been telling me all about Charlene."

"I know most of it, the worst of it" said David. "But I won't waste time telling it now. We've got to get moving. I'll stay here and lie to the police when they turn up, as they will. Any breathing space we have will be courtesy of the Chief of Police. We can't expect that to last very long."

"Are you with me Dad? We may need fuel in the Ace and the only place we'll get it is at the NATO Base. They'll have drained Ace's tanks for sure. If I can find the Navy's tanker at sea we could fill to the brim but we'll need some just to get out of the harbour. Let's hope we can."

"I can fill up a couple of Jerry cans with road fuel at our usual garage."

"That's good. That should keep us going for at least three minutes," said Chas jokingly. "We may need it but Liefsson's been running the engines so there must be some fuel on board."

"Of course I'm with you. What about crew? Two of us is not enough."

"Can you get word to John, David? Tell him to get down to the Base sharpest."

"Yes certainly, I have his telephone number."

"Jonny?"

"He's not a sailor, he's too old and he gets seasick. It's better to leave him behind. He's more value to us at the Base with access to the Commander. He's been organising our arms."

"Is this going to turn into a shoot out?" said David. "The FO doesn't want that. Although I agree you should prepare for the worst. There's Krause and the coastguards to think about. You don't want to be entirely defenceless and what will you do about Liefsson?"

"We may have to take him with us, hopefully without a struggle," said Chas.

"Now transport."

"The Land Rover's where I left it, outside. Let's move it Dad."

"Not so fast. The harbour might be swarming with police by now. The Ace isn't alongside any more. She's on a mooring."

"I can slip the anchor. We've got a spare."

"It will be secured, probably padlocked."

"There's more to this skulduggery than I expected," said Chas. "I'll have to lie low for a day or two while you guys get some kit together. I'll make a list. At the top will be one of those mini-acetylene torches."

"OK, you make out a shopping list and we'll get it together. We'll need another car. All the embassy cars are known."

"That will be a bit of a problem," said David. "All the dealers will be told what to watch for. So will the taxis. Anyone who owns a car will be told to lock it securely at night."

"What about the Base. Maybe that's something Jonny can arrange. We only want it for an hour or so. We can buy it if necessary."

"The Base Commander will need some convincing. It's in his interest not to cut across the Althing so someone will have to explain the bigger picture. Any volunteers?"

"I'll ring him and at the same time I'll find out what Jonny is up to. Leave that bit to me," said David.

19   THE BASE

Jonny's room at the NATO Base was conveniently sited in the main living block. It was only a few minutes walk to the main armoury and the office building. Yesterday he had discovered that the Adjutant's full name was Archibald Pate but he was warned not to use this. He was told that 'Arch' would do or 'Adjutant'.

There came a tap on his door as he struggled to re-join the world after his short night.

"Come in."

A young man entered carrying a mug of coffee and some clothes across his arm.

"Good morning sir. Here is a uniform for your stay here, courtesy of Arch. It will help you to get around the Base. I hope it all fits. If not just ring on 900 and I'll come running. OK?"

"That's very thoughtful, my compliments to the Adjutant." After breakfast in the officer's mess on the ground floor he went to see him, not hurrying unduly since haste might breed anxiety and that might put up the price of the kit he was engaged in assembling.

Seeing the building ablaze with light in the early morning darkness, he went in without ceremony. Making his way towards Arch's office, he entered a large open area. Seated at their desks were numerous operators. He noted their smart American style khaki uniforms, similar to his, decorated with the NATO shoulder flashes. Nearly everybody was wearing a headset and talking into a mouth-piece. At one long desk there were three men sitting with television screens in front of them.

"Can I help you sir?" enquired a young woman as she walked towards him.

"I've an appointment to see the Adjutant."

"Just a minute sir, I'll get his secretary for you."

While he was waiting he stood behind one of the men tapping the keys in front of the cathode screen. He did not realise the importance of this new technology, which would soon change the whole of NATO procedures and render obsolete all the Soviet systems east of the Iron Curtain. A secretary approached,

"I'm sorry sir; the Adjutant is tied up this morning. He won't see you until late today or tomorrow."

"My case is too urgent for that. Haven't you been told? The CO offered us full co-operation. Perhaps there is someone else I can see."

"You can't go past Arch, Sir. No one will talk to you unless sanctioned by him."

"Well if I can't talk to anyone here I'll have to go to the CO or, if that fails, I'll work via NATO in the UK," Jonny bluffed. "Hank's orders came straight from the White House, no kidding."

"Just a minute sir. You can wait in my room. Follow me. I'll see what I can do."

"I'll follow you anywhere lassie." Jonny thought as he watched her slender figure walking away.

Half an hour later, he entered the Adjutant's spacious office. The large window gave a panoramic view of the Bay and the NATO Harbour. He walked round the desk to greet Jonny. They shook hands.

"So you're the mysterious Jonny."

"May I call you Arch, sir?" he replied.

"Sure, everybody else does. We don't make exceptions here but if we are with the CO, the General, call me Adjutant. We do things American style on the Base."

"There's nothing mysterious about me, I assure you. I'm just a plain ordinary ex-policeman, now pensioned off."

"That's not what I heard. I think we need Felix. I've got him on standby. Shall I call him across?"

"By all means, Sir, Arch I mean."

The secretary brought in three large mugs of strong coffee. Felix entered.

"Good morning Sir."

"Hi, Felix. You two have met I believe."

"We have indeed." Felix replied. "Swell to meet you again Jonny. We know the score. I put it all in my report. Celia confirmed that Charlene has been taken. Its odds on that she is to be used as a pawn in the game Krause is playing. He will know by now that Chas is on the run from prison. We have Vilbert to thank for that."

"Chas will make a break with the Ace." Jonny said. "She is moored in the old harbour. It will be better for us if he encounters the coastguards at sea but before he can set course for Scotland he will need to pick up fuel and arms from here. In addition to that, we need a car, or the use of one, to get Chas and his father down to the harbour. The transfer will have to be at night and it will help a lot if we can get you to cut a hole in the wire fence on the quay."

"Not so fast. I don't want my men to be involved."

"Maybe not but the President promised full co-operation. Without that you may have to say goodbye to your Base here. The Icelanders are on the point of breaking diplomatic relations with Britain. All we need is for the coastguards to start using live ammunition and the Base will be as good as lost. So my advice is not to let a wire fence stand in the way.

Oh and while I'm at it please can you lend us a seaman to assist us moving the Ace round the coast? An engineer would be ideal."

"See here, I don't like the sound of this. Do you want to run my show here?"

"I'm not one to engage in argument. Perhaps we need to involve the CO in this."

"Don't worry, I will. Just leave your shopping list here. OK?"

"Thanks. Now I would be grateful for a secure line to the Residence."

****

Jonny picked up the telephone in a small private office.

"David, hello, good morning."

"Good to hear you Jonny. What news?"

"It's mainly good news so far. The Adjutant, Arch, has got my shopping list, so far so good. I'll keep you posted. I think we've got an extra crewman. Three can move the Ace but an engineer will be very handy. I've got a bit about Charlene. Krause has definitely taken her. Felix has confirmed it."

"My God. What do we do now? I've a good mind to call the whole thing off and confess everything to the police."

"You don't mean that. Your career would be finished without any guarantee that you will find her. Krause has nothing to gain by harming her. She's being used as a lever to get you to aggravate the Icelanders. Already they are on the point of breaking diplomatic relations. Put diplomacy on the back burner for a while and throw a party. Lucy's good at that and invite all your friends and the drivers from the Althing. Charlene will turn up when the dust has settled."

"What do you mean by that?" queried David.

"Take my word for it. I've not been idle for the last few weeks. Our trawlers will withdraw because international opinion is against us and this so called war will end. Good relations will be restored and anyone in prison will be released or in Charlie's case, forgiven. Charlene will be released one way or another."

"How complacent is that? Jonny you amaze me."

"Don't do anything rash and least of all don't go to the police. That will put her in real danger. Thanks to your wife, we have excellent relations with the police, at least with the Chief of Police."

"You don't have to remind me," said David icily.

"Well then, let it rest."

"All right, I will for now . . . Listen. Charlie has scheduled departure for the night after tomorrow. I couldn't afford to keep Chas here, at the Residence, for more than an hour. I got him to take over your room at The Grand. As I expected, the police came knocking only half an hour after Chas got away on foot. We just hope that no one in the hotel will realise that he is not the man who checked in. I gave him your room keys and, I hope you don't mind, I told him to use your sweater."

"That sounds OK. Let's hope it works. Arch has a meeting with the CO at the moment. They'll be going over my list. We've got to have the means to knock out their helicopter otherwise there's no point in making the run."

"You mean the Stinger."

"How do you know about that? It's on their top secret list."

"Word gets around. It's just a name to me but they're testing them at the Base and using them for training. We'll be very lucky to get our hands on one because they're not even in service yet."

"What about cost?"

"Cost is not an issue at the moment. We can leave that to the top brass to sort out. If this op. is successful we might even get everything ex gratia."

Nice talking to you David. I've got to go. Arch is on his way back. I hope he's the bearer of good news. Bye now."

"Bye Jonny and good luck."

****

It was late afternoon before Jonny was able to obtain an interview with Arch and the CO. The outcome of his work so far still lay in the balance. Arch was of the opinion that collaboration with the British trawler, The Ace of Spades, would put classified information in the public arena. The CO on the other hand took the view that the East Germans should be prevented from bombing a British trawler and that the use of the Stinger was the only way to do it. The US President had stressed the need to co-operate fully with NATO's plans.

"Come in Jonny, sit with us while we argue this one."

He entered the private office, not normally frequented by staff, and sank into a low chair.

"Whisky?"

"No thanks, water's fine."

"I think we've talked this through Jonny very thoroughly. Arch is very concerned that if we use Stinger the world will know that we possess a very important tactical weapon. Frankly, we are not ready for such a step. Stinger is still a very closely guarded weapon because it is, at this stage, unreliable. We have a limited supply here, on the Base, for training and experimental use. They are not armed, in other words there is no explosive capability. It would be possible to use a stinger 'in anger' but for it to be effective the missile would have to make contact with the target. A close call would be ineffective. Do I make myself clear?"

"Quite clear General."

"Apart from the cost, they are scarce. They would be even more scarce but for being able to recover most fired in training without the warhead. We can release two missiles provided you are willing to take from those that have been used once.

196

The accounting procedures are quite flexible. I don't want to interrupt our training procedures for this venture and that might jeopardise our good relations with this government."

"OK Sir, I understand your concern but the activities of the East Germans, encouraged by the Russian Politburo, are designed to close this base. This is no idle threat. However the presence of European and British trawlers in Icelandic waters will end, as surely it must. The British trawler owners are reconciled to losing the Icelandic fishing grounds. International opinion is against them. It's all a question of when and on what terms. Britain and Iceland have always been friendly. Nobody wants to change that. When the present crisis is settled in Iceland's favour, normality will return. Iceland has always depended on the British market but with the ban on their landings they've gone to Russia. Recovering that may not be so easy."

"So, where would that leave us?" asked the General. "Our relations with the Althing will be severely damaged if we assist the Ace and Chas Forbes to escape justice. I can't afford to take that risk."

"It's all a question of weighing the risk. Whether to risk offending the Althing or risk that the East German helicopter will provoke a shooting war between the coastguards and the British navy. If you want my advice, you can solve this problem by giving Chas the fuel he needs and a Stinger to defend himself and inform the coastguard when they will be sailing."

"That sounds like treachery. I don't think I could live with myself if I did that."

"You will have to tell Chas what you are about and why. It will be no secret anyway. He can't stay on this base for ever. He will have to sail sometime so you won't be telling the coastguards anything they can't find out for themselves. You should know that the Althing is split down the middle. The present coalition only just has a working majority controlled by the Communists. You'll make good friends of the Conservatives, the so called Independence Party, if you can demonstrate that your actions are designed to end the trawling dispute".

"You're very persuasive. Put like that it makes good sense. The immediate problem I have now is to teach the Ace's crew how to fire the damn thing."

"Good and thank you Sir. I'll relay the good news to the Ambassador."

****

Jonny got a secure line to the Residence for the second time that day.

"Charlie, I've got everything we asked for, food, water, oil, diesel, powerful torches and arms. The arms I'll tell you about later. We've also got an engineer and the use of a car. We'll do it all tonight. OK?"

"That's a bit short notice. I need a bit more time to get all the stores."

"All right, but it's got to be tomorrow night at the very latest. For one thing there's a new moon and some rough weather forecast. Felix's dancing partner has told Max it will possibly be in three or four days at the earliest. So with luck the patrols will be light if you can get away before then."

"What we want is thick mist for 24 hours. I can't commit Chas into sailing within two days. We've too much to do however much help we get. He's not too bothered about patrols so long as their Catalina is grounded."

"The CO is concerned about the reaction of the Althing. The longer you hang about the more explaining he will have to do. The Minister of Justice is convinced the Base is assisting Chas escape justice."

"The truth is, Jonny, we're removing a threat by the Communists at the real risk of our skins. Tell that to the Conservatives."

"All right then, nuff said. Now as to the arrangements, I'll drive the car, first stop the sculpture museum near the Grand and then you. Arch has arranged for a GI to cut a hole in the fence. What about Liefsson?"

"He's the least of our worries. If he's on board he'll be sailing with us."

"Nothing's guaranteed, but we think he'll be in his own bed. I want Chas to be standing on the pavement near the sculpture museum on Sigtun. I want you to have our gear at the gate of the Residence. You did get the acetylene, didn't you?"

"Yes, no problem with that. My local garage have sold me their cutting torch but not till tomorrow."

"Good, then I'll be with you at ten minutes to one exactly. The whole op. should take less than half an hour. I'll take the car back to the Base. That leaves you, John and Chas to move the Ace round to Keflavik. Hank's arranged for the pilot boat to meet you off Garoskagi. The light flashes every five seconds. He'll escort you in."

"I hope charts are still on board. They were."

"The sea entrance to the Base is mined so you need the pilot. That's all fixed up with Arch. Now you must be away from the old harbour well before dawn. Get John round to your place and get a good meal, we've a long night ahead."

"Did you get the artillery?"

"Yes two, and I've spent a lot of time learning how. It's pretty complicated. They're not armed but I'll tell you all that later. The Quartermaster is going over it with you three tomorrow. I'll go now and leave you to put Chas in the picture."

"That's fine. Leave that to me. He'll be ready, you can count on that."

****

"Do these cars actually work?" Jonny asked the mechanic in the Base garage.

"So long as you treat them kindly," came the reply.

Jonny slumped into the Skoda's driver's seat and started the engine. He smiled up at the mechanic.

"Thanks for your help. I'll be back in three hours or so." Jonny waited while the sentry lifted the barrier at the main gate. He covered the forty miles to Reykjavik in just over an hour. He reached the Grand Hotel and saw Chas waiting as instructed on the pavement at the museum. Without wasting time on greetings, Jonny drove to the Residence to collect Charlie and John. They found them waiting just inside the front door. The cache of stores was soon loaded into the car's boot.

"We must have been spotted." Charlie said as he got into the front seat. John and Chas sat in the back.

"How do you know that?" queried Jonny.

"They've had a round-the-clock-watch here since Chas went missing. There's usually two on the first floor of that office opposite. Unless they've gone to sleep our movements will have been relayed back to police headquarters. We can expect trouble." Five minutes later, Jonny stopped their car near the quay on Geirsgata.

"Keep your voices low and move about without making a sound," said Chas. "Can anyone see the Ace?" The night was black outside the immediate lit areas around the harbour. No one answered.

"There's a man under the light at the end of this jetty. He's smoking a fag. We can't steal a tender with him there."

"Leave him to me," said Jonny. "He's probably just a lookout."

They watched as Jonny walked toward the man and challenged him.

"Who are you?"

"I'm supposed to be waiting for some limey bastards. Orders from General Thorne."

"You're the fellow we want. Give us a hand. We've got a pile of stores to get on board. You must be the engineer."

"That's how it is. I'm Uncle Sam's right hand."

"I'll move the car up. You'll see a group of dinghies and hopefully a hole in the fence. If Liefsson's aboard, our dinghy will be out there." Chas climbed out of the car and greeted the American.

"Hi, I'm Chas, this is my Dad, Charlie. Did you cut the hole for us?"

"Sure did, Bud. Name's Wayne."

"OK, and thanks Wayne. Can't see a thing at the moment," said Charlie.

"You'll soon get your night vision Dad if you don't look at the lights."

"Don't waste time Chas looking for Ace's tender, just take one, any one," said Jonny.

"There's no oars, I'll have to swim for it. The Ace's boat's not here." Chas peeled off his clothes and slid silently into the black water. The near zero degrees took his breath away.

Jonny said, "There's a raft of trawlers out there. I've seen them in daylight, about six at my last count all moored together. Just climb on the dinghy you find first and row back but hurry."

While John and Charlie carried the stores down the steps to await Chas returning, Jonny left them to it and set off back to the Base. An hour later he stopped once more at the guard house and reported his return.

"This is too easy Dad," said Chas as he rowed across the harbour, the dinghy loaded to the gunnels with stores. It's as if they want us to escape. We haven't seen anyone manning the harbour office or any police at all anywhere. It's eerie."

"Soon they reached the moored trawlers. The Ace was sandwiched between two others. There was a short accommodation ladder near the stern. The stores were transhipped and taken below except for the small oxy-acetylene bottles. Chas was shivering in the night air and went below into his cabin to change into some dry gear. There was no sign of Liefsson or the Ace's lifeboat.

"Who's got the lighter?" said Chas regaining the bridge deck. Nobody had.

"This is unbelievable. John there must be some matches or a lighter in the galley."

"I'll have a look."

"It's nice to be home again," he remarked to his Dad.

"It will be home to you but not to me, I have to say. Let's get out of here."

John returned a few minutes later with matches.

"Thanks John. We'd be really sunk without a flint or a match." Chas said. "We can't go anywhere until I've cut us adrift. There are three chains coming over the bow and one over the stern. I just hope there aren't any others I haven't seen."

Chas said to himself, "If the burner doesn't wake up the harbour patrols nothing will."

He turned on the acetylene bottle and lit the escaping gas. Quickly adjusting the oxygen he brought the flame down to a small brilliant blue jet. It was the work of a moment to cut the chain which had been wound round the main winch. The cut end he slid into the harbour. Picking up the bottles and acetylene torch he started for the bow. On the way he said to John,

"Everything OK below?"

"There's a padlock on the engine room door. You'll need to burn that off as well. Liefsson must have the key."

"No wonder they think there's no need for a harbour patrol. I wonder what other glitches the harbour master has dreamt up. I'll take care of that next. Bring a fire extinguisher. I'll get this open and then Wayne can have a good look at the engine and if it's good then start her up." In the confined space below, the torch had them coughing. The oil in the padlock burnt away with a smoky flame which soon filled the passage and engine room.

Ten minutes later Chas returned to the bridge having cut the three chains which secured the Ace to the other trawlers and to the main anchor which he rightly guessed would be firmly embedded in the mud. Chas looked around the mess on the bridge deck that used to be his pride and joy.

All the electronic gear had been stripped out, Decca, Radar, Gyro Compass, Sonar, radios. Everything was gone except a multitude of loose wires that spewed out of the gaping holes that should have connected the ship's navigation systems.

"The autopilot's gone too which means we'll have to steer all the way home. I've a magnetic compass in my cabin. Let's hope they haven't found that, and I've a hand held radio direction finder too which we can use to locate the lighthouses."

Wayne shouted from below.

"Everything's fine here, Skipper. Shall I press the tit?"

"Go ahead Yank."

The main engine roared into life. Chas throttled back onto tick-over and with the engine engaged in slow ahead he manoeuvred from between the other trawlers. Clear of them, he opened up to full ahead. The Icelanders on the harbour launches gave them a wave as they passed. John took the helm. It started to rain.

Chas said, "Steer for the light on Grotta, John. Without our radar you'll have to judge distances. Aim to go round at about three miles and then steer 230 degrees. Distance to Keflavik is about thirty miles. We should pick up their pilot two miles out. We can't talk to anybody until we get VHF. Let's hope the Base will give us one."

"Aye aye Skip." Two and a half hours later Chas came into the bridge from the open wing.

"The pilot launch should be dead ahead. Do you see her yet John? White light over red."

"Not yet Skip. Viz must be down to about a hundred yards in this. It's a dirty night to be sure."

Suddenly, without much more than two minutes warning they all saw the Keflavik pilot boat heading straight for them. She came alongside. The pilot put his megaphone to his lips."

"What ship, what ship."

"Trawler Ace of Spades," Chas shouted across the narrow gap between the two vessels.

"Welcome Ace. What's wrong with your radio?"

"Gone, along with the rest of the electronics."

"Follow me. I'll take you through the mines."

Chas acknowledged the instruction with a wave of assent and retired under cover once more. Later, steaming at two knots, the pilot came aboard and took the helm.

"There's a boom across the entrance, I've arranged an opening at 0600 hours for three minutes. Just drift around here for the next fifteen minutes. They'll open on time. They always do, to the second. There's a sub. due in at 0630 so I can't stay here with you. Good Luck. The pier master will get you alongside, just watch for his signal lamp. I've told him you have no radio."

Chas brought the Ace alongside a wooden jetty. He saw, with some relief, the fuel bowser alongside just ahead. Then he saw Jonny, striding down the quay towards him.

****

With the lines secure Jonny stepped on board. Chas, Charlie and John were on the bridge to greet him. Chas turned to Wayne as he stepped ashore.

"Many thanks for your help Wayne. I'm sure John's taken all on board that you told him."

"How'd it go then," Jonny asked

"No trouble, no sight of the coastguards at all. They must have all been asleep, Chas replied with a one sided smile."

"That they were not. I promise you. I was listening to their VHF. I got a girl in the office to translate for me. I was lucky.

It should have been her knocking off time. They monitored you all the way."

"Indeed. I wonder what they had to talk about. The harbour police let us sail right past them."

"They're playing a devious game Chas. That's for sure. This is getting to be blown up into an international incident. Your uncle is going to have some explaining to do."

"I thought that Hank was to do the explaining. He can talk to their Prime Minister. Letting us go will reveal what the East Germans are really about. If Krause succeeds in fermenting trouble between our navy and their coastguards a shooting war will almost certainly break out. The most urgent task is to get our Government to withdraw the navy altogether."

"They are talking, which is a step forward. The navy is to be withdrawn."

"But when?" queried Charlie.

"Our PM, is trying to negotiate a settlement as we speak but it's up to the FO and the Fisheries Minister, Reynir Josefsson to agree a maximum fishing tonnage. I've been asked by the CO to keep your intervention very low key," replied Jonny.

"But the Yanks want the East Germans off the carpet, don't they," said Chas.

"And so does the Independence Party," said Charlie

"The coastguards know where you are. That's for sure and they know you will be sailing soon. The best time for you will be in thick weather, whenever that might be. I can get Felix to feed a bit of misinformation to Celia, said Jonny."

"Yes, but be discreet about it," said Charlie. "Any news of Charlene?"

"Celia says Max has set the whole thing up without Krause's say-so. They know where she is and so does the chopper pilot."

"When I get back here we'll get the police and take the consequences," said Charlie. "Meanwhile we've a job to do . . . discreetly."

"There's nothing discreet about murder," he protested. "We've been set up. As soon as we poke our nose out of here we'll be sitting ducks. The Ace has lost all her navigation aids. Unless we get some equipment here, I'll be navigating by the seat of my pants."

"What have you got?"

"A magnetic compass, not swung, a radio direction finder, the old ship's patent log, Saxon's sextant and sight reduction tables, charts, tide tables et cetera."

"So what's the minimum to get you home?" asked Jonny.

"Decca and radar would be ideal and a VHF set, if that's OK."

"I'll see what I can do. I must say the CO is being very co-operative, not so the Adjutant. Your main aid to survival however is very secret. It will arrive at about midnight tonight in a large box. It is man-handle-able and you must stow it out of sight. I suggest in the chart room in case you need it in a hurry."

"OK, that bit should be easy. When do I get to find out how it works?"

"After breakfast. I'll come for you all in the morning. Now I must go and I'll have another session with the Adjutant, to get your stuff. We want to see you home, safe and sound after your encounter with Krause, which we think is inevitable."

"Bye then for now. See you at nine Jonny."

"Great. Bye then. Get some sleep. You must need it."

****

Jonny ushered the trio, Chas, his father Charlie and John into a classroom. A missile lay on a raised platform near one end of the room and several rows of chairs occupied the main floor area. Chas laughed. "I feel as though I'm back at school."

"Meet the Quartermaster," said Jonny. He's going to explain this bit of artillery. You're very lucky to have the chance to see this weapon, let alone use it. The CO has persuaded the Pentagon to supply you with two development rounds but they will be unarmed. That means the rocket will have to hit the target. A near miss won't do. Without the war head we can recover the round and use it again. I'll let Q explain."

"Good morning gentlemen," Q opened. "This session will take about an hour. There's no point in supplying you with this very expensive equipment unless you are familiar with its use. We cannot let you fire one this morning. So everything I say you will have to take on trust. I'm sorry we don't include the warhead, the explosive bit. If we had known sooner what you wanted, we could have got one shipped in; never mind. These gadgets are very accurate. Feel it," he said. "It weighs about forty pounds and is designed to be fired from the shoulder. It's best to have two soldiers, one to fire and one to indicate the target. The missile itself weighs twenty-two pounds and the launcher eleven pounds. The propellant is solid cordite so initially the rocket is propelled by compressed gas which is cool until clear of the operator. The navigation computer receives an infra-red signal from the target's engine and homes in on that. The soft-ware is very sophisticated and will find your target despite any manoeuvres it might make. Would anyone like to ask a question?"

"Yes," said Chas. "Is this the sort of equipment we will find difficult when under pressure, in other words a panic."

"That depends on how easily you panic. But seriously, it takes about two to three minutes to fire up the software and mount the launcher so it's wise to prepare if you think an attack is imminent. Let me assure you it is easy, dead easy. It has to be when you consider the many situations the soldiers under attack find themselves. There are batteries to drive the computer which need care. For the short time you will be interested, the batteries are fully charged and ready. They won't cause you any trouble."

"How much training does the GI get on this?"

"About as much as I'm giving you now in the classroom and then he has the chance to launch one missile. The range is about four miles and the height of climb about three miles travelling at more than twice the speed of sound. If it's helicopters you're after it will be a duck shoot. Incidentally, I'm supplying you with two. I had a spare which won't be missed."

****

"Let's go through the check list again, Dad."

"Leave it to John and me Chas. You've done nearly all the work so far. Take it from me, if its checking then a fresh mind is more likely to see any flaws."

"OK then thanks. I'll put in some time on the new gear. If they ask us to pay for it I'll have to ask David to give us a sub until we get home."

John said, "Suppose we don't get home."

"Shut up, John," exploded Chas.

****

Charlene had a rough night. The wind had been howling round the lodge threatening to lift the roof clean off the old timbers for the last twelve hours. When she woke it was still dark. The snow was piled high against the windows on the north and west facades. The room heater was cold. She switched the bedside lamp but there was no illumination. Trying several other lights, she found that the power was off. With a lighted candle she went into the kitchen and lit the stove to make a mug of early morning coffee. In recent days Charlene and Emil had been taking it in turns to perform this ritual.

She tapped lightly on Emil's door, then harder. Then she put her ear to the woodwork, no sound.

"Emil." No answer. "Emil". This time a little louder. She placed the candle on a table and pressed down the handle slowly opening the door. Suddenly it was wrenched from her grasp.

"Boo," he said. He stood within an inch of her smiling broadly.

"Emil, that's not funny. I could have easily spilt this."

"Oh, thanks. Why the candle?"

"The power's off. He stood silent for a moment to digest this. Then almost spitting the word,

"Scheisse."

"Emil, please. What do we do now? Swearing won't do us any good."

"What can we do? Stoke up the fire and when the fuel runs out we'll have to go to bed."

She smirked and pulled a long face. Then stroking his face she said,

"You'd like that. You've been testing me out, haven't you?"

"You've been testing me . . . Don't pretend you haven't."

They stood half way into his bedroom. He put out an arm and encircled her waist. She did not resist. She broke the spell of the moment saying.

"Its ten days since Claus came. We've no milk, not even powdered and the bread's green with mildew. It's not fair. They're going to let us starve."

Charlene sank on to the sofa, dabbing her eyes. Emil sat beside her and put a protective arm around her shoulder.

"Let's stoke up the fire and get a really good blaze going. There's enough canned food for a month and we have plenty of coffee powder."

"When will they come? If we go mad and run out of fuel, what then?"

"Then we start to burn the furniture. Come on. He might come today. Let's have a good breakfast in front of the fire and maybe we can do another message like the one we did before."

Charlene turned towards him and buried her face in his warmth.

"We can't do that; the snow's nearly a metre deep. It's not possible . . . We've been imprisoned in this room for nearly a month. I don't think we're going to get out alive. How else will they hush it up?"

The following morning they heard the familiar cracking beat of the Kamov helicopter. Emil opened the outside door and was greeted with a cascade of powdered snow. Pushing it aside he moved forward and stamped it down soaking himself in the process. The machine came into view around the rocks and hovered over the helipad, gradually setting down and creating a miniature snow storm. The pilot slid back the door. He did not get out but shouted,

"Get your things we are going home."

Charlene shouted,

"Where to?"

"A house in Reykjavik."

"That's not home. I want to see my Dad."

"Tomorrow we shall have a rendezvous with your Dad. It's all arranged."

Emil said,

"Come on Charlene. Do as he says and don't argue. It's our only chance of getting out of here."

"I want to know where he is taking us. For all we know he's got orders to bump us off, me at least if not you too."

"I'm going to take that chance. You stay here if you want. I'm going."

"You can't go without me."

"You watch then and see."

"You leave me no choice. If I stay here I'll die, either of the cold or else starvation."

Soon they had gathered up their few possessions and pushed their way through the drifting snow.

"Pull me up Emil."

"Close the door Claus it's freezing." With a roar from the engine the snow, stirred up by the fast rotating blades, blotted out all sight of the lodge, the helipad and the surrounding mountains. Rising above the artificial snow storm, the gale threatened to force the machine on to the nearby rocks. Charlene screamed,

"Look out we're going to hit." Then Claus banked away down the narrow valley to get below the snow line.

He set down at a house near the East German Legation where Max greeted them. In his hands he held a short length of black cloth. Before anyone could get out he reached in and ordered Claus to blindfold Charlene. Then he passed a roll of sticky tape with which to bind her hands. She cried out, again and again,

"I want my Dad, I want my Dad."

Max said,

"Come, you are not in any danger and we shall take you to your father tomorrow."

"Why not now?"

Your father is at sea. We don't exactly know where he is but in daylight we should be able to locate him."

"Why do I have to wear this?"

"When you meet your father tomorrow you will want to answer his questions. When he says, 'Where were you?' we don't want you to be able to tell him. Now then Charlene. Play it my way and don't be difficult and no harm will come to you."

"Emil, where is Emil?"

"I'm here Charlene."

"Are you wearing a blindfold too?"

"No."

"Then you're one of them."

"Not really. No harm will come to you if you do as they say. I'll stake my life on it. I love you and what ever happens after today I will find you. Please believe me."

Charlene was led into a small windowless room. The blindfold and the tape were removed. On a table set against one wall there were place settings for two. On the other side was a narrow bed.

"Dinner will be served soon," said Max.

****

"Did you really mean . . . ?"

"Of course. I don't tell lies. I love you very much and I want to be with you always."

"I love you too Emil but if we got married I would not like to live in Leipzig. I would want to stay in England."

"That's honest at least. I don't mind. Eastern Germany is not such a big deal these days. The communist government is incompetent. A country which relies on secret police can never succeed. Western Germany is far ahead of us. I would be glad not to be going home. Let's see what tomorrow brings."

20   HOMEWARD BOUND

Chas, Charlie, John, Jonny and Hank were sitting in the officer's bar going over the details of the Ace's ad hoc re-fit.

"Sorry about the radar Chas," said Hank.

"That's OK, we'll manage. It would have been a luxury."

"Moves are afoot to make peace. The way things are going there might be some sort of a settlement by the end of the year," said Jonny.

"We can't wait that long," replied Charlie.

"No, I agree you can't. I'll be listening for you and I'll get help from the coastguards if necessary. Hank has told me I'll be welcome on the Base until you get home."

"Thanks Jonny for everything. We couldn't have managed without your help."

"Tell us Jonny, why aren't you sailing with them."

"I'm not a sailor Hank. With the exception of the Southend ferry I've never been on a boat. Taking me would be a mistake. Chas knows that, don't you old man! I can be of more use here, mainly because of Charlene. The search goes on for her. We may have to involve the police if David fails in his efforts to contact Krause," said Jonny

"I'm going to fly back here as soon as we touch land," said Charlie. "David and I will make a direct appeal to the

Icelandic authorities and blow the consequences. David tells me that their Legation has denied all knowledge. If its money they want we'll pay the bill."

"Let's get moving chaps. Sparks should have the radio in by now, said Chas.

****

Jonny, Arch and Hank were on the jetty as the harbour pilot came aboard. Charlie and Chas cast off the warps. With full tanks and the new instruments in place, John on the helm started to reverse slowly off the quay. Hank gave them a smart salute and said,

"I hope all goes well for you guys."

"We all say amen to that General," replied Chas. "Very many thanks for all your help, sir and Jonny, make sure Uncle David sends off our telex to the FO."

"Will do, Chas. God speed," replied Jonny. He gave one more farewell wave. As the Ace cleared the end of the jetty the pilot turned her round and made for the channel through the minefield and the open sea.

"Steer to clear Garoskagi, she flashes every five seconds, John. Thank God for the mist. I reckon the visibility is down to about half a mile, probably less."

"Aye aye skip. Are we sticking to our plan then? No change in the weather tonight."

"Until we have a better idea, we will. The coastguards have the Catalina to search for us. I hope they will only spend a day or two looking. If they take longer the rest of the fleet will be having a field day. If this weather holds we should be outside their area tomorrow. I've streamed the log. After the point, head due west. When we get two hundred miles offshore I'm banking on the coastguards losing interest in us."

Charlie interrupted.

"We don't really want Krause to lose interest. He'll not be happy until we hit Davy's locker and we won't be happy until we see his damned helicopter fall out of the sky."

"OK, then," answered Chas. "But at least we'll only have him to contend with. I think we can manage that."

"That remains to be seen. Why don't you get some rest then? You've been up twenty four hours."

"Good idea Dad. It's no use being fagged out. In this calm we should all take our rest.

Are you OK John?"

"I'm fine Boss."

"I'll take four hours. Say we do four hour watches with two dogs in the afternoon, agreed?"

"Aye aye," they both said together.

"As soon as we're out of danger we'll set a course for Pentland."

"But we want to get Krause first, irrespective of the danger, Chas."

"Understood Dad. You were always one for excitement. Being a GP didn't really suit you. Did it?

****

At first light the following morning Chas called Charlie and John to the bridge.

"Sorry to disturb your beauty sleep guys. John you may have sharper ears. Can you hear a chopper to the south?" John went out on to the wing bridge and stood there for a few minutes.

"Not at the moment."

"What about you Dad?"

"Let's just wait a few minutes to see if he comes any nearer," Charlie replied.

"What course are we on Boss?"

"Without Decca we'll have to navigate by dead reckoning. Allowing for wind and tide steer 275 degrees, OK?"

"Aye, aye. If this calm holds I should be able to hold steady."

"Listen," said Chas with a degree of urgency in his voice. "There it is again, I'm sure. With this low cloud base we won't see him until he's on us. He'll have Radar."

John said, "I think I can hear it now but it's not to the south of us . . . It's more easterly; I think."

Charlie said, "Fog does funny things to noise. For all we know it may be coming from the north."

To the south the sky was lighter. A breeze started to pick up. At mid-day Chas set a southerly course.

"We've been going four hours at eight knots. I reckon we're about thirty miles off the Garoskagi light. It dipped below the horizon about two hours ago. At least there's no fog to the east of us so we should see the chopper. Can you guys hear it yet?"

"Off and on," John said. "We can't see it in the east although it's fairly clear weather there so it's my guess they're to the north of us at the moment."

"OK then. Throttle back to tick over. We'll just drift for a while and let them come to us. So long as we are out of sight of land and there are no other vessels about we can expect some action."

"Dad, are you ready for some action?"

"I got you into this so I'll be on the Stinger. OK?"

"Now we can hear him," said Chas. "Can either of you see any signs?"

"Not yet," shouted Charlie. "Shall I fire one off? It should find the target wherever it is."

"Don't be so rash. Suppose it's one of ours?"

"OK then. I bow to your judgement."

"It's not a question of bowing. Look, its common sense. We'll have to fire at very short range. Without the warhead it's not lethal unless we actually score a hit."

"Belay that," shouted John. "Here they come . . . from the north as I said." The words were no sooner out of John's mouth when the helicopter suddenly loomed out of the low cloud and circled the Ace.

"It's a Wasp, Don't fire Dad." Charlie had raised the Stinger.

"Don't fire. It's ours, one of ours Dad. It's a Wasp." John left the helm for the wing and thrust out his arm compelling Charlie to lower the missile. The Wasp hovered for a brief moment while the navigator waved a greeting. The VHF crackled into life.

Chas waved back. *"Greetings from Jupiter,"* sounded out loud and clear on the VHF.

"Great to see you out here Jupiter, Channel 12, over" Chas responded.

"Channel 12. Going up"

"Hello Jupiter. We are expecting a visitor before dark, over"

"My control told me about that and to locate you and report. Why are you stopped?"

"We're waiting for him to find us, over"

"Understood. I'm returning to Base for more fuel, out."

"Thanks for your visit Jupiter. Tell the Base we're OK, out." Chas said,

"Blast and damnation. That's all we need. The bloody Navy keeping an eye on us. How the hell did they get to find out we are out here, Dad? This is supposed to be a covert operation. Do they think we've had clearance from the FO to start a private war?"

"Thank God I didn't let fly with the Stinger. Now that would have started the war," said Charlie.

"In some ways I wish you. Dad. An honest mistake—friendly fire. Ha."

"They've got more fire power than we have," said John.

"Don't worry John. Just joking. It's going to be dark in an hour. Unless they attack in the night we might as well revert to watch-keeping. What do you say?"

"OK by me."

"And me," said Charlie. "I'll do the first till mid-night."

217

As night overcame the day, the wind started to pipe up from the north-west. There was a sharp chop on the water which was soon superseded by large smooth rollers. The Ace started to roll. Laying across the wind the motion was sickening.

"John, check the engine for us. We'll have to steam slowly into this. We're going to have trouble with an early warning of the chopper. They've got Radar and we haven't and Dad if you hear anything or even if you only think you do, then wake us both."

"Aye, aye," Charlie and John both said together.

****

In the early hours of the following morning with John on watch the radio crackled into life.

"Ace of Spades, Ace of Spades." A voice with a thick German accent came over the radio and filled the whole bridge deck with sound.

"This is Kamov Ka 60, air tender to MV Kerenski, do you read me, over? I repeat, Ace of Spades, Ace of Spades . . ."

"Yes, I can read you Kamov/Kerenski. Channel twelve please." John replied. He released the transmit button. "Charlie, Chas, quickly. They've found us," he almost shouted into the ship's telephone.

"Channel twelve." The German voice continued on twelve after a short delay.

"Have you Dr Charles Forbes with you?"

Seconds later they came on deck.

"Hell fire John. Didn't you hear them?"

"What with the engine and the wind, I didn't hear them until they called us on sixteen, sorry"

"Yes, we have." Suddenly the Ace was flooded with light, almost blinding them.

"Dr Forbes, I am sure you will wish to know that we have your daughter with us, here on board. She would like to wave to you."

218

"Hello Kamov, switch off the flood lamp. It's blinding. We can't see anything . . ."

"They've got Charlene . . . bloody bastards."

"I can hear as well as you. We can't fire the Stinger . . ."

As the helicopter circled the Ace they looked up, Charlie with binoculars. Framed in the open door they saw Charlene with Krause behind her. Her legs overhung the edge. It looked as though Krause had a firm grip of a cord around her waist. She waved as if she was enjoying the ride.

Chas was overcome with emotion.

"What next Her Krause?" The words almost stuck in his throat.

"Here, give me the mike," said Charlie. He grabbed the microphone from Chas who was now choking with emotion.

"Take her back to the British Embassy please."

"Hello Doctor. I have to tell you that is not in our itinerary. I wish to trade. How about a young life for an old life?"

"What do you mean?"

"Think about it Doctor but think fast. We shall run out of fuel if we delay. Then we shall be forced into going, taking your daughter with us."

"All right then, send her down by wire."

"Just what I have planned. We have her hooked on ready. All you have to do is to jump over the side of your vessel."

"What good will that do?"

"It will do you no good at all, mein herr. As for me, I have been looking forward to this moment for over ten years."

"And if I don't?"

"Then I am sure your lovely girl will not object to taking your place in the sea."

"You're a devil. A murderer."

"Be careful of your language, mein herr. I am trying hard to control my temper."

"Dad, put on this jacket, its inflatable. We'll pick you up as soon as Charlene is with us. Take this torch. It's waterproof.

219

I'm going to put a Carley Float over the side hoping the bastard doesn't see it."

"Hurry, hurry doctor. On a count of ten please. ONE."

"I don't trust him. He's bound to be armed. How do I know he's as good as his word? If I'm saving Charlene, of course I'll do it."

"TWO."

"Krause, I'll do it if you can guarantee the safety of my daughter."

"Nothing is guaranteed in this life, doctor. THREE."

"Offer something, for heavens sake."

"You offered me nothing, mein herr. Neither you nor your brother—in-law. He is next on my list."

"He is not involved at all."

"FOUR. He was very much involved."

"John, are you listening to me?"

"Every word, Charlie."

"Make sure the Stinger is ready. As soon as Charlene hits our deck, shoot him down. If he's still alive when he hits the water, leave him to me."

"Sure thing. Everything's ready."

"FIVE."

"OK. Krause. Give me time. You must winch her down as soon as I am in the water."

"You don't dictate terms to me, doctor. SIX".

"I need to know. It's me you really want. You gain nothing by killing the girl."

"SEVEN. I thought the English were renowned for fair play. I didn't think you would kill her to save your own skin."

"I've no intention of saving my skin, only my daughter's."

"Very laudable, I'm sure. EIGHT."

"I'm jumping."

Charlie ran to the stern where the freeboard was low. Having inflated his life jacket he lowered himself into the freezing water.

"Bloody hell. I can't take this. Where's Charlene?"

"Still in the chopper Dad."

"Too bloody cold. I won't last long in this. Tell them you'll shoot them down if they don't release her straight away."

"Go ahead Ace. Get away from the doctor. Two cables, four hundred meters at least before I release the girl."

"We've got to leave you Dad. He won't release her until we've moved away."

"I heard. That's OK Chas. On your way. Where's the float? Quickly. I want to see her on your deck before I pass out."

Reluctantly Chas put the Ace into slow ahead and ran to the stern to take one last look at his father before he disappeared. He saw him struggling to get on to the Carley float and then he was lost in the Atlantic swell.

"Now you will see that a German is as good as his word. Honour is satisfied." Krause's voice came over the VHF Radio. Guided by the experienced hand of Claus, the Kamov manoeuvred over the Ace and lowered Charlene slowly down. She screamed with alarm as she swung overhead and collided with the radio mast. Chas gripped the hook and unhitched the wire. Charlene threw herself into his arms, trembling with exhaustion and fright. She watched with alarm as John lifted the missile launcher and screamed,

"Don't shoot. Think of Claus, the pilot. He is a good man. He tried his very best. I couldn't understand everything but I know he was trying to get Krause to change his mind," she said.

"I'm sorry Charlene, I really am but none of us will sleep while that man is alive. Think of Uncle David. He's their next target. Now we've got business." Turning to John, Chas shouted,

"Shoot, shoot now. John. Let's see what these American gadgets will do, quickly before they're out of range."

They looked up and saw the helicopter. Not content with letting the arctic water do it's deadly business, the chopper circled round to take one last look at Charlie. Krause found him lying on his front, arms and legs outstretched, appearing unconscious. The down-draught from the blades flattened the sea around him.

John swung the rocket launcher onto his shoulder and pressed the firing button. The compressed gas propelled the missile to a safe distance before the rocket motor fired with a roar. They watched, spellbound, as it homed in towards the Kamov. They saw the fiery trail pass within inches of their antagonist. Then it sped upwards into the low cloud and was lost to view."

"Oh God, I've blown it. The bloody thing missed them," John shouted.

"Missed John. One last shot. It's all we've got. Charlene, help John. Hold him steady. I'm turning us round to go and look for Dad." Without looking round at the missile, Chas ran aft and climbed into the bridge deck. While he was manoeuvring the Ace on to a reciprocal course John was coolly securing the second missile into the launcher and with Charlene's help hoisted it on to his shoulder. Meanwhile the helicopter had disappeared into the low cloud.

Charlene shouted,

"They've gone. You've let them go."

"This baby will find them. They got lucky with the first shot. It only just missed them. If you're into prayer missy, then start now."

They had one brief view as the Kamov dropped below the cloud. They heard the crack, crack, crack from the machine as a spray of bullets hit the Ace, shattering the glass of the trawler's superstructure. Then John pressed the button. He felt the kick as the compressed gas propelled the missile. Almost in slow motion, his sharpened senses felt the hot draught as the cordite took over and the Stinger took flight with an ear shattering roar. Seconds later the air was filled with flame which knocked them both to the deck. John looked up and saw the helicopter disintegrating as it hit the water. A lone figure came whirling out of the fire ball and fell into the sea. It seemed to struggle for a few seconds and then was lost.

The silence which followed, punctured by the gentle throbbing of the trawler's engine, was almost painful. Charlene sunk to the deck, gut wrenching coughs and cries at the full import of her escape. John helped her climb the steps to the bridge where she fell into the arms of Chas once more. He shouted,

"Bloody good. Got the buggers fuel. Now where's Dad? Take over John. Charlene and I will go for'ard. Keep her on 186. We might just catch sight of Charlie. I don't hold out much hope. He's been in the water for over half an hour unless he got on to the float."

"We're not wasting time, Boss, but I don't hold out much hope either."

"Ten more minutes and then start to circle. I reckon we'll be about over the spot. I'll raise my arm if I want you to stop."

"Aye, aye."

"We'll give it an hour from now. OK? If we don't find him I don't see how he can survive even fifteen minutes in this."

Suddenly Charlene yelled.

"There's something out there. I saw it. I definitely saw it."

"Point to it and keep pointing. Don't take your eyes off it for a second." Chas ran back to the bridge.

"Follow Charlene John. She's seen something out there but in this swell we only catch a glimpse when we're not in the trough."

"How far, skipper?"

"About two cables. She's still pointing. I'll release the dinghy and launch it from the stern when we know for sure."

"It will be a small miracle if it's Charlie, even more if he's still alive."

A shriek from the bow.

"There it is, there," cried Charlene. On the next swell the Carley float was about a cable away on the port beam. Spread-eagled face down was Charlie as if gripping the lifelines. The rubber dinghy's engine started at the first pull of the cord and Chas sped away across the swell towards the raft. Putting a short lanyard on one of the float's rings he towed it slowly into the lee of the trawler hoping that Charlie would not slide off into the sea. He transferred to the raft as John threw a line which Chas secured under Charlie's armpits. John put four turns of the line on an electric winch which hoisted him aboard. In the morning twilight the ship's deck-lights illuminated a gruesome scene. Charlie's features were bloated and a sickly grey-green, his hands deathly white. There was no sign of life.

"He's a goner."

"Come on John. We can't give up now. Charlie's been through some terrible times, near death on several. We owe it to him. Charlene owes it to him. You carry his legs. Get him below; every second counts. Put him on the long table in the mess and get the galley stove going. We need some heat."

Down below they stripped him and wrapped him in blankets and rubbed his hands and feet. Chas felt for a pulse. There was none.

"Come on John. Get some blankets in the oven to wrap him up warm. I'm going up to see how Charlene is coping and then I'll get my shaving mirror." Five minutes later Chas was back in the mess. He placed the mirror close to Charlie's nostrils and watched. He thought he could detect a faint misting on it.

"He's not dead yet John. I've given Charlene a course to steer. When it goes dark again I'll try for a fix with the sextant. Until then it's up to us to work like hell. We've got to warm his guts, mainly the heart and liver."

"Try with some rum."

"That's the very last thing to give him. It would kill him, taking away body deep heat and wasting it on extremities. Are those hot blankets ready yet?"

"Yes Boss."

"Let's get them on him and if there are any bottles about, fill them with hot water and we'll put them under his arms. Hurry. Any bottles, empty them down the sink."

"Aye, aye."

"Next, we must try to get some warm water down into his stomach but we don't want to drown him so we must be very careful. There should be a stomach tube in with the first aid box."

"Chas, I'm sure he's dead. I really am. There's every sign that we are going into a gale. We should be looking after ourselves not trying the impossible."

"I saw the mist on the mirror John. He was breathing then."

"Maybe but is he breathing now? We've done everything possible. There are things to do on deck.

The dinghy to stow and a host of small tackle to secure. The Yanks may want us to hand back the Stinger—launcher. Charlene's been on watch for four hours at least. She must be worn out after her ordeal. We're still inside the fifty mile zone. We can't risk the coastguards arresting you again."

"OK John. You've said enough. You go about your duties. I'll stay here with Dad for a while longer. Give Charlene a break when you can. If I can't get a sign from him inside an hour or so, I'll come topsides. We'll organise four hour watches. I'll set a course when we're clear of Reykjanes light. For the moment steer180. When the light bears 63 degrees change on to 105."

"I've seen men die from hypothermia before, when I was in the 'Wavey'. It only takes half an hour in freezing water. He's a goner Chas. Take it from me."

****

225

Charlene came into the mess rubbing her eyes and shaky through lack of sleep.

"What's going on Chas? John didn't tell me anything. He's on the fish deck making all the loose gear safe. He told me we are in for a blow. I'm scared."

"I said bunk down in the chart room Charlene. There's a comfy bunk in there and you'll be able to help out if we need you in a hurry. I'll do the next watch."

"What about our Dad? I can't sleep. I want to see him."

"He's dead Charlene. We tried but he was dead before we brought him aboard."

"Oh God, Chas. That's terrible." Charlene swayed on her feet, sank to the deck and buried her face in her hands, sobbing. "He was in his prime. Oh God. I can't live with this. The whole thing was my fault."

"Not your fault . . . That bastard Krause, you know in your heart. You mustn't blame yourself."

"I shouldn't have even been here. I got on the wrong plane in Manchester. I believed Emil who met me. I was so stupid, stupid, stupid. I should have realised he was a fucking plant." Chas dropped to his knees and enveloped her in a bear-hug. Great sobs shook her frame. In uncharacteristic way, Chas started to cry too. Together, brother and sister stayed hugging each other for a long time.

"Charlene, don't torture yourself." Chas muttered softly in her ear. "Please don't cry any more. I love you. Go and lie down and get some rest. We can talk about it later. No amount of recriminations will bring him back. Try to console yourself with the thought that you were cheated, all the way along the line. How were you to know what their plan was and how it would turn out?"

"I could have jumped."

"Of course you couldn't have jumped. Krause won that round but they won't win any more. When this stupid war is over I shall return."

"I want to see Dad."

"He's not a pretty sight. Don't see him now. Wait till we get back to Hull. Come on sis. Let's go and get us back on course."

John climbed the companion into the bridge just as Chas and Charlene reached there.

"All's squared off on deck and made fast Boss . . . Hello, what's been going on? Charlene are you OK?"

"She's distraught at us losing Dad, devastated."

"Of course we are. We all are. He was a great man and he went giving himself for you Charlene."

"It was my fault, all my fault." She screamed. "Bugger Krause, bugger Chas, hell to you all . . ."

"There, there lassie. Don't fret yourself. If blame there is, we're all to blame. Go down that 'if-only-road' at your peril 'cos there's no end to it. The man to blame is dead and good riddance."

"John's right there. Now go on and get some rest. I'll bring up some hot soup when you wake."

"Are we going to be all right?"

"Of course."

"I liked Claus. He was nice. I liked Emil too."

"Who the hell is Emil?"

"Emil and I had over three weeks together. We were in a shooting lodge owned by the Germans, the East Germans. Emil came from Leipzig. I got to know him pretty well."

"I bet."

"It wasn't like that. He was supposed to be my jailer after I was kidnapped but it turned out that he was just as much a prisoner as I was. He vowed to find me again. He wants to marry me."

"So you did get to know him pretty well, very cosy."

"I don't want to talk about it but I just wanted you to know that they're not all bad, just Krause and now he's dead. Claus was a good man."

"There now, please get some rest, Charlene. There's a mattress in the chart room. We shall need you to stand a watch later. Its about six hundred miles to Sula Sgeir. That's about three days steaming and the wind is getting up."

"I feel sick. This rolling has me beat."

"You'll feel better if you lie down."

"I'm going to be sick."

"Not in here. Go out on the wing. On the lee. Move it."

"OK Chas. I'm whacked. I'll go and lie down. Wake me if you need help."

"John, what's the wind speed?"

"I guess about twenty, from the north, gusting near thirty but with the wind on the quarter we should be fine. We'll be in the lee of the island soon."

"OK. I'll stand the rest of this watch, another hour say. I'm starving. Could you rustle up some sandwiches?"

"Good idea, leave it to me. What about Charlene?"

"Let her sleep. She'll be OK. We'll keep on 180 until we're across the Reykjanes ridge and then we'll be clear to set a course for the Storhofoi light."

Twenty minutes later John climbed the companion to the bridge with a parcel of sandwiches and fruit.

"I had a look in the mess. Charlie's body has slid off the table. Rigor mortis has set in since we warmed him up. If it's all the same to you, I would like to put him in the freezer."

"That's OK John. We'll do it in due course but just for now cover him up where he lies and put a turn under his armpits so he stays put this time. It'll be easier when he's loosened up in a couple of days or so. I'm going to get some kip in my cabin after a sandwich."

"That's OK."

"Give me a buzz if you see any ships. It's about 35 miles to the Eldeyjarbooi rock. We must change course before then when the Reykjanes light bears 64. Give me a shout before we get there. If you see another ship, southbound, follow her through the gap. It's only four miles wide. South-going ships keep to starboard. Once we're through we'll make for Storhofoi."

"I'll ring you in three hours."

****

With Charlene sleeping Chas and John shared the watch-keeping, along the south coast of Iceland. They reached Storhofoi just after midnight. Chas summed up the position with John,

"That's the light all right, three flashes every twenty seconds. When it bears due north we turn to 112 and I'll set the log to zero. That can be our point of departure. It'll be the last light until Sula Sgeir. Someone took our lights book, so I don't know the characteristics from now on but there's a massive light on Cape Wrath. Ideally I want to get there in the morning so we get daylight along the north coast. It's about four hundred and eighty miles from where we change course. That's about 60 hours or two and a half days. So we should get there late morning if we average eight knots. See how it goes. We can always add a couple of knots."

****

Chas rolled out of his sleeping bag, pulled on his sweater and sea boots and went forward to the bridge.

"Hi John. How's it going?"

"No problems. The engine's as sweet as a nut, running like a sewing machine. The wind has abated to about four I'd say."

"OK then I'll take over. Please read the log and enter it in the book. Anything from Charlene?"

"Not a squeak, sleeping like the dead."

"Don't say that. It's not a good simile."

"Sorry, not thinking."

"Let her sleep on. I'll do her watch. Check the engine and then get some rest yourself."

"We've done 34 miles since Storhofoi."

"Well done John. What's it like back there?"

"Fine, nothing adrift. We're taking the occasional sea over the ramp. Some of it will be finding it's way below so I'll give it five on the bilge pump and then turn in."

"OK then. See you in four hours."

****

Next time John came on deck he found Charlene at the helm.

"Hello little one," he said, "How's it going?"

"I'm tired John. I've only been here for an hour and I'm tired already."

"That's to be expected. You've had a shock. A terrible shock. We all have. I remember when we were off the coast of Israel in '49. A quiet night, looking out for immigrant ships. As things turned out it was anything but quiet. The first salvo from out of the darkness blew the First Mate's head off, clean off. I caught him as he . . ."

"John, its kind of you to help me stay awake but I don't want a story just now. Not like that one any way. Would you like a hot drink?"

"Chocolate will suit me fine." On the way to prepare two mugs, she stooped and raised the corner of the blanket covering her father. She turned a sickly pale. Putting her hand to her mouth she ran into the galley and vomited into the sink.

"You were a while," chided John.

"I made a mistake. That's all."

"What was that then?"

"I had a look at Dad. It turned me over."

"I'm afraid that's how a person looks when they die of hypothermia. I'm sorry you saw him like that.

I wanted to put him in the freezer but Chas wouldn't hear of it. We'll do it when he comes on watch."

"I couldn't bear to see him again."

"Not pretty, poor Charlie . . . The chocolate's good. Thanks"

"Do you know where we are John?"

"You take the helm and I'll go aft and read the log. Subject to wind and tide we're on the track, steering 122 degrees. Another 36 hours and we should be looking out for the light on Cape Wrath. Chas is putting into Scrabster."

"Oh, why?"

"Several good reasons. We're all tired. Your father's body and the empty hold to say nothing of the damage, bullet holes, shattered windows and the like, the lack of a crew. It will all have to be explained. So we need a coherent story. I just hope that we will get a friendly policeman. Chas doesn't want the authorities to know about your mother and aunt swapping identities, or the stinger, or your kidnap. If the full details ever reach the newspapers you'll have reporters camping on your lawn for months to say nothing of the international fallout."

"What fallout?"

"Well, it's not every day that a trawler shoots down a helicopter belonging to another nation-state. The Americans will have a lot of explaining to do if that ever comes out and we don't want to embarrass Hank."

"Who's going to embarrass Hank?" said Chas coming into the bridge.

"I was just explaining to Charlene why we're going into Scrabster."

"I see. Well we need more crew, some charts and we need to navigate Pentland. That's the tricky bit. We'll have to deal with everything else when we get to Kingston. I know Scrabster well and without charts I would rather lay over there for a couple of days to get sorted out."

Charlene said, "I'm tired, worn out."

"John do you mind taking over the watch?"

"No problem."

"OK. That's good. Get some more kip Charlene. Come on watch when you can."

"Are we going to make it?"

"Two days from now we'll be snug in Scrabster. We've nothing more to be worried about Charlene. The weather's staying moderately settled. Nothing can go wrong. So go and get your head down."

"Boss, we've several days to go yet. Let's put Charlie in the freezer before she goes."

"OK, no time like the present. We'll get him down to minus five and then transfer him to the hold."

Leaving Charlene at the helm, they went below. Chas switched on the fish room lights and stood transfixed looking at a red cylindrical canister supported on three short legs in the centre of the hold. It was about the size of a can of beans.

"John."

"Yes Boss."

"Belay Charlie. Come and have a look at this."

John descended the short ladder and stood beside Chas on the fish room floor.

"I know exactly what it is. At least I think I do. It's a bomb. A shaped charge. If it exploded now we would be struck deaf and the cone in its base would be propelled through the bottom leaving a neat hole through which the ocean would swamp us."

"Good God. Through the two layers of plates and the insulation?"

"No trouble with that at all. Those gadgets will go through two inches of armour and kill everyone in a tank . . .

"How come we never saw it before?"

"No one's been in here before now, ever since the old harbour."

"That's unbelievable."

"Why should we? I wonder what Liefsson knew about this."

"We should have searched the entire vessel."

"Too late to regret that now. The clamps were on the door. I never thought . . ."

"Why hasn't it gone off then?"

"I reckon it was to be a nasty surprise, care of Krause, only we got him first, just . . . I expect there is a device on board to set it off by radio."

"So what do we do now then? Chuck it over the side?"

"Let's get out of here for a start, Boss and don't slam the door. I vote we leave Charlie where he is for the moment."

"I suppose you think it could go off at anytime."

"I won't put money on it. It may have a time switch or a trembler which will prevent anyone touching it."

"So what do we do? Damn Liefsson. He must have known about it."

"Not necessarily. He had the odd night ashore and that thing would go into a large pocket. All the bad man needed was a screwdriver, a couple of screws and the wooden floor. For my money, Chas, leave well alone until we can beach the old girl at high water somewhere. We can get the local TA to set it off. There shouldn't be too much damage. There are several dry docks in Hull who could repair the hole."

"You make it sound very simple, John."

"Well it is quite simple. If your Dad was alive he would know all about it."

"Would he? That's as may be."

"Well he spent most of the war clearing minefields, didn't he? If it goes off, we'll have about half an hour at the most to get off, more like twenty minutes."

"Whatever happens we mustn't scare Charlene."

"I'll send her below and then we can decide how to deal with it," said John.

They climbed back up to the bridge and John took the helm. Charlene went to Chas's cabin flung herself on the bunk and was sound asleep with her second breath.

"This is serious stuff John. Our VHF doesn't reach land from out here. Come to think of it, why didn't the trembler set it off in all that bumpy weather?"

"Because it's not sensitive or because the switch is in one of the legs. I think it could be fatal to touch it. Let the TA do it. They have the know-how."

****

The Ace of Spades steamed on through the night. The reliable Mirlees engine thumping away and never missing a beat. Charlene slept round the clock, Chas came into his cabin a few times just to check she was all right. As he looked at her tumbled hair he thought, "If she wasn't my sister I think I could fall for her." She came on deck as the sun was going down on the following day.

"There you are Sis," said Chas. "Just like I said. See the harbour lights? That's our journey's end in sight.

Half an hour from now we'll be alongside."

"Thank God. I'm scared."

"No need to be scared now. We're almost home. Nothing can touch us now. I'm going to wind in the patent log."

****

As Chas turned the boat inside the breakwater there was an ear splitting crack which shook the vessel from stem to stern. The reaction to the explosion in the fish room came upwards through the superstructure. The flash from the exploding gases followed the remains of the bomb and shards of red hot metal. The steel deck beneath their feet bulged up under the force of the explosion but remained intact. The red hot fragments set alight the furnishings throughout the officer's cabins. Chas,

234

John and Charlene picked themselves up and stood, looking dazed and defeated.

Chas was the first to recover but John pulled a fire extinguisher off the wall bracket and sought to kill the flames now licking the companion way to the bridge.

"Belay that John. We've lost her. I can smell diesel. Get out of here. Charlene, over the side and quick."

"Where to Chas?"

"Down the ladder on to the mess-deck and run to the stern. Take the lashings off the lifeboat. John, she's going to capsize, grab the log book and follow Charlene. I'll be right behind you."

"Aye, aye skipper but the engine's still running. I can beach her. You take the logbook and put the life boat over the side and get her aboard."

"No chance. You do that. I'll give myself ten minutes but no more. The only place I can pull alongside is by the ice shed."

****

Epilogue

That is the end of my tale. What happened next? At this point the record becomes uncertain. We know that Chas took the Ace into Scrabster but, for some reason never explained, the bomb went off as the ship listed rounding the breakwater. She rolled over and sank within ten minutes. We don't know what caused the bomb to detonate. The lifeboat was damaged. Chas, his sister, Charlene and Mr Fowler swam to a flight of stone steps and watched as the Ace settled on her beam ends taking all their hopes with her. An edited version of the story gradually unravelled.

Charlie's body and the missile launcher were removed from the wreck one night with the co-operation of the Scrabster Harbour Master and the Royal Navy's diving team, sworn to secrecy by the Foreign Office. Charlie was taken to Hull for interment by the Thurso undertaker. The launcher was probably returned to the U S Navy via a destroyer visiting Weymouth on a goodwill mission. The fate of Oskar Krause and his collaborators was never revealed. Max disappeared and it is thought that he was drowned at sea serving with the fishing fleet from East Germany. The loss of their helicopter was explained by a sudden local storm at sea. At the first opportunity Emil Molte left the German legation in Reykjavik and flew to Manchester. He and Charlene were married in June 1976.

In the previous September there was a meeting of family and friends at Belvedere. Sir David and Lady Lucy, Jonny, John Fowler, Chas and Susan, Charlene and her captor, Emil, were present. David had been posted to Bangkok so he and Lady took no further part in the investigation which followed. Chas swore Charlene and John to secrecy and never revealed the truth, how his father came to be in the water off the coast off Iceland. It was assumed to be due to the same storm which caused the loss of the Russian helicopter. His body was recovered and a burial service held in Kingston Parish Church. He was buried in a plot arranged by the Royal Mission to Fishermen. Susan broke down under the stress of losing Charlie and lost no opportunity in pointing out that she had been against the project from the beginning. She was confined in a nursing home where Chas and Charlene could visit. John missed the Ace and Charlie. He felt it was time to retire. Needing to keep in touch with Susan he moved to Bolton where he was able to visit her also and talk over old times. She made a slow recovery from depression. Five years after Charlie's death they married. Chas vowed to return to sea as soon as his claim for insurance had been met. His case has gone to arbitration and is still pending.

The Ace was sold by the insurers as she lay to a salvage company based in Indonesia. The newspapers were presented with a severely edited version of events. The Second Cod War ended with a provisional agreement. Protective naval forces were withdrawn on the 30th September 1973. It was a disaster for the fishing industry. The trawler owners considered the settlement to be yet another sell-out by the British Government. Fishing was to be allowed only for the next six months subject to a reduction of the size of the British fleet. It was later announced that all freezer vessels were to be excluded from Icelandic waters.

The 200 mile fishing limits were eventually adopted by the EEC, the Americas, Scandinavia, Russia and other countries. For the Forbes family however it was a relief. Official enquiries into the circumstances leading up to the loss of the Ace of Spades were quietly dropped.

The new British ambassador in Reykjavik soon restored friendly relations with the Althing. A new treaty guaranteed the presence of the NATO Base. The Icelandic newspapers were never informed of the Ace's dramatic escape from the old harbour and the visit to the NATO base to pick up fuel for the voyage homeward.

Here is a transcript of the Eulogy given by Charles Forbes (the younger, known as Chas) at the service of Commemoration to his father.

Dear Friends,

We are assembled today to celebrate the life of my beloved father, Charlie, and to say in our hearts one last 'goodbye' to a man many of us love and all of us admire. Some of you have undertaken long journeys to be here on this sad occasion, others have been prevented by illness or, dare I say it, old age. Eliza, his mother, most regretted being unable to witness her son's last journey and meet all those who treasure their memories of one of our nation's heroes.

Charlie was never in any doubt whose side he was on. He was British through and through. Even in his teens he joined himself, quite voluntarily, to the national struggle at Dunkirk, and later to fighting the Cold War and more recently, to neutralising one of our country's enemies. At heart he was a pacifist, never having fired a shot in anger at any one, although if called upon, I am sure he would have done. He preferred to dodge the bullets rather than fire them. Thrice seriously wounded he was restored to life by the skill of modern surgery.

Charlie was born on the sixth of May 1921 in Grimsby's Dock Street. Even at the tender age of ten Charlie was fascinated by his father Jack's work and pleaded to be taken to sea in one of their three herring drifters. Jack was killed at the battle of Dunkirk in 1940. Although Charlie's vessel was sunk, he survived and made a daring escape by the rivers and overland to Switzerland.

His first encounter with Susan, my mother, occurred in 1936 and then by a remarkable coincidence they met again in Blackpool in 1937. They were separated by the war and reunited in Switzerland where they married in 1944. Charlie helped to inaugurate the famous 'pipeline', the undercover and highly secret work of helping allied airmen escape from Nazi Germany for which he was awarded the George Cross in 1945. As a doctor and lieutenant in the Royal Army Medical Corps he endured extreme danger to free important dignitaries from the Eastern Block at the time of the cold war and latterly his actions off the Icelandic coast did much to terminate the infamous Cod War and to secure the NATO base at Keflavik.

Charlie is a national hero by any standards, a great man who has devoted his entire life to promoting the interests of the country of his birth.

****

END

Author's Note

This is a work of fiction. For the sake of dramatic effect, I have been fairly free with the real history of the Cod Wars. The actual dates were as follows:-

DATES		LIMITS IN MILES
		Changed from/to
1. 1-9-1958	to 11-3-1961	4 to 12
2. 1-9-1972	to 3-10-1973	12 to 50
3. 14-11-1975	to 30-6-1976.	50 to 200

Acknowledgments

1. To my wife, Mary, who has once again helped and encouraged me in completing my trilogy,
   Black Diamond, Isosceles Triangle and Imperfect Circle

2. My especial thanks to Skipper Ken Knox and Alan Hopper without whose extensive and detailed information I would not have been able to write this book.

3. Also to Myrrah Stanford Smith for valuable advice; to Bettina Frances and Steph Mason for language advice;

4. Also to Joy Mawby and Doctor Fiona Haslam for detailed editing and corrections.

5. Also to Julie Roberts for creating the front cover

6. Thanks also to many others, too numerous to mention here, whose help has been of great value.

****

Bibliography

Trawling   by Raymond Anderson
Trawler   by Redmond O'Hanlon

The Royal Navy in the Cod Wars by Captain Andrew Welch
Cod Wars and How to Lose them   by Sir Andrew Gilchrist,
                                  Ambassador in Reykjavik
                                  at the time.

Men Apart   by Camilla Sacchi Field, about the
The work of the Royal National Mission to Deep
Sea Fishermen And 'Network',   The Mission's Magazine

Other Sources

The 'Arctic Corsair': The Museum Ship alongside
in the river Hull
The Hull Maritime Museum
And
Museums in Dundee and Iceland.
Various Icelandic Fishing Harbours whilst
on a cruise there.
Hepworths Shipyard, Hull

From the Web:
The Holy Trinity Church, Kingston upon Hull
Beverley Guildhall and Museum
Nimrod Aircraft
'Trawler Celtic Explorer'

From Wikipedia:-
NATO (The North Atlantic Treaty Organisation)
Decca and Loran Navigation systems
Wasp and Kamov Helicopters
The Stinger Guided Missile
The Carley Float
Hypothermia and Rigor Mortis
The Beaufort Scale (Wind Speeds)
Shaped Explosive Charges

The North of Scotland Pilot Book
Admiralty Charts, Iceland to Scotland

Trawling and Trawlers: Detailed technical and industrial
information supplied by:-
Ken Knox (ex Kingfisher Charts, Hull and retired fishing
skipper) and Alan Hopper (Naval Architect)

The Fox and the Hound

By

Skipper Ken Knox

The gunboat Thor patrolled the ground,
A certain trawler just had to be found.
He'd searched and searched, his one intent,
To find the skipper, he had his scent.

The trawler he hunted, to live and to die for,
Was new and named after a famous author,
Its skipper was also known by name,
A legend based on his knowledge and fame.

For years this skipper trawled Iceland's grounds,
Catching the prime fish, the flat and the round.
Cod-fish, haddock, plaice and sole
The more the better, his only goal.

This notorious skipper had given him hell,
A damned elusive pimpernel.
The search had gone on long enough
He'd set a trap and he'd make it rough.

The limit line was like a fence,
To go inside by law an offence.
Three miles, six miles, twelve miles, more,
For trawler skippers like closing a door.

To open that door and go inside,
Enticement too much, "let's open it wide".

The Thor was the hound and he'd choose a box,
He'd lure this skipper, this clever old fox.
The place he chose was a well-known ground,
And many ships trawled all around.
He knew his prey was among this group,
So he made his plans to make his swoop.

His ten man Gemini he'd leave in place,
Six men and first officer would lie in wait.
Fifty horse power and thirty knots,
Far too fast for our clever old fox.

"While you lie in wait in the fjord so calm,
I'll steam away to a set false alarm.
Out of sight from their radars I'll wait.
Before the dawn we'll seek his fate.
As soon as you see him, on your radio call,
Here we'll snare him, our own net will fall".

The call for assistance far down the south side,
Had left them alone, the doors open wide.
The fox among others saw the gunboat leave,
Disappearing off radar, new plans to conceive.

Two hours later and the coast looking clear,
The fox went inside with no sign of fear.
With minimal lights the fjord dark and calm,
He'd pay out his nets for the codfish and prime.

The officer saw the loom of the lights,
"Call the Thor on the radio, we have him in sight".

In the quiet the fox heard the Gemini start,
"Get them nets back on board we must depart".

On the surface it floated, fishing line wrapped in weed,
Fouled the Gemini's screw, abruptly stopping its speed.
Then an act of nature with Iceland's freak weather,
Brought a wind down the fjord, all acted together.

The Gemini disabled and to the officer's grief,
He and his men would soon be on reef.
He called the Thor and to his dismay,
Fifteen miles distance, too far away.

The experienced fox, a seaman of old,
Surmised the danger, it left him cold.
"Engines full, from this fjord we'll flee,"
Instead he put Gemini safely under his lee.

He took them onboard with their craft made secure,
No dangers now do you have to endure.
Have a rum and some food, there's plenty more,
I'll soon have you back to your mother ship Thor.

At thirteen knots for fifteen minutes,
He met with the Thor right on the limits.
They tied up close, both fox and the hound,
"You'll need these men that I've just found."

Two captains looked across the gap,
One with gold braid the other flat cap,
The fox with eyes so brown and intent,
The Icelanders blue, no sign of contempt.

"Look on your chart skipper, you'll see a red line,
One side's yours the other side's mine.

This special time I'll overlook,
You're a seaman special, not for my log-book.

Thirty years later and both retired,
Two old seamen sat weary and tired.
With whisky in hand, their second round,
They toasted themselves,
The FOX and the HOUND.

This poem is 'loosely' based on the exploits of Skipper Dickie
Taylor, notorious for fishing inside the limits.